The DOG who saved the WORLD

Also by Ross Welford

Time Traveling with a Hamster

What Not to Do If You Turn Invisible

The 1,000 Year Old Boy

The
DOG
who saved the
WORLD

Ross Welford

schwartz & wade books · new york

Text copyright © 2019 by Ross Welford
Jacket art copyright © 2020 by Tom Clohosy Cole

All rights reserved. Published in the United States by Schwartz & Wade Books, an imprint of Random House Children's Books, a division of Penguin Random House LLC, New York. Originally published in paperback in the UK by HarperCollins Children's Books, London, in 2019.

Schwartz & Wade Books and the colophon are trademarks of Penguin Random House LLC.

Visit us on the Web! rhcbooks.com

Educators and librarians, for a variety of teaching tools, visit us at RHTeachersLibrarians.com

Library of Congress Cataloging-in-Publication Data
Names: Welford, Ross, author.
Title: The dog who saved the world / Ross Welford.
Description: First edition. | New York: Schwartz & Wade Books, an imprint of Random House Children's Books, 2020. | Audience: Ages 8–12. | Audience: Grades 4–6. | Summary: "A girl and her dog set out to save the world from a deadly plague by time traveling into the future"—Provided by publisher.
Identifiers: LCCN 2019043233 | ISBN 978-0-525-70748-6 (hardcover) | ISBN 978-0-525-70749-3 (library binding) | ISBN 978-0-525-70750-9 (ebook)
Subjects: LCSH: Dogs—Juvenile fiction. | Time travel—Juvenile fiction. | Epidemics—Juvenile fiction. | Science fiction. | CYAC: Dogs—Fiction. | Time travel—Fiction. | Epidemics—Fiction. | Science fiction. | LCGFT: Science fiction.
Classification: LCC PZ7.1.W4355 Do 2020 | DDC [Fic]—dc23

The text of this book is set in 12-point Whitman.
Book design by Stephanie Moss

Printed in the United States of America
10 9 8 7 6 5 4 3 2 1
First Edition

The DOG who saved the WORLD

Whitley Bay, Not Many Years from Now

I've got this framed poster on my bedroom wall that Dad got me for my birthday. I see it every morning and every night, so I know it by heart:

THE WISDOM OF THE DOGS
Don't trust anyone who doesn't like dogs.
If what you want is buried, dig and dig until you find it.
Don't bite if a growl is enough.
Like people in spite of their faults.
Start each day with a wagging tail.
Whatever your size, be brave.
Whatever your age, learn new tricks.
If someone is having a bad day, be silent, sit near,
and nuzzle them, gently.

It's all true. Every single word. As I discovered last summer, when the world nearly ended.

Introduction

Ladies and gentlemen, boys and girls, allow me to introduce (drumroll . . .):

MR. MASH: THE DOG WHO SAVED THE WORLD!

I love him more than anything. I know that sounds harsh on Dad and Clem, but I think they'll understand, especially after what happened over that summer.

We don't know exactly how old he is, how he became a stray, or even what sort of dog he might be. He's got shaggy fur—gray, brown, and white—and ears that flop over at the ends. He's got a cute, inquisitive face like a schnauzer; big soft eyes; and a strong, *very* waggy tail like a Labrador.

In other words, he's a mishmash. When we got him from the St. Woof's shelter, the reverend said I could name him, and so I said "Mishmash," which sounded like "Miss Mash," but because he's a boy dog, he became Mr. Mash.

Mr. Mash: my very best, very stupid friend. His tongue

3

is far too big for his mouth, so it often just lolls out, making him look even sillier. He's completely unable to tell if something is food or not, so he just eats it anyway. This, in turn, means he has what the vicar calls "a gas problem."

You can say that again. "Silent and violent," Dad says.

"Disgusting," says Jessica, but she never liked him much anyway.

Without Mr. Mash, the world might have ended.

Really.

PART ONE

Chapter One

It's six o'clock on a warm summer's evening and Ramzy Rahman and I are staring at the back entrance of the Spanish City entertainment center, not daring to knock. Mr. Mash has just scarfed down a Magnum ice cream bar that someone dropped on the pavement and is licking his chops, ready for another. He even ate the wooden stick.

There's a massive double-height steel door in the white wall—one of those doors that's so big that there's a normal-sized door cut into it. In the middle of the normal door—looking totally out of place—is a knocker like you'd see on the door of a haunted mansion. The metal is green and in the shape of a snarling wolf's head.

Mr. Mash looks up at the wolf's head and curls his lip, though he doesn't actually growl.

Around the corner, on the seafront, men in shorts push babies in strollers; cars with dark windows hum along the coast road; and people pedal FreeBikes in the bike lane.

Ramzy nudges me to point out Saskia Hennessey's older sister, in just a bikini, flip-flops, and goose bumps, shimmying toward the beach with some friends. I keep my head down: I don't want to be recognized.

Above us, the sky is the intense blue of late afternoon, and it's so hot that even the seagulls have retreated to the shade. Ramzy is doing his familiar shuffle-dance of excitement, and I feel I should calm him down.

"Ramzy," I say patiently. "We're just visiting an old lady. She's probably lonely and wants to give us tea and scones or something. Scroll through photos of her grandchildren. And we'll be polite and then we'll be off the hook. That's *not* an adventure, unless you're very odd."

Ramzy gives me a look that says, *But I am very odd!*

Eventually, I lift up the wolf's head, which hinges at the jaws, and bring it down with a single sharp rap that echoes much louder than I expected, making Ramzy jump.

His eyes are shining with excitement and he whispers to me, "Tea, scones, wolves, and *adventure!*"

Dr. Pretorius must have been waiting, because no sooner have I knocked than we hear several bolts sliding back on the other side of the door, and it opens with a very satisfying creak. (I see Ramzy grin: he would have been disappointed if the door had *not* creaked.)

Now, to complete his delight, there *should* have been a clap of thunder and a flash of lightning revealing Dr. Pretorius in a long black cape, saying, "Greetings, mortals," or something.

Instead, it's still bright and sunny, not even slightly stormy, and Dr. Pretorius—as long and as thin as a cat's tail—is wearing the same woollen beach robe as when we met her this morning.

She just says, "Hi," in her throaty American accent. Just that: "Hi."

Then she turns and walks back into what looks like a large dark storage area. With her white hair on top of her thin dark body, she reminds me of a magic wand.

She has gone several steps before she stops and turns to Ramzy and me.

"Well? Whatcha waitin' for? The last train to Clarksville? Come on in. Bring the mutt if you have to."

On the other side of the cluttered storage area is a narrow flight of metal stairs leading up to a platform with a handrail. She doesn't wait to see if we are following, so I peer round the high, dusty space. It's piled with boxes, bricks, bags of cement, ladders, planks, a small cement mixer, a leather sofa propped up on its end, and a builder's dumpster filled with rubble. There's other stuff too: a horse's saddle, a car seat, bar stools, an exercise bike, a huge machine for making espresso, and something the size of an old-fashioned wheelbarrow on its side, half covered by a dusty blue tarpaulin.

Ramzy pokes me in the back and points to it. "*Psst.* Check out the copter-drone!"

I have heard of copter-drones, obviously, and I've seen people demonstrating them on YouTube and stuff, but I've never seen one for real. I'm thinking that Clem would be dead jealous that I've seen one before he has. Then I remember that I'm not supposed to tell anyone that I'm here.

Dr. Pretorius is saying: ". . . my green wolf knocker—d'you like it? It's called *verdigris.* From the old French, green of Greece. It's copper carbonate caused by the brass tarnishing in the salty air. Same as the Statue of Liberty. But you knew that, didn't you?"

We say nothing, following her up the stairs, both of us casting curious glances back at the storage area and what might—or more probably might not—have been a copter-drone.

She stops at the top and turns. *"Didn't you?"*

"Oh aye. Definitely," says Ramzy, nodding enthusiastically.

"Liar!" she snarls, and points her long chin at him. I notice that the white halo of her Afro quivers when she talks, then goes still when she stops. "What's the chemical formula for copper carbonate?"

Ramzy's poor face! His mouth droops. Ramzy is clever but not *that* clever. "Erm . . . erm . . ."

Dr. Pretorius turns again and marches along the metal

landing, her beach robe billowing behind her. "It's $CuCO_3$," she calls over her shoulder. "What do they teach you at that school of yours, huh? Is it still self-esteem and climate change? Ha! Come on, keep up!"

We trot after her, Mr. Mash's claws *click-clacking* on the metal walkway.

She halts by a pair of double doors in the center of a long, curved wall and faces us. She takes a deep breath and then starts a coughing fit that goes on for ages. At one point, she is almost bent double as she hacks and coughs. It kind of spoils the dramatic moment, but then, as suddenly as she started, she stops and straightens up. Her face softens a little. "Ah! Don't look so scared, fella. I'm just gettin' old is all. What's your name?"

"R-Ramzy. Ramzy Rahman. Ma'am."

The side of her mouth goes up and she chuckles. "*Ma'am?* Ha! Well, you got better manners than I have, buddy. Invitin' you into my place without even a proper introduction. So we've got Ramzy Rahman and . . . ?"

"Georgina Santos. Georgie for short." I don't do the *ma'am* bit. I can't carry it off like Ramzy.

"OK, Georgie-for-short and Ramzy-ma'am. That was my little test, see? But from now on no more lies, huh? From here on in, I'm trusting you. Did you tell anyone you were here?"

Ramzy and I shake our heads, and both say, "No."

"*Noooo*," she drawls, and takes off her thick glasses, bending down to peer at us with her pale eyes. "So is it a deal?"

We both nod, although I'm not at all sure what the deal is exactly.

"Deal," we say together.

Seemingly satisfied, she turns round and flings open both doors, growling, "Well, ain't that dandy? We've got ourselves a deal! Welcome, my little chickadees, to the future! Ha ha ha *haaa*!" Her laugh is like an arpeggio, each bark higher than the one before, ending on a loud screech.

Ramzy catches my eye and smirks. If Dr. Pretorius is pretending to be a weird person, then she's overdoing it. Only . . . I think it's real.

Mr. Mash gives a little whine. He doesn't want to go through the doors, and I know exactly how he feels.

Chapter Two

I've tried really hard to work out where the whole thing started. By "the whole thing," I mean Dr. Pretorius's "Future-Dome" stuff, the campervan explosion, Dog Plague, the million-pound jackpot . . . everything. And I think it started with Mr. Mash:

Don't trust anyone who doesn't like dogs.

That's number one on my Wisdom of the Dogs poster. I know it sounds a bit final, so I've come up with some exceptions:

1. People (Ramzy's aunty Nush, for example) who have grown up in countries and cultures where dogs are not pets. So it's not *really* their fault.

2. Mail carriers and delivery people who have been attacked by dogs, though it's really the owner's fault for not training the dog properly.

3. People who are allergic. I have to say that because of Jessica. More on *her* coming up soon.

But, exceptions aside, I think it's a pretty good rule. Dogs just want to be with us. Did you know that dogs have lived alongside humans for pretty much as long as we've been on earth? That's why we have the expression "man's best friend." (And woman's, and children's as well, obviously.)

I was born wanting a dog. That's what Dad says, anyway. He says my first words were "Can we get a dog?" I think he's joking but I like to pretend it's true.

Next to the poster on my bedroom wall I've got a collection of pictures of famous people with their dogs. My favorites are:

- Robby Els and his poodle.

- G-Topp and his (very cute) chihuahua.

- The American president and her Great Dane.

- Our king with his Jack Russell (I met the king once, when I was a baby, before he was the king. He didn't have his dog with him, though.)

- The old queen with her corgis.

Anyway, eventually we got a dog. It was March last year, not long after Dad's girlfriend, Jessica, moved in. (Coincidence? I don't think so.)

I knew *something* was up. Dad had taken a couple of calls from his friend Maurice, who used to be a vicar and now runs St. Woof's Dog Shelter on Eastbourne Gardens. Nothing odd about that, but when he answered, he would say, "Ah, Maurice! Hold on," and then leave the room, and once when he came back in he was smirking so much his face was nearly bursting. Of course, I didn't even dare to hope.

I asked Clem, but he'd already started his retreat to his bedroom, otherwise known as the Teen Cave (a retreat that is now more or less complete). He shrugged. To be fair, getting a dog was always my thing, not my brother's. If it doesn't have a smelly gas engine, Clem's not all that interested.

Not daring to hope is really, really hard when you're hoping like crazy. I'd look at the calendar on my wall—*12 Months of Paw-some Puppies!*—and wonder if we'd get one, ranking my preferences in a list that I kept in my bedside drawer:

1. Golden retriever (*excellent with children*)

2. Cockapoo

3. Chocolate Labrador

4. Great Dane (*I know, they're massive. "You may as well buy a horse," says Dad.*)

5. Border collie (*v. smart, need lots of training*)

I even tried to work out what was going on in Dad's head. It was like, *Jessica's moving in, Clem's growing up, Georgie's not happy about any of that, so let's get her a dog.*

Which suited me fine. And then . . . I came back from school one Friday, walked into the kitchen, and Dad was there. He said, "Close your eyes!" but I had already heard a dog whining behind the door.

I have never, ever been happier than when Dad opened the door to the living room, and I first saw this bundle of fur, wagging his tail so much that his entire backside was in motion. I sank to my knees, and when he licked me, I fell instantly, totally in love.

Dad got him from St. Woof's, and we didn't know his age. The vicar (who knows about this sort of thing) estimated him to be about five years old. Nor did he fit anywhere on my list of favorite dog breeds.

So I made a new list, where "mutts" was at the top.

It lasted a month. Twenty-seven days, actually. Twenty-seven days of pure happiness, and then it was over. Trashed by Jessica, who I try *so hard* to like—without success.

Chapter Three

It wasn't Mr. Mash's "gas problem" that was the issue.

I for one would have put up with that. Although sometimes the smell could make your eyes water, it was never for long. No: it was Jessica, one hundred percent.

It started with a cough, then wheezing, then a rash on her hands. Jessica, it turned out, was completely allergic.

"Didn't you *know*?" I wailed, and she shook her head. Believe it or not, she had simply never been in close enough contact with dogs for long enough to discover that she was hypersensitive to their fur, or their saliva, or something. Or maybe it developed when she was an adult. I don't think she was making it up: she's not that bad.

OK, I *did*—occasionally—think that. But after Jessica had an asthma attack that left her exhausted, and her hair all sweaty, we knew that Mr. Mash would have to go back.

It's probably unusual to have the best day and the worst day of your life within a month, especially since I was still only ten at the time.

I cried for a week, and Jessica kept saying she was sorry and trying to hug me with her bony arms, but I was furious. I still am sometimes.

Mr. Mash went back to St. Woof's. And the only good thing is that he is still there. The vicar says I can see him whenever I like.

I became a St. Woof's volunteer. I'm way too young officially, but Dad says he persuaded the vicar to "bend the rules."

Actually, it wasn't the *only* good thing. The other good thing was that there were loads of dogs at St. Woof's, and I liked them all.

But I loved Mr. Mash the best, and it was because of him that—fifteen months later—Ramzy and I ended up meeting Dr. Pretorius.

Chapter Four

It was morning, about nine, and there was a cool, early mist hanging over the beach. There was me, Ramzy, Mr. Mash, plus two of the other dogs from St. Woof's.

I had let Mr. Mash off his leash, and he'd run down the steps and across the sand to the shore, where he likes to try to eat the white tops of the little waves. Ramzy was holding on to ugly Dudley, who can't be let off the leash because he has *zero* recall, which is when you call to a dog and he doesn't come. Dudley once ran as far as the lighthouse, and would probably have run farther if the tide hadn't been in.

So there was Mr. Mash down by the shoreline, Dudley straining on his leash, and Sally-Ann, the Lhasa apso, sniffing the stone steps very reluctantly. Sally-Ann's a "paying guest" at St. Woof's and I genuinely think she's snobby toward the other dogs there, like a duchess having to stay at a cheap hotel.

At the bottom of the steps was a tall old lady cramming a

load of white hair, bit by bit, into a yellow rubber swimming cap. I nudged Ramzy. "It's her," I whispered. "From the Spanish City." At that stage, we didn't know her name, and hadn't even met her, although we had both seen her before.

We hung back at the top of the steps. The old lady snapped on a pair of swimming goggles, shrugged off a long beach robe, and started walking across the sand toward the sea. The tide was in, so it was a short walk, but long enough for us to stare in wonder.

Her one-piece bathing suit matched the vivid yellow of her cap and made her long legs and arms—a rich dark brown—seem even darker. She had almost no flesh where her bottom should be: just a slight swelling below the scooped back of the swimsuit. She moved confidently but slowly and didn't stop when she got to the water, just carried on walking until the sea was at waist level; then she bent forward and started a steady swim out toward a buoy about fifty yards away.

What happened about fifteen minutes later was Mr. Mash's fault. By now, Ramzy and I were on the beach. We'd seen the old lady come out of the water and walk back up the sand to where her stuff was. She was a bit scary-looking, and I didn't want to have to pass her as we went back up the steps, so we stayed by the shoreline.

I have no idea what Mr. Mash could have found even

slightly edible about a yellow swimming cap, but suddenly he was running up the beach to where the old lady had dropped it, and he had it in his jaws.

"Hey! You! Get off that!" she yelled, and then I was running too.

"Mr. Mash! Off! Off! Leave it!" I yelled.

"Give it to me!" shouted the old lady, and that was it. Mr. Mash leaped up at her with the swimming cap in his mouth, and over she went onto the sand, banging her wrist on the steps as she fell. I heard something scrape and the old lady exclaimed in pain.

"I'm sorry, I'm sorry! He's just being friendly!" I cried, and the lady sat upright, sand sticking to her wet skin where she'd fallen. She rubbed her wrist while, behind her, the silly mutt slowly chewed her bathing cap.

On her wrist was a big watch, one of those ones with pointers and numbers, and she was looking at it. Then she held it up to show me a wide scratch on the glass front.

"Your dog did that," she said. "And what the *heck* is he doing to my swim cap?"

"I'm really sorry." It was pretty much all I could think of saying. I just wanted to run away.

Ramzy, meanwhile, was wringing his hands and shuffling in the sand like he needed to go to the bathroom, his mouth pulled tight into a line of fear. His skinny legs were trembling and making his enormous school shorts shake. Dudley was yapping with excitement on the end of his leash, while Sally-Ann sat nearby, facing the other way as if she was trying to ignore the commotion.

The woman looked at me carefully as she got to her feet and pulled on the long woollen beach robe that reached to her ankles. "You're lucky my watch isn't broken," she said to me in her strange, low-pitched American accent. Then she added, "You're the two I saw a few weeks ago, aren't you?"

I nodded. "I . . . I'm sorry about your wrist. Is it OK?"

"No, of course it's not OK. It hurts like heck and there's a great big scratch on the crystal of my watch."

"I'm very sorry."

"Yeah, yeah, yeah, so you said. I get it. You're sorry. Jeez, is that dog gonna eat the whole darn thing? It sure looks like it." Her white Afro bobbed as she talked. She stretched her sinewy neck to peer at me and I think I squeaked in surprise when I saw her unusual pale blue eyes: I don't think I'd ever seen a black person with eyes like that, and it was difficult not to stare. I dragged my gaze away to look at Mr. Mash.

"Stop it, Mr. Mash!" I said. I tried to pull the cap from the dog's mouth, but it was ruined. "I'm sorry!" I said again. Then, "Stop that, Dudley!" to Dudley, who had a dead seagull in his mouth. It was all pretty chaotic.

The old lady replaced her thick spectacles; then she

folded her skinny arms with their papery skin. She looked me up and down. "How old are you?" she snarled.

"I'm eleven."

"*Hmph*. What about Mr. Madrid over there?" She jerked her thumb at Ramzy, who was still hopping from foot to foot with anxiety. He was wearing his black Real Madrid soccer jersey, although—so far as I know—he doesn't follow the team. It's not a real jersey: it's made by 'Adadis' but I don't think he cares.

"He's ten," I said.

"And five-sixths," Ramzy chipped in, then immediately looked embarrassed. He's the youngest in our class.

A trace of a smile appeared on the old lady's face: it wasn't much more than the slight lifting of one side of her mouth. I didn't know then that it was an expression I would get used to. She flexed her wrist and winced. "Five-sixths, huh? Well, ain't you the big fella?" She took a long breath in through her nose as if she was making a big decision about what to say next.

"I really don't want to have to report all this," she said, staring out at the sea, and then her eyes flashed to the side, measuring my reaction. "You know—a stolen swim cap, a potentially serious injury, a damaged watch, an outta control dog . . ."

"Oh, he's not out of—"

23

"Like I said, I don't *want* to have to report it. That would be a drag. But you two could help me." She turned round to face us and put her long hands on her narrow hips. "You know the Spanish City?"

"Of course." I pointed to the big dome a little way in the distance.

"Yeah, course you do. Go there this evening at six, and we may be able to forget about all . . . this. And don't tell anyone, either."

Ramzy was nodding away like an idiot, but that's because his aunty Nush, who he lives with, is super strict about good behavior. I think he's on his last chance or something, so he'd agree to anything. Me, on the other hand . . .

I half raised my hand and said, "Listen, I don't mean to be rude, only you said *don't tell anyone*, but we don't know you, and . . ."

She stared at me, unblinking, and her large glasses seemed to magnify her pale eyes.

"There's a rule, honey, and I know that you know it: if a grown-up you hardly know asks you to keep a secret from your mom and pop, it is *always* a bad idea."

I nodded, wishing she'd stop staring, but I was unable to take my eyes away.

"It's a cast-iron rule," she said. I nodded again and swallowed. "Which I'm gonna ask you to break."

She let this sink in. "See you at six this evening." She turned and, in one movement, gathered up her sandals and yellow beach bag and stalked off up the steps. Then she turned. "Pretorius. Dr. Emilia Pretorius. Good to meet ya."

Beside me, Mr. Mash threw up the pieces of bathing cap, then started to eat them again. (Later I added bathing cap to the ever-lengthening list of things Mr. Mash has eaten.)

"What d'you reckon?" asked Ramzy, watching her go.

I thought a bit and then pointed to his soccer jersey. "How many ladies of her age would recognize Real Madrid's away uniform?" I said, impressed. "Plus . . . Mr. Mash quite liked her."

Which meant I was prepared to give her a chance.

Chapter Five

So here we are, the evening of the same day, back in the Spanish City.

"Ha ha ha *haaa!*" cackles Dr. Pretorius again, and I honestly don't think she's acting. I think she's just excited.

Beyond the double doors it's dark—I mean, totally dark—till Dr. Pretorius barks, "Studio lights!" and brilliant pinpoint lights flicker to life on thin metal rails that crisscross the domed ceiling high, *high* above us.

We're in a vast, round, windowless room with walls clad entirely—floor to ceiling—with a dull dark green . . . foam, I suppose? It looks spongy, although I don't dare touch it. The ceiling and floor are matte black, and in the center of the room is a single deck chair: the old-fashioned type with red-and-white-striped canvas. That's it.

We are inside the dome of the Spanish City—the mosque-like building that dominates the seafront of Whitley Bay—and it is *huge.*

"You like?" says Dr. Pretorius, sweeping a proud arm into

the blackness, and her voice echoes round the vast empti-
ness.

"Yeah!" I say, and Ramzy nods, but before I've finished
my syllable, she turns and glares.

"Liar! How can you? You have no idea what this is. I
warned you: you must tell me the truth, and only the truth!
Now, I'll try again. You like?"

"Erm . . ." I don't know what to say this time, and I'm
scared I'll get it wrong again. This Dr. Pretorius is pretty intimidating. Ramzy rescues me.

"To be honest, Dr. Pretorius," he says, "there's not a great
deal *to* like. But I'd certainly call it impressive. Striking.
Erm . . . *remarkable*."

"Ha! You're learning! That's more like it. You know a lot
of words. Where are you from, kid? That Northeastern accent's mixed up with something else, isn't it?"

Ramzy hesitates. "Well, my home country doesn't really
exist anymore. There was a war and, well . . ."

"I get it, kid. We're all lookin' for a home, huh? Well,
this is mine. Welcome to my *lab*-ratory, or—as you English say—my la-*bor*-atory, ha! Come this way. Stay to the
side. And . . . hold up a second." She sniffs the air. "Can you
smell . . . burning rubber?"

"I'm sorry. That, erm . . . that's Mr. Mash. He has a slight
erm . . . digestive problem."

Dr. Pretorius's hand covers her face and her voice is

muffled. "You don't say!" She looks at Mr. Mash and then her gaze flicks to the door as if she's considering sending him out, but she doesn't. It makes me like her a little more.

My eyes have become accustomed to the gloom, and we follow her round the side of the circular room. She pulls aside a thick green curtain to reveal a narrow doorway, and the three of us, plus Mr. Mash, squeeze through.

"Control-room lights!"

Blue-white strip lights come on to reveal a long room with white tiles on the floor and walls. There are work-benches, sinks, a big fridge, an eight-ring stove, and a black iron grill. It's obvious that this was once a restaurant kitchen.

Along one wall, above a wooden desk, are three huge, blank computer screens and a large keyboard with colored keys—the kind they have in the tech lab at school. And everywhere—on every shelf, on every surface—are endless bits of . . . *stuff*. Boxes of wires, components, tiny tools, rolls of gaffer tape, a soldering iron, boxes of screws and nails, and a selection of eye-shields, helmets, gloves, and glasses for use with virtual-reality games. Some of them are dusty and look years old, with different names on them. Google, Vis-Art, Apple, Ocean Blue, Samsung . . . Some of the names I recognize but most I don't.

On one aluminum worktop lies a computer and a monitor—an old one, from the last century, with its insides spilling out as though it's been dropped and no one has swept up the pieces. I don't think anyone has swept anything, to be honest: the whole place is pretty rank.

Below the desk are several cabinets, housing—I suppose—the actual workings of the computers. A few lights blink but they make no sound, not even a hum.

On a worktop next to a sink is a wooden board with a wrapped loaf of bread and some butter and cheese, plus a load of dirty cups. Mr. Mash has found some crumbs and snuffles around, trying to locate some more.

Dr. Pretorius eases her long body into a wheeled desk chair, adjusts her spectacles, and taps the keyboard on the desk, which makes the middle screen come to life.

"Sorry about the mess," says Dr. Pretorius, but she doesn't sound sorry at all.

Her fingers tap and type while page after page scrolls up on the screen. The two other computer monitors light up with images that flash by, too fast to see properly, before they stop on a picture of a beach.

It's a moving image, from three different angles, one on each screen.

I look at Ramzy, who has been silent since we walked in. He gazes at the screens, his mouth hanging open.

"Don't worry, guys," says Dr. Pretorius behind us. "It gets better. Here." She holds a bicycle helmet in each hand and waits for our reaction. "Well, put 'em on," she says eventually. "Adjust them so they're a good fit, and make 'em tight: tighter than you'd normally wear."

A tiny earbud plugs snugly into each ear. She helps us with the straps and buckles, fiddling and pulling, till Ramzy says, "Argh! It's too tight!"

"Can you breathe?"

"Yes."

"Then it isn't too tight. OK—follow me. The dog stays here." She leads us out of the control room and back into the studio, and we stand with our backs to the foamy green wall.

I look down and realize for the first time that we're standing on a kind of path that runs round the whole of the circular floor. The floor itself is a huge disc filled with . . . what? I bend down to look closer.

"One-millimeter matte-black ball bearings," says Dr. Pretorius beside me. "Billions of them, half a yard deep. You can walk on them—it's OK. They're packed tight. You won't sink."

She stands before us, checking the helmets and finally lowering a curved steel bar that attaches to the helmets like a visor. It rests above our eyes. "That's the 3-D generator," she says. "It'll dazzle a bit but you'll get used to it. You'll probably also feel a little discomfort on your scalp, but it's nothin' to worry about."

Ramzy says, "This is just like the Surround-a-Room at Disney World!"

I get the impression that that was not the right thing to say, although I can't be sure. Dr. Pretorius blinks slowly and takes a deep breath through her nose, as though considering her response. Eventually, she says, "Dead right, sonny. Only this is *waay* better. This is a game that's gonna change the world. OK, this way."

She leads us toward the deck chair. The ball bearings feel odd underfoot, like walking on soft gravel. "When the program starts," Dr. Pretorius says, "the floor will shift a little beneath you. It might feel strange at first but you'll get used to it." She turns and goes back into the control room, pulling the curtain behind her and closing the door with a *thunk*. In my ear, there's a crackling noise; then I hear her say, "Ready? OK—let's do this!"

It is only then that I realize I have *no idea* what I'm doing. I have just gone along with this unquestioningly, strapping on a weird bicycle helmet, stepping onto a floor made of tiny balls, beneath a vast dark dome, while outside people stroll around and eat ice cream, and . . .

I have exactly the same feeling as the first time I went on a roller coaster. I must have been about six. I was with Dad, and we were in the front car. It had crawled up a steep slope, and it was only when we got to the top that I looked down and realized that I was much higher than I wanted to be.

Five minutes before now—less!—I was banging on the big double door with a wolf-head knocker and now I'm about to test some new . . . what? A game? *Who IS this woman?*

I am terrified. How, I am wondering, did I end up *here*?

"Ramzy? I don't like this." I reach out and grip Ramzy's hand; then I call out, "Stop!" and then louder, "STOP!"

But it's too late. The pin lights in the ceiling all go off and everything goes dark.

Chapter Six

Exactly where we're standing in the Spanish City was—till very recently—a restaurant, although I never went inside it. Years before that it was a ballroom, then a discotheque, with cafes and amusement arcades; outdoors there was a permanent carnival dominated by a huge white dome, and the whole thing was called the Spanish City.

Granda, who grew up here before he moved to Scotland with Gran, says he remembers an ancient, rattling roller coaster made of wood and iron called the Big Dipper. By the 1990s, though, the Spanish City was almost a ruin, and it stayed like that for years apparently.

It was all refurbished a few years ago, and there's no carnival now, and no Big Dipper. But there are still ice cream shops and cafes in another section—swanky, expensive ones like the Polly Donkin Tea Rooms that make Granda suck his teeth and go, "You're kidding! *That* much for a pot of tea! I tell you, when I was a kid . . . ," and so on.

The king visited the Spanish City once, before he was the king. I was a baby, and there's a picture of me and Mum, and the king looks like he's smiling at me, although that's just the angle of the picture. He was smiling at something else. It's in a frame in our hallway.

Anyway, last winter the restaurant under the dome closed down. No one knew why. Saskia Hennessey's mum worked as a waitress there and one day she was called in and told she no longer had a job. But . . . she was given a boatload of money. The family all went to Florida and had brand-new laptops when they came back, and Mrs. Hennessey got a job at the Polly Donkin Tea Rooms.

It was the same for everyone who worked there, according to Sass.

One day: busy restaurant. Next day: removal vans being loaded with tables and chairs. Week after: builders moving in with sledgehammers and dumpsters.

It all still *looks* the same from the outside. But no one knows what's going on inside. Well, no one *knew*—till Ramzy and I met Dr. Pretorius.

Once, before the October half-term, Ramzy and I were walking home from school and I was talking to him about all this, and about me meeting the king, wondering out loud what on earth was happening, when he just marched up to a guy in an orange jacket and a hard hat who was pushing a wheelbarrow full of bricks and broken wood by the big back doors of the Spanish City building.

"Excuse me, sir—what's happening in there?" Ramzy asked him, while I cringed with embarrassment. (*Sir!*) Mr. Springham, our teacher, says Ramzy has "no social filter": he'll talk to anyone.

The man seemed glad of the chance to rest his load.

"Haven't a clue, son. Perfec'ly good restaurant, aal ripped oot! Big shame, if y'ask me. Looka that. . . ." He pointed at a large slab of shiny stone in his barrow. "Big piece of Italian marble, that is. Come to think of it, I'll have that for meself, like. It'll make a nice garden table!"

"So . . . what's going in instead?" says Ramzy.

The man took off his hard hat and wiped his brow with his forearm. He looked up at the dome. "Dunno, son. Some sort of music or film studio, I reckon. There's a load of fancy equipment goin' in next week. Y'know: lights an' projectors, an' computers an' that." He nodded to an elderly looking lady in a hard hat who was crouching and checking the labels on a stack of silver canisters like fire extinguishers. She turned and stared at us fiercely.

"Aye, aye. Can't stay here gabbin' wi' yous. Ol' Dr. Wotsit over there'll be on to us." He picked up his wheelbarrow and resumed his work.

Ramzy turned to me. "See? You've only got to ask!"

As we walked away, I looked back, and the old lady had stood up and was still staring at us. She was tall and thin, and I looked away. A few yards farther on, I dared to glance back again, and she was *still* looking at us, and I felt as though I'd been caught doing something wrong.

I recognized her: I had seen her sometimes down on the beach, swimming. Even in the winter.

Whatever she was building was huge as well. The silver canisters I recognized as Liquid Weld: Dad uses it in his car workshop, but he only has one of them. The old lady must have had about twenty.

I looked back again, and something happened. A look? A connection? I don't know, but I had the definite feeling that she was watching us both for a reason. I think she even smiled to herself, satisfied with something, or perhaps I was imagining it.

Chapter Seven

Back in the dead-dark dome, without warning, the curved metal band above my eyes glows a dazzling blue-white—a light that is so sharp it almost hurts. I squint, and as the brilliance fades away, shapes begin to form in front of me. Within seconds, long, thin poles become palm trees, and the dark floor turns white as it's transformed before my eyes into a tropical beach.

And I mean a *real* beach: not some corny yellow virtual-reality beach, with clunky graphics, viewed through a heavy headset. This is much, *much* more realistic than anything I've ever seen in any VR device.

I let go of Ramzy's hand and he says, *"Whoaaaaa!"*—a long sigh of amazement.

In front of us is the deck chair, and now, to either side of it, stretches a wide crescent of creamy-white sand, fringed with palm trees, leading down to a rippling turquoise ocean a few meters in front of us.

I turn round 360 degrees. The illusion is *perfect*. I look up, and the blue sky has little clouds in it, and there's a darker gray cloud on the horizon.

Then I notice the sounds: the breeze; the scratching noise that palm leaves make in the wind; the breaking of the little waves; an old moped going past on a distant road. From behind me is the sound of tinny music. I turn, and there's a shack selling drinks where the music is coming from. Behind the counter stands a grinning barman. I smile and lift my hand in greeting.

He waves back. His movements are not at all jerky, although his arm becomes a little pixelated, and there's a slightly dark outline around him.

OK, I think. *This is pretty good. No, it's more than pretty good—it's* excellent, *but, you know . . .*

I don't want to sound cynical and spoiled, but I mean, I have played virtual-reality games before. This is good, and *definitely* better than the one at Disney World, but . . . well, *why the big secrecy?*

"It's pretty good!" I say out loud, looking around again.

" '*Pretty good*'?" shouts Dr. Pretorius through the earpiece, and it makes me jump. In just a few seconds, I'd almost forgotten that I was actually inside a large dark dome in Whitley Bay. " 'Pretty good'? Is that the best you can do? '*Pretty good*'?" Her normally deep voice has become a squeak.

"I . . . I'm sorry. I mean, it's excellent. It's . . ."

"Touch the sand! Go on—it won't bite you! Touch the sand!"

I hunker down, stretch my hand down into the sand, and give a little squeal of amazement. You see, I *know* that under my feet is a half-meter-thick layer of tiny metal balls. But that's not what I touch. Instead, I touch . . .

Sand. At least, that is what it feels like.

The grains trickle between my fingers. I gasp and hear Dr. Pretorius's throaty chuckle. "It's better than 'pretty good,' isn't it?"

I nod. "Yes. It . . . it's perfect!"

"Ha! Not quite, but thank you anyway. Touch the sand again and feel it carefully."

I reach out and pick up another handful of sand. Ramzy does the same and says, "It's . . . cold? Shouldn't it be warmer from the sunshine?"

"Hmph," she says; then there's a rattling of the keyboard. "How is it now?"

Suddenly the sand is warmer. "Not too warm?" she asks, and I shake my head, stunned into silence.

"What the . . . ?" I look over at Ramzy and his face is contorted in pure terror. "Georgie! Behind you!"

I swing round and I scream. About five yards away, a scorpion the size of a coffee table is raising its huge pincers at me, its quivering tail arched over its back, and it's advancing toward me.

Chapter Eight

I have only ever seen scorpions in pictures and on TV. They're not—I'm very glad to say—native to the northeast coast of England. But I know this much: they're no bigger than your hand, and they're usually poisonous.

This one reminds me of a huge, shiny black lobster, tinged with red, with an extra-long jointed tail that curves over its back. There's a dark orange bulb at the end with a long spike. Its claws are like a crab's and they snap together menacingly as the scorpion scuttles forward and then sideways on its eight jointed legs. I can see slight imperfections at the scorpion's edges: a bit of blurring in the movement, like when the barman waved at me before.

Unfortunately, knowing that it's a virtual-reality scorpion doesn't make it much less scary.

"Dr. Pretorius!" I shout. "Ramzy!"

Ramzy is frozen in fear, and all I hear in my ear is Dr. Pretorius muttering, "Oh, for cryin' out loud: not *him* again."

The creature takes two scuttling steps toward me and I aim a desperate kick at it. To my astonishment, my foot connects with its claw. I feel my foot kick it—but still it comes forward. Without thinking, I run up the beach, away from the scorpion, which has raised itself up on its legs. It doesn't appear to have eyes: instead, there are raised mounds on top of its head like glistening black half-footballs, but still—they seem to be looking right at me.

I notice a strange sensation as I run: it's not *exactly* like running on sand. More like running on a bed of tiny metal balls, which shift beneath my feet, although right now I'm more interested in putting distance between me and a massive black scorpion.

"Dr. Pretorius! What *is* that thing?" I yell. Ramzy has picked up the deck chair and throws it. His aim is good, but the chair passes straight through the scorpion, as though it is a ghost.

"*Tsk.* Don't worry," says Dr. Pretorius through my earpiece, sounding more frustrated than anxious. Then she says, "Why, you little . . . ," but I think she's talking to the scorpion.

Together, Ramzy and I retreat farther up the beach, but still the scorpion comes at us, scampering through the sand two or three little steps at a time.

Then, without warning, it opens its pincers, rises up on its jointed, hairy legs, and starts to sprint toward me. I turn to run and stumble forward, landing with my face in the sand at the exact moment that the band above my eyes goes dark.

Everything is silent.

When the pin lights come on again in the dome a few seconds later, I'm still in the center of the studio, panting. Ramzy is kneeling next to the upturned deck chair on the black floor where the scorpion was. Dr. Pretorius comes out of the computer-control room and walks toward us over the floor of tiny steel beads, beaming with delight as I blink and pant.

"Welcome to MSVR—multisensory virtual reality, kiddos! And congratulations on being the first people in the world to experience it." She clasps her long hands together and shakes her head, her halo of white hair quivering. "Nearly there," she says. "Nearly there!"

I'm still breathless after my encounter with the huge scorpion. Dr. Pretorius notices and adds, "Aw, hey, honey. Sorry about Buster! He's kind of a bug in the system. I must do somethin' about that. He wouldn't have hurt ya." Then she adds, "I don't think, anyhow, ha!"

Ramzy and I sit on the long desk in the control room while Dr. Pretorius bashes violently at the multicolored keyboard like she's playing Whac-A-Mole. In front of us we each have a can of supermarket cola and cookies from a packet. If Ramzy is disappointed—I promised him homemade scones—he doesn't show it as he crams another two cookies in his mouth. At our feet, Mr. Mash snuffles around for dropped crumbs.

Dr. Pretorius doesn't look at us while she speaks.

"You"—*bash-bash-tap*—"just sit there"—*tap-tap-BASH*—"and I'll be with you in a minute"—*tappity-tappity-BASH-BASH*—"darn you! No—not you. Ah, the heck with it: I'll sort it out later." She whacks the keyboard one last time and turns to us in her swivel chair. "It's that darned scorpion. He's gettin' ahead of himself. He shouldn't even be there."

Ramzy and I nod as though we understand everything she's saying.

There's a slightly awkward pause before Dr. Pretorius says, "So how *was* the Disney World Surround-a-Room?" She practically spits the words and turns back to her keyboard as if the answer doesn't matter, although it obviously does.

"It was awesome," I begin, and then decide to backtrack. "I mean, 'awesome' is probably overstating it. It was good. Very good. Pretty good. I mean, there are probably better ones. That is . . ." I'm jabbering and I'm not even sure why.

Ramzy rescues me. "Do you *know* Surround-a-Room?" he asks Dr. Pretorius, more conversationally.

"Know it? A little." She's pretending she doesn't care.

Ramzy and I exchange looks. For some reason, I think she knows it more than a little.

"I just wrote some of the code, that's all," she says. "The program that created it? The visuals, the audibles . . . that sorta thing. The massive goggles you had to wear. The rain forest Surround-a-Room is . . . well, it was like a child to me. A child that never grew up."

Dr. Pretorius gets to her feet suddenly and her voice is louder, the words tumbling out. "Remember the sand you touched? Remember how you could feel it—even though there was *nothing* there?" I nod. "And the scorpion—when you kicked it, your foot connected, yeah? You *felt* it. But when *you*"—she points at Ramzy, who jumps—"threw the deck chair at Buster, and it went straight through him? Did you wonder about that?"

"Yes?" we both say slowly. I mean, I *did* wonder about it, but it was just one bit of a load of wondering I've been doing in the last ten minutes.

Dr. Pretorius picks up the bicycle helmet that I was wearing and turns it upside down. The inside surface is dotted with tiny metal bumps.

"Everything we see and hear and touch is processed in the brain. Without our brain, there's nothing. Are you with me?"

Ramzy and I glance at each other, unsure where this is going, but Dr. Pretorius isn't even looking.

"But your brain can be tricked. Optical illusions, magic tricks, déjà vu—they're all tricks of the mind. We've been doing it since we lived in caves. And now *this*!"

She holds the helmet aloft like a trophy, glaring at us.

"*This*, my friends, is the greatest illusion of them all. Or *will* be. The projector here"—she runs her finger round the curved metal band that sat above my forehead—"deceives your eyes into seeing whatever scene is programmed. No more heavy goggles! But it is *these* that make the big difference. These nodes here, and here, and here . . ." She's pointing out the little metal bumps on the inside of the helmet that connected with my skull. "They send signals to the parietal lobe, and—"

"Wait," says Ramzy. "To the what?" I'm glad Ramzy's here. For once, his habit of questioning everything is not an annoyance.

Dr. Pretorius looks unhappy to be interrupted, but then she says, "It's OK. It's taken me a lifetime of study to understand this. The parietal lobe is the part of your brain that deals with touch and sound and the other senses. With careful programming, the computer here can deliver signals to these nodes that will in turn send little electrical impulses to your parietal lobe and trick your brain into feeling, say, heat from a virtual sun. That's actually an easy one. Sand is much trickier: to actually *feel* very fine grains running through your hands? That's quite an illusion. I'm rather proud of it. Another cookie?"

I give her a blank look. I'm still trying to process this, and cookies are not going to help. Ramzy, on the other hand, clearly thinks that they *will* help and takes two more.

"So when I kicked the . . . that scorpion thing, it was what—a trick of the mind?"

"Exactly! Just like the sand. The program tricked your brain into believing the scorpion was solid, and your foot felt it, just like your hands felt the sand—even though neither was there."

"And when I threw the deck chair," says Ramzy, spitting crumbs, "obviously, the chair just went straight through it."

Dr. Pretorius winks. "Smart kid. Though that's something I'm working on." Then suddenly she claps her hands and gets to her feet. "Enough for today! There's a lot more I have to do before it's complete."

"You mean it's not finished?" queries Ramzy, taking the last cookie as he hops down from the desk.

She says no more. Ramzy and I are silent as we follow Dr. Pretorius out of the studio with Mr. Mash and down the metal stairs to the empty loading bay. Instead of going to the door we came in, though, she doubles back and unlocks another door with a large, old-fashioned metal key.

"Shortcut," she says.

The door opens into the interior of the Spanish City arcade. There's a noisy room full of slot machines and kiddie rides, the gelato parlor (which is just ice cream if you ask me), the expensive fish-and-chip shop, and the Polly Donkin Tea Rooms. It feels like we've come through a secret entrance, although it was just a locked door.

The main arcade is a few yards in front of us, and we push through the crowd, but then I have to stop. Sass Hennessey's mum has just served a plate of chips to a table outside the cafe when she catches my eye.

"Hi, Georgie!" she says as if Sass and I are best friends. Ramzy grins at her, even though he doesn't know her, I don't think. "Nice to see you, dear. And, er . . ." She looks at Dr. Pretorius curiously, probably wondering who she is.

I mumble, "Hi."

"How's St. Woof's, Georgie? Saskia's told me all about it," says Sass's mum, gathering glasses from a table. I'm already hurrying toward the entrance and don't answer. There is something in the way she looked at Dr. Pretorius that has unnerved me.

I could be wrong. Maybe she does know who she is. Maybe Dr. Pretorius is a regular in here. What do I know?

Dr. Pretorius leads us out onto the busy street. "Come back same time tomorrow. And don't forget: this is our secret! You ain't seen nothin' yet." She turns and goes back the way we came, and Ramzy and I watch her white hair bobbing above the crowds.

"Well. *That* was pretty adventurous, wouldn't you say, Georgie? Hey—Earth to Georgie!"

I'm miles away, staring up at the blacked-out upper windows of the Spanish City dome.

"What can she mean, Ramzy? 'You ain't seen nothin' yet'?"

"Dunno. We'll probably get to test out some weapons or something: the Battle of the Giant Scorpions! Or—"

"No. I don't think so. This isn't about games. This is about something else."

Ramzy gives me a quizzical squint. "You don't trust her?" he says.

I think about this.

Don't trust anyone who doesn't like dogs.

Dr. Pretorius was OK with Mr. Mash. She definitely didn't *dislike* him. She even tolerated his smelliness. (He dropped what Dad calls "a proper beefy eggo" in the control room and she pretended not to notice. That was nice of her.)

On the other hand, we only met her this morning, and she's already sworn us both to secrecy.

"I don't know," I say to Ramzy eventually. "But there's something going on."

"Well," he says, "let's find out. Same time tomorrow. It'll be an adventure."

I smile at him. "OK."

So that's that. We're trusting her, for now.

And mad scientists have to be mad for a *reason*. Right?

Chapter Nine

For the next few weeks, our afternoons after school with Dr. Pretorius settle into something of a routine. She never calls us on our phones, and we have no way of contacting her other than thumping on the door with the wolf-head knocker at a prearranged time and day. It is all very "old-school" as Ramzy says, clearly thrilled.

Once inside, we sometimes test a new MSVR environment. Other times, though, we just hang out in the control room, watching, mesmerized, as she programs her computer to create new worlds for us to explore.

Once I had a headache afterward, but it didn't last long. Ramzy too. Dr. Pretorius didn't seem overly concerned and gave us each an aspirin.

(It turns out that it's definitely a copter-drone under the blue tarpaulin, by the way. One day it was uncovered and lying flat: a bucket seat in the middle of ten spokes, each with rotor blades attached. It's obviously homemade: there are exposed wires and lumpy welding, and one bit beneath the seat is made from the bent lid of a cookie tin. Dr. Pretorius saw me staring and said, "Yup. That's my next project. Solar-powered too: unlimited range.")

And all the time we're there, in the dome, Dr. Pretorius keeps telling us that we "ain't seen nothin' yet." That there's going to be a Big Experiment, although she won't say what it is. She does check that we are keeping it all secret, though, by saying things like:

"No one knows, huh? You two—my co-conspirators!"

"We're the only three people who know about this—what a gas that is!"

And if this all sounds a bit sinister written down, it doesn't *feel* like it. As Ramzy says—so often that it's now a bit annoying, to be honest—it feels like a huge adventure.

As for visiting Dr. Pretorius, that requires deception, which I'm not keen on—but, as it turns out, I don't *actually* have to lie:

1. I've got St. Woof's, plus I'm a library monitor, so I'm often late back from school.

2. Jessica is at work all the time these days and hasn't ever taken much notice of what I'm up to at school.

3. Clem has been doing his exams and only emerges from the Teen Cave to dump his teacups in the sink, so he never even asks.

4. And Dad? Dad's just happy if I'm happy. Which I
   am, so, you know—yay!

Ramzy has it tougher. It's not his dad: he drives a truck and is away on long deliveries most of the time. It's his scary aunty Nush, who I've only met once. She looks after Ramzy and his two little brothers and speaks hardly any English. She's super strict. Ramzy has to lie a lot. It's usually about doing extra credit at school.

"Ramzy, you're only ten. There is no extra credit at school."

We're walking to the corner shop after school, Ramzy's school shorts flapping in the breeze. He looks a little ashamed. "I know, but she's not going to phone the school to check, is she? She can hardly get past *hello* as it is. Anyway— you're my study buddy. Just so you know."

"Thanks a lot! So now I'm a part of your lies?"

"I haven't got a choice, Georgie! My aunty's a nightmare. She used to make me carry an electronic tracker till it sort of accidentally broke. She'd install one on my phone if it wasn't such an antique." He holds up his ancient pay-as-you-go phone, which looks like it comes from the nineties.

We've reached the shop, where the owner, Norman Two-Kids, is sweeping the pavement outside. He glares at us and follows us in. He glares at everyone, not just us. (And

Norman Two-Kids is not his real name. Everyone just calls him that, thanks to his rule that no more than two school-children can enter his shop at any time in case they steal all the sweets or something. He's always shouting, "Nor-man two kids at once!" in a high-pitched voice with a strong accent that we can't place.)

Ramzy buys a top-up for his phone, which he pays for with a bag of loose coins, making Norman mutter under his breath with annoyance.

I always end up feeling a bit sorry for Ramzy. It's his big puppy eyes, I guess, and his teeth, and his ears, and . . . well. I find myself taking off my library monitor badge and handing it to him. "Here. You can say you're on the Library Committee as well. That should be good for a few after-school excuses."

He grins his rabbit-tooth smile. "Thanks, study buddy!"

"Just don't let Mr. Springham see you wearing it."

He pins the badge to his faded school shirt. "Let's not forget," he says, "that Dr. Pretorius is old and she's *lonely*! We're doing a service for the community!" and that removes any remaining guilt I might have had at my slight deception.

We head to the Spanish City, as we always do.

We go to the dome, as we always do, and Dr. Pretorius sits at the computer, as she always does.

We play a game in the virtual-reality environment, as we always do.

But then, when we take off the helmets, Dr. Pretorius says something she *doesn't* always say.

"I guess you want to know what this is all about, huh?"

We stare at her. Of course we do. But neither of us can think what to ask.

She gives a final, decisive whack on her keyboard to begin a rendering of a huge Roman arena, with gladiators and chariots; then she swings her chair round and looks at us hard.

There's a silence while we wait for her to speak, and I study her old, lined face. Her sky-blue eyes are as sharp and captivating as ever, but her skin seems paler, duller, and I immediately understand when she coughs violently and says, "I may not have long left, kiddos. I'm engaged in a battle against time, and there's stuff I need to complete before I . . . before I leave you."

Ramzy frowns. "Aww. Are you moving?" I roll my eyes at him. Even I knew what she meant, but she doesn't seem to mind.

Instead, she barks, "Moving? Ha! Do I have to spell it out, kid? I'm dyin'. A fatal heart condition that the finest physicians in the land are powerless to combat. And before I check out, I need to know that my life hasn't been wasted, you know?"

Ramzy just goes, "Oh," and looks at his scuffed shoes.

"Yep. *Oh* indeed. You ain't seen nothin' yet!"

There it is: that phrase again. *You ain't seen nothin' yet.* What on earth could it be that is so big and important?

"I tell ya, kids, it's going to be extraordinary. You'll be the first to experience it."

I think she wants us to go "Wow!" or something, or even just say thank you, so I do.

"Wow," I say, but I don't think I'm very convincing. The silence afterward is a bit awkward, so I fill it by saying the one thing that I have been wondering.

"Why *us*?"

She grins her wolfish grin. "You wanna know? You wanna know the whole truth?"

When someone asks you that, there's only one answer you can give, even though the outcome might be uncomfortable. I shrug one shoulder and say, "I guess?"

She turns back to her keyboard and taps it a few times till a series of still photos appear. They're satellite pictures of the street outside—Marine Drive—which leads to our school. A few more clicks show pictures of Ramzy and me, taken from a distance, but pretty sharp. The pictures scroll down, one after the other: Ramzy in his thick, too-big coat in the winter; the two of us riding FreeBikes one day; me in my red, white, and blue costume for the school's International Flags day . . . and so on.

Ramzy speaks up, a touch of indignation in his voice. "You . . . you were spying on us?"

I have to say, it's all a bit creepy.

"Aah, relax, kid! Look: what do you notice about these pictures?"

We peer at them, but I can't think of anything (apart, obviously, from how strange it is to be photographed without knowing it). Eventually, Dr. Pretorius says, "Look, guys—you're the only two on your own! Every other kid is with a parent, or babysitter, or whatever. Well, those who don't get a car or a taxi home."

It's true, of course. Ramzy and I are pretty much the only kids who walk home alone.

"That told me something. And then when you started to quiz my builder that day? I figured, *Hmm—curious kids*. You see, you kids are all so darn protected these days. You don't play out in the street. You get taken everywhere—everybody except for you. I'd see you on the beach with those dogs and walking home on your own. And well . . . it turned out you were just what I needed. Also, you don't wear glasses. Multisensory virtual reality requires near-perfect vision."

"So . . . that day on the beach, when we met?" says Ramzy suspiciously.

"All kinda engineered. Well, apart from your dog eating my swim cap. That was a piece of luck."

"Your watch?" I say.

"Already scratched."

"Your wrist?"

She averts her eyes and even looks a bit embarrassed. "Sorry." She glances up and sees our shocked expressions. "Hey, don't bail on me now. We're so close."

"So close to *what*?" I say. I can't keep the impatience from my voice. Dr. Pretorius narrows her eyes.

"You'll see. Trust me, kid. You'll see. It's nearly time for the Big Experiment."

"Today?" says Ramzy, who's still buzzing after shooting down an attack helicopter containing scary-looking aliens.

Dr. Pretorius doesn't answer directly. She just says, "Gimme a week, kiddos. One week. I'll take you somewhere no one has ever been before." She unlocks the door that leads through to the Spanish City arcade and the tea rooms. I do a quick check for Sass Hennessey's mum and am relieved that she isn't there. She has seen me a few times, I'm pretty sure—and although she hasn't said anything, I still worry that she might.

Although, as it turns out, there are bigger things to worry about.

Because this is the week that everything goes wrong.

It is the week everybody learns about the plague.

Chapter Ten

First, though, I need to explain about St. Woof's.

The old parish church of St. Wulfran and All Saints—known to everyone as St. Woof's—is a smallish church not far from the seafront, and old, with a short, fat steeple. Except it's not a church anymore—at least not one with a congregation, and a choir, and weddings and stuff. Now it's just a building in the shape of a church. It's got heavy wooden doors, and together with the thick sandstone walls, they do a good job of holding in the noise made by twenty-five dogs.

It is also my most favorite place in the whole world.

I first took Ramzy to St. Woof's at the start of last semester. I wanted him to know what I'd been talking about (or, as he put it, "boring everyone senseless with"—*thanks, Ramz*).

The first thing a newcomer notices about St. Woof's is the noise: the howling, the barking, the yapping, and the snuffling. I love the noise almost as much as I love the second thing you notice—the smell. I was horrified to see that Ramzy had clapped a hand over his nose.

"Oh by goodness," he said through his pinched nose. "It stigs!"

"You get used to it." I hardly even notice it anymore, to be honest. Dogs *do* smell a bit, but they usually smell nice: sort of warm and woody. And—fun fact—their paws smell of popcorn. Honestly!

(I know their breath can be a bit fishy and I'm happy to admit that their poop really is foul, but then—sorry to say this—whose isn't?)

Anyway, it was a Saturday morning, just before we start the weekly clean, when I turned up with Ramzy and that's when St. Woof's smells the strongest.

"Good morning, Georgie!" said the vicar. I like the vicar: he's quite old, probably seventy. He's sort of lean with shaggy gray hair like an Irish wolfhound. That day he was wearing a huge, hand-knitted sweater and fingerless gloves. He sat at the long table just inside the door. "And who do we have here, perchance?" he said when he saw Ramzy. He talks like that. You get used to it.

Without waiting for me to answer, Ramzy clicked his heels together and saluted. "Ramzy Rahman, at your service, *sah!*"

The vicar was a little taken aback, but then lots of people

are when they first meet Ramzy. After a few seconds, though, he returned the salute and smiled.

"Welcome aboard, Private Rahman! I suppose you've come to help, ah . . . Sergeant Santos?" He removed his glasses and reached under his baggy sweater to extract an untucked shirttail to polish them on. Ramzy nodded enthusiastically.

"Top-notch! Tickety-boo! Many hands make light work, eh?" He replaced his glasses and peered at a worksheet on his desk. "You are on your usual station, Georgie. Clean first, brush afterward, and remember . . ." He held up a finger, his eyes looking humorous for a moment. We said it together:

"Whatsoever ye do, do it heartily, as to the Lord!"

"Jolly good, Georgie. Off you go!"

Ramzy's face was contorted in puzzlement as we walked away. "What the heck was that?" he said, easily loud enough for the vicar to hear.

"*Shhh!* No idea. It's old Bible stuff. The vicar likes it. It's kinda fun, and he—"

"Wait. He's a *vicar*?"

"Used to be. He doesn't wear the gear. Grab that bucket there. This was his church. Then I guess no one came anymore, so they turned it into St. Woof's and allowed him to stay on."

Most of the old wooden church seats have gone. Instead,

in the center of the church is an indoor exercise pen covered in sawdust. Around the sides are all of the kennels. It's pretty awesome.

My station, the vicar had said. I love that. It's like the four dogs in the adjacent pens on the first level actually belong to me. My name goes on the board like this:

STATION 4

SATURDAY VOLUNTEER: GEORGINA SANTOS

and I feel a little surge of pride even though it's just handwritten on a whiteboard.

The dogs on Station 4 are some of the longest residents at St. Woof's, who have a promise that they will never, ever "put a dog to sleep."

That's what some other dog shelters do. If they can't rehome a dog, or find its original owner, then after a few months the vet comes and . . .

Do you know what? Even thinking about it upsets me. That's why I love St. Woof's. They will try to rehome dogs, but if they can't, well . . . they become long-term residents.

With Ramzy following me, I gave him a tour and I just couldn't help sounding a little important as I pointed out the cages, and the care sheets hanging outside each one. It's quite old-fashioned: things are written down by hand on the sheets, like fresh-water top-up (check, with a pencil on a string), daily brushing (check), stool analysis (check), and so on.

And as for the dogs themselves:

1. **Ben.** Jack Russell mixed with something else, possibly spaniel. Black, white, and brown. Age— about six. Quite snarly with new people, which is why he hasn't found a home yet.

Ben bared his teeth at Ramzy, who backed off.

"It's OK," I reassured him. "His bark really is worse than his bite."

"He bites as *well*?"

"No! Not usually. He gave me a little nip once, but I think he was playing."

Ramzy didn't seem reassured and kept his distance while I topped off Ben's water, picked up a poo with a poo-picker, and put it in the bucket that Ramzy was holding at arm's length.

2. **Sally-Ann.** Sally-Ann's a "paying guest" because her owner, Mrs. Abercrombie, is very old and is often in a care home. She's brown and white, very hairy, and always has a haughty look on her

flat face. (The dog, that is, not Mrs. Abercrombie, although come to think of it they are quite alike.) Sally-Ann is a purebred Lhasa apso.

3. **Dudley.** A brown Staffie/bulldog cross who *looks* terrifying because half of one ear is missing, plus some teeth, one eye, and a patch of hair on his side. We think he was in a fight and he's now very timid.

He shrank away from Ramzy, trembling. He's OK with me, though, and I felt a little smug when he let me pat him. And finally my favorite:

4. **Mr. Mash.** You've already met him, but that day he was especially friendly, wagging his tail and rolling onto his back for a tummy rub. I think Ramzy fell for him too.

The other people at St. Woof's are also nice. They're all older than me, but they don't treat me like a kid. Well, apart from Saskia Hennessey, who *is* older than me—by a whole eight months—and treats me like I'm about five, even though she only walks the dogs and certainly doesn't have her own station.

I happen to know (from Ellie McDonald at school) that

Sass's mum *pays* her to be a volunteer dog-walker, which if you ask me is totally weird. It's not volunteering if you get paid for it. On top of that, I don't even think Sass likes dogs all that much.

That day she was standing by the poop chute in the old vestry when Ramzy and I came in with the bucket, and I felt my good mood deflate just a little.

The poop chute is a wide, square tunnel that leads to a big pit outside, where all the dog poo goes. You lift the lid of the hatch and tip the poo down it, and then add a cupful of activator, which breaks down the poo into compost, which the vicar then spreads on his allotment. (I've only just found this out. We've been eating his home-grown stuff for years. Eww.)

You can imagine: twenty-five dogs produce a *lot* of poo, and doing the poop chute is the only bit of St. Woof's that I don't really like, although, because of Ramzy, I was trying not to show it.

Sass is in our year at school but looks about fifteen. She's already got boobs and hips, plus a double chin and a round belly to go with them. She's really strong and can lift up the twins, Roddy and Robyn Lee, one under each arm.

My stomach fluttered when I saw her because, although she's not exactly a bully (Marine Drive Elementary has a zero-tolerance approach to bullying), she still manages to be scary.

"Wow—look who it isn't!" she said, fixing her small eyes on Ramzy. "You two make a happy couple walking up the aisle together!"

I gave her a tight smile, pretending to find her comment funny, but I didn't say anything, which I find is usually the best approach. Sass crossed her arms and tilted her chin toward Ramzy. "Is that your *school shirt* you're wearing? At the weekend? You are allowed to change, you know."

I hadn't noticed till then, but Ramzy was indeed wearing his blue school polo shirt under his too-big jacket. Ramzy shrugged and murmured, "It's clean. And I like it."

She's quite intimidating, and as I lifted the lid of the poop chute, Sass took a step forward and said, "Careful you don't fall in."

It made me flinch, as though she was going to push me. I kept quiet as I tipped the contents of the bucket down the hatch. Ramzy, though, never keeps quiet.

"At least she'd fit," he murmured. *Ramzy,* I thought. *That's not necessary.*

"What was that? Are you making fun of—" She was cut off midsentence by the vicar, who came in, rubbing his hands.

"Ah! Good work, good work! *The hands that removeth the dog poo are blessed in the eyes of the Lord.*"

"Is that the Bible?" asked Ramzy.

"No, no—that's just one of mine," said the vicar.

As Ramzy and I left, Sass scowled at us.

That's the thing with her. You know that expression "If you can't say anything nice, say nothing?" Well, Sass seems to have got it the wrong way round: "If you can't say anything mean, say nothing."

It was a mean comment by Sass Hennessey that, a few weeks later, nearly caused the end of the world. And if you think I'm exaggerating, then let me explain.

You see, up until recently, all of the dogs in St. Woof's were healthy. And now . . . well, now they're not.

And it is all down to me.

Chapter Eleven

It has become a big thing in the last year or two: Disease Transmission Risk. At school it's DTR this, DTR that, and the only good thing about it is that you only need to cough in class to get sent home.

Last year, every classroom at Marine Drive Elementary had a hand sanitizer installed by the door. I think it was a new law.

So one of my jobs when I'm at St. Woof's is the maintenance of the sani-mats and hand-sans in the quarantine area. The sani-mats are wet, spongy mats that clean the bottom of your shoes when you go in and out of the quarantine area, which is where dogs go when they're sick.

Anyway, it all happened a few days after our first visit to Dr. Pretorius and the dome.

I had topped up the disinfectant in the sani-mats first; then I went into the quarantine section to see Dudley, who had a tummy bug. It wasn't his first time there, so I wasn't especially worried. If you remember, he'd been gnawing on a dead seagull at the beach, and I thought that might have been the cause.

He was behind a fence of wire mesh that comes up to my chin. There were rain boots and rubber gloves by the entrance gate, which I put on before I went in. He wagged his bent tail weakly.

"Hello, you funny old thing!" I said. "Are you feeling better?" Normally, I'd let Dudley lick my face, but we're not allowed to do that with the quarantine dogs, so instead I gave him a good old tickle on his tummy. It wasn't quite the same with rubber gloves, but he didn't seem to mind.

A family had been in to see him a few days before, perhaps to adopt him, but I think he was just too odd-looking.

"The little girl thought he was cute," said the vicar, "and she said something to her mum in Chinese. Then they all had a long conversation that I didn't understand—except the dad was pointing to Dudley's eye, and his teeth and his ear, and then they left."

Poor, ugly Dudley! I thought of the little girl from China falling in love with him and then her dad saying he was too strange-looking.

Secretly, though, I was very relieved. I *know* it's better for a dog to be with a family rather than in St. Woof's, but I couldn't bear it if Dudley was adopted.

I looked at him carefully. He didn't seem very well, poor doggie. He hadn't eaten much of his food, but he had drunk his water and done a poo in the sand tray, which I washed out and sanitized, and I did everything right, exactly according to the rules. Then I threw his soggy tennis ball for him a little, but it didn't excite him very much and anyway I bounced it too hard so that it went over the fence and rolled away and we had to stop.

I was coming out of the quarantine area, I'd done the sani-mats, and I was about to do the hand-sans (which were empty) and who was standing there but Sass Hennessey. She did this little hair flick and stood with one hand on her hip.

"*Hiiiii!*" she said, but there was *zero* warmth in her eyes.

"Hello, Saskia," I said.

"I was just saying to Maurice that he's got the place looking really nice now," she said.

Maurice? *Maurice?* Nobody calls the vicar Maurice, apart from my dad, who's known him for years. Everyone else calls him Reverend Cleghorn. It was so typical of Sass to call him by his first name, though. I was annoyed already, and what came next was worse.

"That ugly old mutt in there," she said with her head to one side, all fake sorrow. "It really would be kinder just to put him down, don't you reckon?"

That was it: the mean comment I mentioned before. It

took me a few seconds to realize she was talking about Dudley. *Dudley—my second-favorite dog in the whole of St. Woof's!* I could feel my jaw working up and down, without any sound coming out.

"Are you OK, Georgie?"

"Yes, I'm fine, Sass." But I wasn't. I was furious. In silence, I refilled the hand-sans, removed my gloves, and put some of the gel on my hands, rubbing it in angrily while she just stood there. Then I took off the boots.

"Look, I didn't mean—"

"You know we don't do that here. So why did you even say it?" I was furious.

"But if he's very ill and old—"

I snapped, loudly: "He's not *that* ill and he's not *that* old. All right?"

I could tell Sass was a bit taken aback. She said quietly, *"Ooo-kaaay,"* and I thought for once I might have got the better of her.

She bent down and gingerly picked up Dudley's spit-soaked ball, which had rolled toward the door. She handed it to me and I was forced to say "Thanks." It was an odd sort of peace offering.

I turned the ball over in my hands as I watched her walk away, and then tossed it back to Dudley, shutting the quarantine door behind me.

I was still mad when I got back to my station. Ramzy was waiting for me, and he was holding Ben, the snarly Jack Russell, who was trying to lick his face.

"Look!" he laughed, all proud. "I've made a friend!"

"So you have," I said. "Good boy, Ben," and I let him nuzzle my hand. Then I went round the rest of the dogs in the station, giving them a final pat before I left.

"Bye, Vicar!" I said, pulling on the big door.

"Goodbye, Sergeant Santos and Private Rahman!" said the vicar, giving another salute. "Jolly good work!"

So that was it. Damage done. I had started the End of the World.

Obviously, I didn't know it at the time. I've kept the secret till now: how I handled the tennis ball that was infected with Dudley's germs, germs that he had picked up from the little girl who had wanted to adopt him. I then passed on the infection to poor Ben by letting him lick my germy hands, and then to the other dogs . . .

Turns out that all the DTR lessons in the world can't stop someone from being stupid.

Or—for that matter—being so furious at Sass's mean comment that my mind was all over the place. Which amounts to pretty much the same as being stupid.

Chapter Twelve

"Give me a week," Dr. Pretorius had said. It was seldom out of my thoughts. Another week of secret-keeping.

Secrets are easy to keep so long as no one finds out.

So long as no one sees you. Someone who knows your brother, say. Someone who has just started working at the Spanish City and notices you coming out of the door at the back of the arcade.

Sass Hennessey's sister, Anna, for example, who is in the same school year as my brother Clem and whose mum had got her a Saturday job at the Polly Donkin Tea Rooms.

Give me a week, give me a week. It was going around in my head, like some annoying song that gets stuck, as I was walking back from the Spanish City, up our lane, swinging my school bag. I was surprised to see Clem come out of Dad's workshop, wiping his oily hands on a towel.

We live in a farmhouse, although it's not a proper working farm anymore. Nearly all of the other farms around us have been sold for development. You can stand by Mum's tree in the top field with the cows and see houses and cranes and half-built complexes in every direction except from the east, where the sea glints silver in the distance. (The cows are not ours, though I wish they were.)

Down the lane from our farmhouse is Dad's workshop where he restores old cars, and a barn with bits of engines, exhausts, and car doors and stuff.

It looked like Clem had been expecting me.

"Hi, Pie-face," he said. He was cheery. He used his nickname for me for the first time in ages. This made me suspicious, but I smiled.

"Been anywhere exciting?" he asked.

The truth? I had been a participant in a medieval jousting tournament, charging toward Ramzy on a virtual horse (made from an old piano stool and the saddle I had seen on the first day in the loading bay).

"St. Woof's," I lied. I hated lying, even to Clem. I could feel my cheeks going red.

"And how is he?"

"Who?"

"That dog. Ben?"

"Oh, fine! We went on the beach. The usual. He's great." Clem was watching me carefully, and I didn't like it.

He paused for what seemed like forever before saying, "Instant recovery, then?"

I gave Clem my "puzzled but innocent" look: half-smile, blinking.

Clem said, "The vicar called me. He's been trying to call you but your phone's been off."

That was true: we always switched our phones off in Dr. Pretorius's studio—something to do with electromagnetism. I'd forgotten to switch mine back on.

"Let's keep this simple, shall we?" Clem counted off on his blackened fingers as he said: "One: some dog called Ben is sick. He's in quarantine. That's the vicar's message. Two: Anna Hennessey's seen you at the Spanish City with your buddy Ramzy Whatsisname and some spooky old lady. Three: you're lying to me, because you're blushing. And four: I want to know why."

"Or what?" You've got to remember: this is my *brother*. He's supposed to be on *my side*.

"Or I'm telling Dad."

OK, so maybe he's not on my side anymore. Clem nodded, pushed his glasses up his nose with an oily hand, and turned to go back into the workshop, expecting me to follow him.

Did I have a choice?

Chapter Thirteen

I've hardly seen Clem for weeks, it seems. He's finished his exams, so he isn't back at school till September. He was supposed to be going to Scotland with his friends, but it all fell through when one of them got a girlfriend. So he hasn't got much to do before we all go to Spain later in the summer.

For the last couple of weeks, he has occupied himself by messaging people, listening to music, helping Dad in his workshop, and growing a patchy beard. He now looks about twenty.

The thing is: I miss him. Something happened to Clem maybe a year ago. The brother I grew up with—the boy who played with me when I was tiny, who let me ride on his back for what seemed like hours, who lied for me *when he didn't have to* when I left the faucet on and the bath overflowed, who told me his screen login so I could watch stuff when Dad said I couldn't, who once laughed so hard at my impression of Norman Two-Kids at the corner shop that he fell off the bed and banged his head . . .

. . . *that* boy had moved out of our house.

In his place had come a boy who looked exactly the same but behaved differently. A boy who hardly smiled, let alone laughed. A boy who wanted to eat different food from us and, when Dad refused to cook separate meals, got shouty; a boy who could spend a whole weekend (I'm not joking) in his room, emerging only to go to the bathroom; a boy whose response to pretty much everything was to roll his eyes as if it were the stupidest thing he had ever heard.

Dad said it was normal.

But . . . there was one good thing about Clem changing, and it was this: I think I succeeded in persuading him not to tell Dad about Dr. Pretorius, and it was all down to his beard. Sort of. Let me explain.

He was full of questions, and the main one was, "Why is she so secretive? If I'd invented something like that, I'd want everyone to know."

"I don't know, really. She says she's got something even better to show us soon, but right now I think she's probably scared that someone will steal her idea."

And then I added something that—not to sound boastful or anything—was utterly and completely brilliant, and I didn't even plan it. I looked at the floor, all sorrowful, and said, "I know it was wrong, Clem. I really should have told a grown-up. But . . . I think you probably count as that now?"

Clem took off his glasses and held them to the light to check for dirt and smears. It's something he does a lot. "Perfect vision required, eh?" he said, obviously flattered by me calling him an adult, and I nodded.

"So she says. It's why she can't test it herself."

"She'll need to figure that out if it's to be commercial. Two-thirds of people wear glasses, you know?" He picked up a wrench from the bench and turned back to the rusty old campervan that he and Dad had been working on, which meant our conversation was over.

"You won't tell Dad?"

"Not for now. But be careful." He actually sounded like a grown-up then.

Now I could worry about something else instead. The vicar had said Ben was sick. What was that all about?

Everything, as it turned out.

Chapter Fourteen

I couldn't worry for long, though, because that evening was Mum's memorial.

Mum: the mother I never knew.

"Mum's memorial" sounds like it's some big event, but it's just a little thing we do every year, mainly for Dad's sake, I think.

Mum died when I was very little. We have lots of photos and a video clip shot on Dad's phone, so I know what she looked like. In the video, I'm lying on a playmat and I am giggling and trying to grab the toy that Dad is dangling above me.

There's music playing in the background: a song called "You Two" from *Chitty Chitty Bang Bang* and Dad is singing along.

"Someone to care for; to be there for.
I have you two!"

Mum's there too: she's pretty, with long hair in a ponytail and a big smile. She's laughing at Dad's groany singing voice, and he's laughing too. Then Clem comes in, and he looked *so* cute when he was five—especially his chubby knees—and joins in the song.

Which makes Mum giggle more, and the camera pans up to her face with this big smile and then the picture stops.

So I suppose it's not *really* a memory, is it? It's a video clip, shot on Dad's phone. I've seen it hundreds and hundreds—maybe even thousands—of times.

"Cow flu" they called it: that's what she died of. Eleven years ago, the virus was carried across the world on people's shoes, in their fingernails, in their stomachs, in infected meat and foodstuffs, and milk. Thousands and thousands of people died, most of them in South America. Thousands more cattle had to be killed to stop it from spreading. Millions of gallons of milk were poured away while doctors and scientists worked around the clock to develop the vaccine: the special injection that would halt the spread of the disease.

They did discover it, of course. Eventually. But it was too late for Mum. She became one of twelve people in Britain to die of cow flu.

(It was also how Dad met Jessica. Every year Dad raises money for the new biobotics research unit to investigate diseases. It's where Jessica works and, as Dad says, "One good thing leads to another. . . .")

So Mum's ashes are buried beneath a cherry tree in the field where the cows usually are. I know that sounds a bit weird, burying someone near cows when they died of cow flu, but Dad insisted.

"She was an animal lover, just like you, Georgie," he said once. "She wouldn't blame the cows."

You can see Mum's tree from our kitchen window, standing out against the sky, bent and buffeted by the winds off the sea and fertilized by the cows beneath it. Sometimes I catch Dad sitting at the kitchen table, drinking his favorite super-strong coffee, and staring at the tree. It blossoms every spring: a beautiful cloud of white like a massive spool of cotton candy, although there has never been any fruit. Dad says it's too cold.

Every year on her birthday, we—Dad and Clem and I—gather by Mum's tree. Only this year Dad's girlfriend Jessica was with us. You can probably guess how I felt about that.

It was evening and the sun was lower and cooler.

"She's looking good," said Dad as the four of us proceeded up the field toward the tree. Dad always refers to the tree as "she."

She'll be losing her leaves in a week or so. . . .

She's done well to withstand that gale. . . .

That sort of thing. I think it's because he likes to imagine the tree as *being* Mum, but I've only just realized that. I mentioned it to Clem about a year ago, and he just rolled his eyes as if I'd just said that I'd discovered that honey was sweet.

The vicar from St. Woof's was already at the tree when our little group got there. He'd come over the back way.

We're not exactly religious, but the vicar is an old friend of Dad's from way back, in that way that adults can be friends even though they're years apart in age. Dad was one of the last people to go to St. Wulfran's Church before it closed down.

That evening the vicar was wearing his vicar stuff—the black tunic with the white collar—under his zip-up jacket.

We gathered beneath the tree's leafy branches, looking back down the hill toward the sea, and we did exactly what we do every year.

1. Dad reads a poem. It's always the same one: Mum's favorite, Dad says, by someone ancient called Alfred Tennyson. It starts like this:

   > *Sunset and evening star,*
   > *And one clear call for me!*
   > *And may there be no moaning at the bar,*
   > *When I set out to sea . . .*

   I don't really understand it, even though Dad has explained it to me. It's about dying, basically, which is sad, but Dad has a nice voice and I like hearing it.

2. The vicar says a prayer with old-fashioned words. I have heard this every year now and can almost remember it all: *Almighty God, we pray for Cassandra, and for all those whom we see no longer . . .* Then my favorite bit: *and let light perpetual shine upon them.* I mouth along with the words when I can remember them.

3. Then Dad takes out his Irish pennywhistle and Clem his big old tenor recorder that he got as a prize in elementary school. They both play an old hymn called "Amazing Grace." Under any other circumstances it would sound awful: the high-pitched whistle and Clem's squeaky and inaccurate playing. But somehow, on that cool evening in summer, the tune is perfect, rising above Mum's cherry tree and floating off into the wind and down to the ocean.

And all the while, Jessica has this face on like she'd rather be *anywhere* else.

While the vicar was saying the prayer, I cracked open my eyes a little and saw her: eyes wide, gazing around everywhere, not praying *at all.* Then our gazes met for a second, and she just stared at me. I'm sorry to say it, but I hated her at that moment.

At the end of the music, I was startled to see that the cows had gathered round us in an almost perfect semicircle. Their huge eyes watched us and their tails flicked over their creamy brown flanks.

Dad took the pennywhistle from his mouth. He wiped his eyes and smiled. "Hello, girls," he said to the cows. "Come to join in?" As if answering him, one of them mooed softly, while another lifted its tail and deposited a loud, splattering cow pie on the ground. It made us laugh, except Jessica, who flinched in horror.

There was one more tradition. In turn, Clem and I stood with our backs against the tree trunk. Dad took out a pocket-knife and cut a notch in the wood to indicate our heights, and we compared. Clem had grown about six inches in the last year. Me? Hardly anything.

Dad smiled as he folded up the knife. "Ah, don't worry, dear: you're due for a growth spurt. You've plenty left in you yet!"

And that was it: Mum's memorial.

Dad clapped his hands and turned to the vicar. "Right, then, Maurice. You comin' back for a drink?"

The vicar looked surprised, although it's the same every

year. "Now you mention it, Rob, that sounds good." But then he took out his phone and read something on it. "Ah. Maybe not."

"Problem?" said Dad.

The vicar pursed his lips and looked to the sky. "Probably not. I've got to meet a vet. Another time, eh, Rob? God bless you all. Don't worry about me—I'm fine to walk."

He saw the look on my face.

"Is it Ben?" I said, immediately aware that I hadn't yet asked him about it. Then I added, "Is it Mr. Mash?" I was scared of the answer I might get.

"I'm sure it's nothing, Georgie. And Mr. Mash is fine. For now," he said, before turning and stalking off purposefully in the direction of St. Woof's, muttering to himself.

For now!

It turned out that the vicar meeting a vet was the start of everything bad I have ever known.

Chapter Fifteen

Right. I think you're nearly caught up, in terms of the things you need to know.

It's now the last week of term, and everyone—including the teachers—seems to be going a bit crazy.

The day after Mum's memorial was no-uniform day: you bring in £3 for charity and you can wear anything you like. The Lee twins came dressed as Thing One and Thing Two from *The Cat in the Hat*. Ramzy came in his uniform. He said he'd forgotten, which seems unlike him. And Mr. Parker, the new headmaster, wore a kilt during assembly, which made everyone laugh when he did a little dance.

Ramzy's eyes were nearly popping out. "He's wearing a *skirt*!" he whispered to me. I tried to explain but it was hard.

He hissed, "So do *all* Scottish men wear them?"

"No! Not all the time! Mostly never, I mean . . ." I was silenced by Mr. Springham's loud throat-clearing and a stern look.

It all meant no one was really listening when Mr. Parker delivered yet another lecture about Disease Transmission Risk.

All I picked up was CBE—something-something Ebola— and with a mouthful like that, it's hardly surprising I didn't really make the connection with St. Woof's, like I should have done.

After school, I was *dying* to tell Dad about Mr. Parker's kilt and I practically ran home. It was the sort of thing that would make him laugh his deep, coffee-scented laugh, and he'd have a few funny lines of his own to add as well. Only, when I got in, Jessica was sitting at the kitchen table along with Dad and Clem. She wasn't normally home from work this early (which usually suits me fine), so something was up. . . .

"Georgina," she said, bringing her sharp elbows up to rest on the table. "I'm afraid I've got bad news." I have to hand it to Jessica: she doesn't beat around the bush. I suppose this is a good thing, but sometimes I wish she wasn't so blunt. Sharp *and* blunt: that's Jessica. The deflation of my mood, which had begun when I saw her, was instant. I felt as empty as a popped balloon.

She said: "You know I've been working a lot lately."

I nodded. Like I said, Jessica works at a medical research laboratory attached to the hospital, helping develop vaccines. She'd been working late for weeks recently, and on weekends.

"All vacations have been canceled for the next month. It's an emergency—this CBE thing is getting out of hand, and, well . . . they need all the expertise they can get."

I'm sorry to say that my first reaction was not concern about a deadly disease—there had been plenty of scares before. But there it was again: CBE. You don't hear of something ever, and then suddenly it's everywhere.

But I didn't know what the letters stood for, or why it was bad, or where it came from—nothing really.

No, my first reaction was entirely selfish. "Does that mean you're not coming to Spain?"

Dad piped up. "We'll still go to Spain, love. It's just that Jessica won't be able to come."

I composed my face into a slump of disappointment, which was the absolute opposite of what I felt. This was to be our first foreign trip in years. I'd bought two new swimsuits already, one with my own money. I had told myself that Jessica's presence was a small price to pay.

And now I wouldn't have to pay it! Beneath the table my feet were doing a little jig of delight.

"It'll be OK, love," said Dad, and he leaned across to give me a little hug. "I promise Clem and I won't be too boysy." He winked at Clem who, bless him, winked back.

I was thinking: *Where's the bad news? It's all good news so far. . . .* And then Dad said, "There is one more thing."

Uh-oh.

Dad took a deep breath and, very quietly, murmured, "No more St. Woof's."

I did this odd thing where I looked first at Dad, then at Clem, then at Jessica, and then all the way around again. Their faces were different: Dad's eyebrows were practically fused together in anxiety—he *knows* what St. Woof's means to me. Clem's eyes were cast down into his lap. At first, I suspected him of having snitched on me, but then he looked up over his glasses and gave the tiniest shake of his head, which said, *Not me.* Jessica's face was cold and hard, like marble.

Dad was speaking. "I'm sorry, Georgie, but it's just too risky. It's only temporary. I've spoken to Maurice, and he understands."

I was hardly listening. I was staring at Jessica's expressionless face, and she stared right back at me. Eventually, I said to her, "This is you, isn't it?"

And Dad said, "Georgie, love, it's not—"

I wouldn't be stopped. "First I have a dog, and then I can't keep him—because of *you.* Now I can't even see him—because of *you!*"

"It's not about me," said Jessica quietly. "It's about you, Georgina. It's about keeping you safe."

"And since when did you care about *that*? You're not my mum," I spat.

Dad said: "Georgie, that's enough."

I pushed my chair back noisily and stomped toward the kitchen door, passing Jessica, whose blank face had not changed.

"I'm sorry, Georgina," she said. "But this CBE thing is serious."

This CBE thing.

"I don't care!"

I should have, though.

Later that evening, Jessica was sitting on the sofa, looking at the television, though the sound was turned down. She's been doing this a lot lately and she didn't even notice at first when I sat down on the other end of the sofa.

I wasn't "making peace," you understand, but the *you're not my mum* thing was perhaps a bit much. And it was Dad who had told me that I wasn't to go to St. Woof's. It wasn't all Jessica.

When I'm upset, I can cuddle up to Dad: he has a big, comfortable belly and warm, strong arms and fat fingers and he always smells of, well . . . of *Dad*. Even if I wanted to cuddle her, Jessica is just not cuddly. Not at all. She's not skinny so much as rigid, and her hands are cool to the touch. She's all edges, really, whereas Dad is curves. She always smells of the soap she uses at work. It's not a flowery soap—it's more medical.

I leaned forward to pick up the remote control, and there was this awkward moment when Jessica thought I was leaning in for a cuddle.

As if!

She opened her arms to draw me in, but then I was back at my end of the sofa and she had to lower her arms as if nothing had happened. I almost felt sorry for her. Almost.

Her eyes were closed, and her mouth was drawn thin with worry, with little lines all around. She has short dark hair, and it's usually gelled up and spiky. Today it was just flat on her head.

"Hello, Georgina," she said. That's another thing: she *never* calls me Georgie. "How was school today?"

"It was OK," I said. I had been rehearsing in my head how I'd tell them about my day, and Mr. Parker's kilt, and the little dance he did, and Ramzy forgetting about no-uniform day, but I wasn't going to waste it on Jessica.

She turned her head toward the window and took a deep breath, as if she was wondering whether or not to say anything. She turned back to look at me and I saw the fear across her pale face.

"Pass me my laptop, please. I want to show you something."

She typed a few words to bring up the page she had been looking at.

INDEPENDENT NEWS CORP.

BREAKING NEWS
New Canine Disease "Spreading Fast,"
says International Health Foundation.

CLICK FOR MORE

I clicked, though I could feel my hand trembling. I already knew that it would be bad news.

Chapter Sixteen

HONG KONG, CHINA

The International Health Foundation has issued a rare Grade 1 Alert, warning countries worldwide to be on the alert for a new and deadly disease affecting dogs.

The illness is believed to be caused by a mutant virus similar to that which caused last year's outbreak of swine Ebola (HGR-66) and resulted in the slaughter of more than half of China's herds of domestic pigs.

That virus posed no risk to humans, but spread rapidly through mainland Asia before scientists discovered an effective antiviral.

Dr. Gregor Zamtev of the IHF told *Independent News*, "This disease—canine-borne Ebola—is potentially far more damaging. The symptoms are slow to emerge, so the disease can spread widely before it is seen."

Outbreaks have so far been confined to Jiangsu Province in eastern China. In the city of Nanjing, authorities have already begun a program of mass slaughter of stray dogs in an attempt to control the spread of the virus.

Dr. Zamtev added, "At present, we do not anticipate a risk to humans, although if the disease were to mutate further, there is a possibility that it will be highly dangerous."

IHF virologists and biobotics researchers in China, the USA, and Great Britain are working simultaneously to discover the cure for this frightening new disease.

I read it again, then closed the laptop.

Jessica's voice was shaky. "Things are developing very quickly, Georgina. It's why I've been working so hard. I'm really rather concerned. If this thing spreads as we fear it might, then . . ."

Perhaps I looked scared—I don't really know. I *do* know that hearing Jessica—cool, quiet Jessica, who never gets flustered—say, "I'm really rather concerned," was like hearing anyone else say, *Oh my God, I'm terrified!*

Anyway, she paused, sighed, and said, "I'm sure it will be fine, Georgina. These things have always worked out in the past."

She wasn't looking at me, so I said, "Do you promise?"

"I cannot promise. It is not up to me. All we can do is work hard, do our best, and hope."

I looked across at her and she was staring out the window while the people on television continued their silent drama. Then her arm came up, the one farthest from me, and she brushed something from her eye that might have been a tear but—knowing Jessica—probably wasn't.

Chapter Seventeen

Two days after Mum's memorial, and I'm missing St. Woof's so badly. Thinking about it distracts me from everything else, even Dr. Pretorius's upcoming Big Experiment, which until now has kind of dominated my thoughts. Though it's very close now—it's been seven days since she said, "Give me a week."

I keep looking at the St. Woof's website, where there's a webcam, hoping to catch glimpses of my dogs. I saw Mr. Mash being taken out for a walk yesterday by Sass Hennessey. *She hasn't been banned from St. Woof's,* I thought, feeling my dislike of Jessica increasing still further. I was so furious I felt myself starting to cry, so I stopped watching.

But at least it's the last day of term.

My last day at Marine Drive Elementary. I know I should be totally excited, and everyone's laughing in the playground, but I feel like there's a heavy weight tied round my feet. If I were a dog, I'd have my tail right between my legs. I haven't even seen Ramzy for what seems like ages.

Mr. Springham's been nice. He got everyone in the class a little present with a personal note attached. Mine was one of those extra-bouncy balls and the note said, *Because you'll always bounce back,* which I thought was cool.

In the afternoon, there's a big assembly, and Mr. Parker—back in his pants, which is a shame—does this speech:

". . . respect for each other's differences . . ."

The sun is shining directly into my eyes.

". . . hard work always pays off in the end . . ."

The kid in front of me has a sweat patch in the middle of his back in the shape of Africa that is spreading.

". . . express your feelings . . . take responsibility . . . becoming responsible citizens . . ."

Yes, yes, we get it. Ramzy and I are due in the Spanish City dome later, and the secrecy thing is still bugging me.

It is not helped by Sass Hennessey's comment in the lunch line.

I was standing with some of the girls in my class who I'm quite friendly with. Sass and Ellie McDonald cut in behind us.

"It's OK," said Sass to the people who objected. "Georgie's let me in: haven't you, Georgie?"

Before I could answer, Sass picked up a tray and edged past me. "Hi, Georgie! Thanks. I was just telling Ellie about our lovely Mr. Mash. I mean, stupid name, but isn't he gorgeous?"

I didn't know what to say. *Our* Mr. Mash? And *I* came up with his name, which is *not* stupid: it fits him perfectly. I swallow hard and continue staring, which must have looked strange, but it didn't shut her up.

"And what about you and Ramzy in the Spanish City, eh? What's your big secret?"

It all *sounded* as though she was being nice and friendly, but there's always something else going on with Sass. I still hadn't said anything, but I looked between the two of them, furious. Sass continued as she loaded a slice of chicken pie onto a plate. "Yeah, my sister Anna saw you. With that weird old lady—what's all that about?"

I had to say *something*. I had been completely silent and I realized I was being weird. In the end, I settled for a long "Ermmmm . . ." Pathetic, I know, but Sass didn't seem to care.

"All the staff at the Spanish City know her. Is she a doctor? I heard she bought the whole dome, and she's got some movie or games studio or *something* up there. My mum's boyfriend knows a guy who worked on it. Have you seen it?"

"Erm . . . no. No. I, erm . . . Ooh, look! Tuna macaroni again. Yum—my favorite." It isn't, but I needed something to say.

"So what *were* you doing there with her?" Sass wasn't

97

being aggressive: she was chatty, but she wanted answers, and wasn't going to be distracted by me pointing at a tray of pasta bake.

Ellie, however, had picked up on my discomfort. "Yeah, apparently, you were seen coming out of the door marked 'private'—what are you hiding, Georgie?"

"Oh! Ha ha! Hiding? There's nothing to hide! She's just, erm . . ." I'm hopeless when caught out like this. My brain just sort of melts. I was actually on the point of saying, "Ooh, look—salad!"

"We just got lost, didn't we? 'Scuse me, Saskia," said Ramzy, who squeezed in between us and sounded as relaxed as anything. "It's a flippin' maze, eh? We went to the toilets at the back and took a wrong turning and ended up in this big loading bay. The door slammed behind us, didn't it, Georgie?"

"What? Oh yeah. Yeah. Slammed shut. Bang! Just like that. Shut. Behind us. Ha ha!" I was overdoing it, I could tell, but Ramzy stayed cool.

"So, yeah. Then this old lady turned up—what did she say her name was, Georgie?"

"Oh, erm . . . Doctor something-or-other." I was improving.

"And anyway, she had a key to the other door and she let us back in." It was a brilliant display of calm, convincing lying. It would have fooled anyone.

"You're lying," said Sass, her eyes narrowing. "There are no public toilets there. They're round the side. I know because I used them just last week. And besides, why would you go to the toilets together and *both* get lost?"

We had finished collecting our food, and, trays laden, we were looking for somewhere to sit. All it took was for Ramzy to say, "Erm . . . ," just like I had, and I knew he wasn't going to think up a convincing get-out this time.

So I dropped my tray. I sort of pretended to trip, then overbalanced and dropped the whole thing: food, plate, glass of water, everything, which fell to the floor with a mighty crash and tinkle, followed by a loud *"WHHHAAAAAYYYY!"* from everyone in the dining hall, which was the usual reaction. And the distraction worked. Unwilling to help clear it up, Ellie and Sass scuttled to the far end of the dining hall, while Ramzy and I got the mop and bucket.

"Good work, fellow adventurer," murmured Ramzy as we loaded the bucket with broken china and macaroni. "See you at four o'clock!"

I had almost forgotten the Big Experiment and suddenly felt a churning in my stomach.

". . . *a big Marine Drive Elementary cheer for our departing students. Hip hip . . .*"

"*HOORAY!*"

Well, that wakes me up from my daydreaming.

As usual, the sound system starts playing that old rock song "School's Out."

And then I'm outside, surrounded by my classmates, who are signing each other's shirts with Sharpies, and I'm grinning and hoping that someone will ask me to do theirs, but no one does, and my smile is becoming a bit fixed. This must be what Dad feels like with the mums at the school gates.

(He stopped coming to pick me up from school when I got to fourth grade. I didn't mind: I used to feel sorry for him, standing slightly apart from all the chatting mums, either looking at his phone or staring into space.)

It's a silly thing anyway, I tell myself. Who's going to wear a shirt with names scrawled all over it?

"Hey! Wanna sign my shirt?"

It's Ramzy and he's waving a marker at me. "How was it? Usual speech?"

"You weren't there?"

"You gotta be kidding. I figured I wouldn't be missed. Instead, I had some quality time on the roof with my girlfriend."

Ramzy's "girlfriend" is his favorite author, Enid Blyton; he had a book shoved in his back pocket. At breaktimes and after lunch, he often sneaks off to a little alcove in the library, which is probably why I haven't seen him lately. The roof, though, is strictly out of bounds, and when I point this out to Ramzy, he just laughs.

"What are they gonna do on the last day, Georgie? Give me detention? Expel me? Now are you signin' me shirt or what? Aunty Nush might kill me, but it's worth the risk." I look at his shirt: it's faded and worn and way too small for him. It's stretched so tight that it'll be easy to write on. He turns his back and I scrawl: *Good luck from Georgie* and then add *X*.

He feels the two strokes of the *X* and says, "Hey! Was that a kiss? I don't mind, G, but you gotta remember: my heart is for Enid only!" which makes me smile. Most kids our age have stopped reading Enid Blyton, but Ramzy doesn't care.

We walk back in silence toward the seafront; then Ramzy says, "Blimey, Georgie—why the long face?" and he starts singing, *"Scho-o-o-l's out for summer!"*

The whole summer stretches ahead of me like a hot, empty road. Even a week in Spain without Jessica doesn't make up for a whole summer without St. Woof's.

When I say this to Ramzy, he says, "Man, that sucks," and I immediately feel bad complaining. Ramzy never gets to go abroad: his dad can't afford it. He can't go "home" either because his home country doesn't even exist anymore, thanks to the war that brought him here in the first place.

("Nowhere-istan," he calls it, which is kind of funny in a dark way.)

We carry on in silence for a bit longer, and then I see her. Dr. Pretorius is waiting for us by the big back doors of the Spanish City.

The Big Experiment is about to begin, and it is too late to back out.

Chapter Eighteen

Dr. Pretorius grins wolfishly, like her door knocker, which sends a shiver through me. I don't mind admitting I am nervous. It is not only the whole "keeping a secret" thing, plus the fact that Sass's sister spotted us. It's also because this visit to Dr. Pretorius has been growing in my head so that I now think of it as:

THE BIG EXPERIMENT!

I don't dare admit it to Ramzy, but I really didn't want to come. I list the reasons in my head:

> *Dangerous.*
> *Risky.*
> *Unsafe.*
> And so on.

I know: all variations of *dangerous*, really, although I have no idea why. To be honest, I think I'm just scared.

I am on the brink of telling him, but his "fellow adventurer" comment earlier made him look so excited that I tell myself I'm being unnecessarily cautious, though I don't use those words. *Stop being a wimp, Georgie* is what I say in my head.

And why is Dr. Pretorius *grinning*? She practically skips like a girl up the metal steps to the studio and opens the double doors without looking back at us. She shrugs on a white lab coat and shouts, "Studio lights!" They flicker on as we follow her to the control room. On the desk is a large bottle of Fanta with three glasses and a plate of foil-wrapped chocolate cookies: definitely an improvement on the cheap cookies and supermarket cola we've had before.

"Hey, wow!" says Ramzy appreciatively, and he reaches out for a cookie. Like a frog catching a fly, Dr. Pretorius's hand slaps his and shoots back again.

"Manners! They're for afterward. To celebrate! I think we oughta sit down, and you had better listen." Then she stops and her brow wrinkles in confusion. "Why have you got writing all over your clothes?"

"It's the end of the semester today," I explain. "It's a tradition."

Dr. Pretorius's eyebrows shoot up above her spectacles. She shakes her head slightly and says a flat "Ha." I can't tell whether she's amused or if she disapproves.

We sit on the stools, and Dr. Pretorius sits in her wheeled desk chair and takes from a drawer the familiar bicycle helmet. Her voice goes very quiet: she is almost whispering.

"I reckon you should know: you two are the first people ever to see this! Apart from me, of course."

Ramzy's eyes flick to meet mine. This is getting weird. The three of us sit there, gazing at the helmet. Seconds tick by until eventually I break the silence.

"B-but we *have* seen it. Haven't we?"

Her voice is still hushed and husky. "This is different. So very, very different."

There's a long pause, while Ramzy and I wait for her to tell us. We both jump when she barks at us: "Well? Aren't you gonna ask me how? Jeez, you kids today! So *incurious*! I spend my whole life making this thing that's gonna—"

"How?" says Ramzy to shut her up, I think. "How is it different?"

Dr. Pretorius stops midsentence. "You wanna know?"

"Of course we do. That's why we're here, isn't it, Georgie?"

I nod vigorously. Evidently satisfied with our enthusiasm, Dr. Pretorius takes a deep breath.

"This," she murmurs, "is going to change the world." She strokes the curved top of the helmet as though it were a cat and seems to be gazing at her reflection in the shiny surface.

We wait, and eventually she begins talking again. She looks up at me, and it's as if a light has gone on behind her ice-blue eyes. Her skin seems to glow and she talks urgently as she stares at me.

"You! Have you ever wondered what it would be like to see the future? To know what's going to happen tomorrow? Or next week? Or next year?"

The truthful answer would be a half-shrug, but I guess that would upset her, so instead I say, "Yes. All the time," which isn't strictly true, but it satisfies her. She grins and gets to her feet, waving the bicycle helmet at us.

"Well, now you can."

Chapter Nineteen

Ramzy—as always—is bolder than me. When Dr. Pretorius asks him if he ever tries to imagine the future, he says: "Not really."

"Nonsense!" she snaps. "Everybody does! What's the weather gonna be tomorrow, hmm?"

Ramzy looks a bit scared, and I begin to feel sorry for him. It's as though he's being picked on. "I'm not sure, but apparently it's going to get even warmer after the weekend."

"Exactly! Weather forecasts! We've been predicting the future for years! But tell me this, young man: is it *definitely* going to be warmer?"

"I don't know. I don't think weather forecasts are definite, are they?"

"No! They're just guesses. *Educated* guesses—but guesses all the same. Hundreds of people gather the data from around the country. Air temperatures, sea temperatures, wind speed, atmospheric pressure, heck—from around the *world*—and they punch it into computers, and the computers do their thing and—hey presto!—we can tell you exactly what the weather will be at the weekend. Is that right?"

Ramzy says, "Yeah. Sounds right to m—"

"Wrong!" She says it so loudly that we both jump. "All they can tell us is what the weather will *probably* be at the weekend. So the woman on the television or the guy on the radio—they're not predicting the *actual* future, just the *probable* future."

(*Probable.* Remember that word. It's going to be important.)

"So imagine if a computer could gather *all* of the information about everything around us: not just the weather, but the movements of people, of vehicles, how plants grow, how a leaf blows in the wind, how somebody speaks . . . *everything*! And then process it all. Every last bit of information. Then what?"

I'm still trying to take in this idea, and don't realize at first that Dr. Pretorius is pointing at me.

"Georgie!" she yaps impatiently. "What can the computer do with all this information?"

Slowly, I ease an answer out. It's just like being in school but scarier. Her eyes are wide, and I really think she might explode if I get it wrong.

"Erm . . . does the computer process it, and predict . . . the future? A *probable* future?"

"Yes!" she yells, grinning. (I think it's my use of the word *probable* that delights her.) "Exactly, kiddo! And then, using multisensory virtual reality, we re-create that probable future, allowing us to experience it as if it's really happening! Forget about weather forecasts—this is a *world* forecast!"

Dr. Pretorius is breathing hard as she paces the control room, delivering this speech with waving arms and wobbling white hair. A light sweat has appeared on her forehead. After a moment, Ramzy speaks up.

"Is this . . . you know . . . real? Does it work?"

Dr. Pretorius nods vigorously. Her hair follows. "Oh yes, it sure works. In theory. It just needs to be tested."

"And this . . . processing. Doesn't it require, like, an *incredibly* powerful computer?"

Good question. I've got to hand it to Ramzy: he's not afraid to ask.

"Indeed it does, my boy, indeed it does. Good thing I have one, huh? Follow me."

She leads us out of the control room, round the studio floor, and pulls aside a thick black-green curtain. Behind it is a circular window painted black. She pushes it open and the light floods the dark space, making us squint, and casts an elongated circle onto the floor. On a flat roof, just below us, is a large satellite receiver, about two yards across and more or less invisible from street level.

"Check *that* out!" she says proudly.

Ramzy and I both go, "Hmmm!" and "Wow!" although to us, it's just a satellite dish. Dr. Pretorius aims her long forefinger at it.

"Every ninety minutes, for about ten minutes, this baby picks up a live, ultra-high-definition video signal from the US military satellite Hawking II. You heard of it?" We shake our heads and Dr. Pretorius gives a little sigh. "Good. It's not supposed to be well known. It's the most powerful satellite of its kind on Earth. Or actually, *above* Earth. And in case you were wondering how I get access to such a signal . . ."

(We weren't. *You forget we're only kids,* I want to say.)

". . . then let me just say, a lot of money buys a lot of favors. Ha!" Dr. Pretorius turns away from us to close the window and I can see she's smiling to herself, pleased with her "lot of favors" quip.

"Come on, don't lag behind." She strides off again, back toward the control room, where she stops and points to a black metal box, about the size of a washing machine, with a couple of blinking lights on it. I had seen it the last time but had not paid it much attention.

"You've heard of quantum computers?" she asks. "Quomps, they're known as? Well, meet the most powerful in Europe, possibly the world. I call her Little Girl."

This time, when Ramzy and I say, "Wow!" it's sincere.

"It . . . it works? For real?" says Ramzy in awe.

Dr. Pretorius takes her time. She straightens up and nods slowly, a look of deep satisfaction giving her dark skin a flush of pride. "She most certainly does, fella! Even those dullards at NASA and Cambridge University are about ten years behind old Emilia Pretorius and her Little Girl." She pats the shiny unit gently and smiles as she moves back to the desk.

Ramzy and I are left staring at Little Girl, the superpowered computer, while Dr. Pretorius starts bashing away at her keyboard.

I find myself putting my hand up as though I'm still at school. Ramzy smirks and I put it down again.

"Excuse me, Dr. Pretorius?"

She stops jabbing at the keyboard and looks up. She's been so absorbed in whatever she was doing that she seems almost surprised to see me there. "What is it, kid?"

"You say this whole thing, this . . . this Big Experiment is new and untested?"

"Yes, yes. What about it?"

"So . . . why don't you test it yourself?"

Her eyes narrow to slits, and her lips purse tight, and I wonder if I have said the wrong thing.

"I can't," she says eventually. "That's what I need you for."

Chapter Twenty

"What's special about us?" I ask.

Dr. Pretorius gets up from the long desk and comes over to Ramzy and me, and my heart starts to beat harder as I wonder whether she'll be angry at my question.

Instead, she grabs the bicycle helmet again and holds it upside down to reveal the little metal bumps and nodules inside. She shakes her head sadly.

"See these here?" She points at the red-colored bumps that are dotted all over the inside, in between the other nodes. "These are receivers. They detect the minute impulses that your brain makes when it imagines things, and feeds them back into the images that the computer is creating. It's my theory that it's these tiny electrical charges that will make the virtual future so real—in fact, practically indistinguishable from reality."

"I still don't get why you can't do it? I mean . . ." I run my finger over the inside of the helmet, straining to understand what she's telling me.

"While your brain is growing, Georgie, these impulses are at their strongest and most numerous," says Dr. Pretorius, speaking very precisely. "A child's elastic mind, eh? We've always known that it's a wonderful thing—a powerful thing, even. But we had no idea of just *how* powerful. Only a very young person can experience what I have created. Only a young person will *see* the future the system generates. I am way, way too old."

I am pondering this when Ramzy claps his hands and exclaims, with shining eyes, "I've got it! You're saying that this whole thing is powered by imagination!"

Dr. Pretorius beams with pleasure and gives her ascending laugh. "Ha ha ha *haaa*! You're right—or at least partly right! What a wonderful way of putting it, young man!"

Ramzy blushes.

"There's only one problem, kiddos." Dr. Pretorius's face straightens again. "I don't have that long left to discover if my research has been worthwhile."

Ramzy then says simply, "Why are you doing this?"

For a moment, Dr. Pretorius regards Ramzy, her expression a mixture of annoyance and contempt. At last, she repeats, "*Why?*"

Ramzy nods. "Yes, why? I mean, I can see why you'd want to know what the weather's going to be like. But why else would you want to, I dunno, *see the future*?"

It's as if Dr. Pretorius has to wait a moment for the full fury to load. Once it does, she unleashes it.

"Can't you understand?" she yells, and we both flinch. She notices—and dials down her attitude. She continues, a little quieter, but the frustration is just below the surface. It's a struggle for her, I can tell.

"This is something that humanity has been seeking since we lived in caves! Throughout history we have yearned to know what the future holds. Astrologists, soothsayers, prophets, those who cast runes, even palm readers at carnivals! Jeez—have you never read your horoscope and wondered if it might be true? Have you? *Have you?*" She doesn't even wait for us to reply. "This goes way, way beyond knowing whether or not to take an umbrella with you."

She marches out into the vast dark studio, barking her words over her shoulder, her hair shaking with excitement. We peer through the narrow doorway: she strides across the ball-bearing floor and stands in the middle of the dome, arms outstretched, shouting up at the ceiling.

"Just think, Georgie, think, Ramzy—imagine the horrors that could be avoided if we knew they were coming! Wars, murders, tyrants, natural disasters—the possibilities of this are endless!"

She's getting louder. She levels her gaze and whips off her spectacles to fix us with her fierce pale eyes, like a husky's.

"This is not some game. It ain't a fancy toy. Do you not *see*? Isn't it *obvious*? This has the potential to be the greatest thing ever created, and I will *give* it to the world! I don't need more money, but if I die knowing I've prevented a war by foreseeing it, then what greater legacy is there? The parents of soldiers will thank me forever that their children are not killed in battle, their broken young bodies left to rot under a foreign sky!"

Is this something that Dr. Pretorius had rehearsed in her head? She strides up and down that green-black studio as if she's delivering a speech to a crowd, not to me and Ramzy, who stand there, gawping. Anyway, however long this could go on (and I suspect she has rather a lot to say on the subject), she is stopped by an urgent beeping coming from one of the computer screens in the control room.

She halts midsentence. "Satellite's overhead. Time for a trip to the future. Come with me."

Now *this* is the point at which I should say no. I should say, "Sorry, Dr. Pretorius, but this is too dangerous. I don't like keeping secrets from my dad, and I have no idea whether this is safe or not."

But then I look across at Ramzy, and there's no hesitation on *his* face. No reluctance. Just full-on, excited enthusiasm.

"Perhaps *you* should do it, Ramzy?" I say, and he grins at me. Before he replies, Dr. Pretorius is alongside us.

"Only one at a time, kiddos, and *I* don't care which of you goes first."

Ramzy, despite his excitement, hesitates. I hesitate.

Dr. Pretorius says, "You know we talked about probability? Well, how about a coin toss? Ha!" She takes out a coin. I call tails.

That's how I end up having the helmet tightened round my head.

Chapter Twenty-One

As I watch in the control room, a progress bar inches along the bottom of the biggest computer screen. A few minutes later, a box appears:

RECEPTION COMPLETE

and then a few seconds after that,

SIMULATION COMPLETE

"Shall we do this?" says Dr. Pretorius, clearly not expecting the answer to be no. I nod, swallowing hard and trying to look braver than I feel.

With Ramzy's help, I check the fastenings on the helmet and lower the metal visor. Pulling the straps tight under my chin, I test the release catch, and it pings loose before I shove it in again. The last thing I want is the catch coming loose while I'm in the studio. I feel the tiny nodes in the helmet's lining poking into my scalp, and entering the studio, my mouth is so dry, it's as though I've wiped the inside with a paper towel.

"Oww!" says Ramzy. "You're hurting me." I look down and realize that I've been gripping his wrist so tightly that I leave a red mark when I release it.

Stepping forward, I put both feet into the ball pit, shuffling through the tiny metal balls till I am standing dead center. Ramzy stands before me and gives a thumbs-up.

So far, everything is familiar. I hear Dr. Pretorius in my ear.

"You good to go, Georgie? We've already lost a minute of satellite time, but that's OK. Now listen up: I've programmed in your starting position and the time, and I've kept it simple. The dome will re-create the streets outside here. Everything will be familiar to you, and it's only going to be one week from now. So it's nothing too drastic, OK? Are you with me?"

I nod, and swallow hard.

"I can't hear you when you nod, and I can't see you until this is turned on. Are you with me?"

I manage to croak yes.

"Good girl. So, once you're there and comfortable, make your way up Marine Drive to the corner shop. There's an electronic display in the window showing the date, time, and weather. That will be our confirmation that the experiment has worked, and I have every confidence in you. Do you know the place?"

It's Norman Two-Kids's shop. The sign in the window is one of those scrolling lines of illuminated red letters.

"Aye aye, cap'n." There's a feeling of excitement growing inside of me. I want to do this.

"Ramzy—come out of there now and seal the door shut." Behind me, I hear the soft *thunk* of the studio door, and the lever sealing it closed so that no sound or light can enter the dome.

"Lights going off, Georgie. Stand by."

Everything is black in an instant.

Have you ever been in total, *total* darkness? So dark that, however long you wait for your eyes to adjust, there's nothing to be seen because there's no light *at all*? You can wave your hand in front of your face as much as you like and you still won't see anything.

That is how dark it is. It's so silent that I clear my throat, pointlessly, just to have something to hear. Then I feel a slight tremor beneath my feet as the ball pit activates.

I am terrified.

"Are you ready to go into the future, kid?"

She doesn't even wait for me to answer.

PART TWO

Chapter Twenty-Two

At first, it's just like before. Like a film coming into focus, pictures of houses appear on the studio walls, then some sky, and some trees. I blink hard, forcing myself to look more intently at what's happening, hoping for something different from when I'd stood here the last time.

As before, the houses quickly take on solid form, the nearest trees seem to move closer to me, and others become more distant as the world about me turns three-dimensional. A car swishes past, and the scene becomes brighter and lighter. It only takes a few seconds.

Above my eyes, the metal band glows brilliant blue. If I look at it too much, my eyes begin to hurt. I am aware of Dr. Pretorius's voice in my ear.

"OK, Georgie. We can see you now on-screen. What's it like?" Her voice is eager, childlike.

Then a more distant voice—Ramzy's—going, "Whoa! Amazing!"

This is what it's like: I'm standing on the seafront. A fully rendered, three-dimensional reproduction of the seafront right outside the dome. "It . . . it's incredible!" I reply.

There are people around me and they are real. I can see the sea and it's real. The sounds are real. *Everything is real!* I look above my head and the sky stretches on forever—as it should.

The VR environments that Ramzy and I have experimented with till now have been amazing, but I always knew that I was in a game. Sometimes the people's movements were a little jerky, or an object would blur at the edges. There were loads of tiny little clues. But not here: this virtual world is virtually perfect.

I take a deep sniff.

Ah. That's odd. It smells just like the inside of the studio. I sniff again, and again. Then I hear Dr. Pretorius say: "You won't smell anything, Georgie. The olfactory simulation isn't complete yet. This is still a prototype, remember? Can you turn around? How's the visuals?"

I'm almost speechless, but I turn right round slowly and manage to say, "Unbelievable!" The people walking past seem perfectly, absolutely real, even though I know they're not. I swing my head rapidly from side to side, and that creates a very slight blurring, as the program takes half a second to catch up with my head movement.

I am living in a computer-generated world and it is . . .

TOTALLY

FREAKING

AWESOME!

No wonder Dr. Pretorius has kept this secret. Another car swishes past on the road to my right, and I hear a child shout, "Mam!" somewhere. So far I haven't moved: all I've done is look around, my head swiveling left and right, up and down, taking in every aspect of this amazing illusion.

"Georgie! Can you hear me?"

I've been so carried away.

"Yes. Yes, I can hear you. It's . . . wonderful."

"OK—walk on over the street, Georgie. We haven't got too much time. And take care crossing the road. I'm a little uncertain how realistic a vehicle impact would be."

Oo-kaay, I think a bit nervously. I carry on, crossing the road (which seems quieter than I would expect) till I can look at the beach as well as the sea. The tide's out, and there are a few people walking—one or two people swimming. It's not *exactly* right: perhaps it's the sea's movement, or the color of the sand, or . . . what? I can't quite put my finger on it, but still: the illusion is almost faultless, and I am transfixed.

I cross back over the road and walk up Marine Drive, away from the Spanish City and past parked cars, past a couple of ladies talking to each other.

"Eee, I know. I says to 'im, you hide that dog if you dare, but he wasn't listenin.'"

"You're wasting your breath, dear. . . ."

All the time I am telling myself, *These are not real people, Georgie.* I don't dare talk to them.

"Dr. Pretorius, can these people see me?" I whisper.

"Speak up, Georgie. Didn't catch that."

"I said—can these people see me?" I say, a bit louder. The two ladies turn to look right at me, and then resume their conversation. "It's OK. I guess they can." I move a bit farther up the street. "Do they *know* they're not real?"

"Big question, Georgie—another time, eh? Right now, we got five minutes till we lose the connection with Hawking II, and I need to get confirmation from that calendar in the window, so get a move on."

There are so many things that I want to take in and be amazed at. A curtain twitching in an upstairs window, the child in the backseat of the car that went past . . .

They are all being created by Little Girl: a supercomputer in a black box a few yards away.

I know this street so well because I walk along it every school day. The big pub over the road with its picnic tables at the front; the garden with the long grass that's never cut because the woman who lives there thinks that cutting grass is cruel (according to Kassie Ruman, whose mum knows her);

and the house where the dog is always chained up and barking, but isn't there today although the chain is.

"Come on, Georgie," I hear Ramzy say. "Don't hang around!"

I pick up my pace and there is Norman Two-Kids's corner shop.

NARAYAN SUPREME STORES

FRESH FRUIT . . . WINES AND SPIRITS . . . GROCERIES

I stop before I get there. There are a few people outside the shop—adults, four or five of them, and Norman Two-Kids is standing in front of them, holding his head up and his shoulders back.

"OK, one more, please!" says a man, who is crouching with a small camera, which flashes. "And the last one please, Sanjiv!" and it flashes again. *So that's his name.*

I edge closer to hear what they're saying. The man with the camera is holding it up as though he's filming.

"So what does it feel like?" the man asks.

Norman looks bashful. He replies, "I am very happy for the person who won it."

I have no idea what they're talking about, but I move a little bit closer anyway.

"Can you tell us what will happen now, Sanjiv?"

"I have no idea. . . ." And so it goes on. It seems as though Norman Two-Kids is being interviewed for the local newspaper or website or something.

"How did it all happen, Sanjiv?"

"Well. He came in me shop, y'know, and bought a ticket. I welcome everyone in my shop; it brings good luck."

He's probably won "Maddest Shopkeeper of the Year" if you ask me, and I smile to myself at my little joke. I'm beginning to enjoy this, I realize.

Nobody is looking in my direction as I get close enough to see the shop window, which is covered with advertisements and other signs. I have been past this cluttered shop window so many times, I never even notice what's there, but it's all familiar. The sign announcing that this is a Parcel Collection Point; the big video ad for the Geordie Jackpot lottery; and the one I'm looking for: the electronic calendar.

There it is, the bright red letters scrolling past:

TODAY IS FRIDAY JULY 27

TIME: 16:52

TODAY'S WEATHER: PARTLY CLOUDY

SUNSET: 21:18

In my ear, I hear, "Terrific, Georgie! Congratulations! There's our confirmation!" Dr. Pretorius sounds elated, and

I'm feeling pretty pleased myself. The sense of danger has more or less gone: I only need to take off the helmet and I'll be back in the studio, and that makes me less scared.

I can hear Ramzy now. "Don't move, Georgie. Stay right there."

"Why?" I ask.

"Just . . . just stay there. Move a bit closer to the shop window."

I do as he asks, without knowing why, and while I'm looking at the window, I shove my hands deep in the pockets of my school uniform skirt with a satisfied feeling, and my fingers curl round the ball that Mr. Springham gave me earlier today. A thought occurs to me.

What would happen if I threw it?

You see, the "real me" is still in Dr. Pretorius's studio (although the longer I stay in this virtual world, the easier it is becoming to forget that fact).

What will happen to the ball if I throw it toward the studio's walls?

There's only one way to find out. I take the ball from my pocket and throw it as hard as I can up the street. My eyes follow it on its normal arc, and then—as though it has hit an invisible wall in thin air, above the road—it bounces back toward me, and bounces again on the pavement, and again, and again, finally rolling to a stop a few yards away.

"Georgie!" comes Dr. Pretorius's voice. "What in the name of heck are you doing?"

"Just experimenting!" I call back. Then I reach for a peach from the rack outside the shop.

Now this peach feels real—the slightly furry skin, the right weight. I run my thumb over the skin, and a little of the surface peels off under my nail. I sniff it: it smells of nothing, and I remember Dr. Pretorius saying that smells have not been completed. Then I take a big bite, and the juice runs down my chin, just like real peach juice. Only . . . it tastes of nothing. I swallow, and still no flavor. Next, I throw the fruit as hard as I can in the same direction up the street to see what happens.

It doesn't bounce back. Of course it doesn't. *It's not a real peach.* It sails through the air as you'd expect it to do, without hitting the wall of the studio.

It comes to land on a patch of earth beneath a tree and splits open. That's when I hear Norman Two-Kids behind me.

"Hey, you! What you fink you doin,' huh?"

"So sorry! I, erm . . ."

The small crowd around him has moved aside. One or two of them are smirking at "the naughty kid who steals fruit." Norman's face, on the other hand, is dark and furious.

"You gon' pay for that or what?" he says, advancing toward me. "Well? You fink you can just come up to me shop an' frow stuff aroun', huh?"

I shuffle backward, away from him. "Bloody kids!" He turns to the group. "See wha' I have to deal wif, huh? No respect!"

"I'm sorry, I just . . ."

I am edging away; then I turn to run and I let out a little scream. Two yards in front of me, but facing the other way, is a giant scorpion—the same one that I saw on the beach simulation the very first time I was in the dome.

Only this time it's much more convincing. And *much* more threatening.

When I squeal, it turns round, its eight legs *clickety-clicking* on the pavement; then it takes a couple of paces back, arching its tail high in the air as if preparing to strike.

Behind me, I hear, "Oh my God. What on earth is *that*?"

For a moment, I feel paralyzed with fear. I try telling myself that it's not real, but when the scorpion advances toward me, I react by grabbing a box of oranges and hurling it as hard as I can at the creature. And missing.

"Why, you little vandal!" yells Norman, and he grabs the hood of my jacket. "I know which school you're at, and . . ."

I wriggle but he's now holding me tightly by both arms. The other people don't seem willing to come to my aid.

"Look!" I say, pointing at the scorpion, which did *not* like being threatened with a box of oranges and is now waving its pincers menacingly, shifting its weight from foot to foot. "Scorpion!"

One of the people—the guy who had the camera—says, "Wow! That's so realistic! Look, Anna—it must be remote-controlled!"

Norman says to me: "What are you talking about? You just frew my oranges on the ground! You gonna pick 'em up and any damages you pay for, you little . . ."

I don't wait to hear the rest because the scorpion lunges at me with its quivering tail-sting, and I scream as it gets nearer.

"Ramzy! Dr. Pretorius! Help me!"

"Who you talkin' wif? And what's this flippin' toy lobster all about? Where did that come from? Who's controllin' it?" rasps Norman, still holding on to my arms.

But I'm not paying attention to him because the scorpion stings me.

I feel a sharp pain in my thigh as its needle-like stinger enters my flesh, and I howl again, and I hear the photographer say, "Eew! What a gross toy."

In my ear, Dr. Pretorius is talking urgently. "Stand by, Georgie. Coming out of the program now. Powering down in three . . . two . . . one."

The scorpion has withdrawn in readiness for another strike when everything goes dark.

Everything is silent.

I sink to my knees in the ball pit, my fingers scrabbling

urgently for the release catch of the helmet. I lift it off my sweating head as the pin lights come on in the studio and there I am, surrounded by the green-black walls, panting and completely confused, the way you are when you wake up from a vivid dream.

I hear the padded door behind me open, and Ramzy and Dr. Pretorius come toward me, Ramzy shuffling as fast as he can through the ball pit.

"Georgie?" he says. "How was it? Are you OK?"

I don't know, but I assume I am. I mean, the scorpion wasn't real, was it? So it can't really have hurt me.

But then I look down and there's a small patch of blood soaking into my skirt from my thigh.

Chapter Twenty-Three

Dr. Pretorius, Ramzy, and I sit in the control room and I gulp Fanta from a glass. I have a headache, and I'm still panting. Ramzy's already on his second chocolate cookie, but I'm not hungry. I've lifted my skirt and Dr. Pretorius is peering at the tiny puncture wound, which at least has stopped bleeding.

She shakes her head. "That's, ah . . . that is *irregular* to say the least. By the way, don't worry about poison, but there is just *no way* that even a tiny wound should happen. It would appear . . . hmmm . . ." and she just stands there, staring at my leg and stroking her chin.

I prompt her. "It would appear *what?*" I pull down my skirt with the now-drying bloodstain, and then I feel a surge in my stomach and throat. I manage to mutter, "Excuse me," before I throw up on the floor. Not a big puke, like when you're ill: just a little one, *hup,* like that, and the piece of peach I ate in the dome comes up and lands—along with some of the Fanta I just drank—on the tiled floor.

"I'm sorry!" I say, and although Ramzy's face says *Eeeew!* Dr. Pretorius looks as though she hasn't heard me. Instead, she eases herself onto her knees and bends down to look at the little pool of orange vomit with a lump of peach in it.

She lifts up her glasses and looks closer, then says, "What've you eaten today?"

I dropped my lunch on the school-cafeteria floor and didn't get another, so I've eaten nothing since breakfast, apart from half a flapjack that Ramzy brought me. And then that bit of peach. I tell this to Dr. Pretorius and she nods slowly, then gets to her feet again. Her knees click noisily. She shuffles off to one of the kitchen counters and comes back with a towel, a small glass dish, and some tongs that she hands to me.

"Put that lump of fruit there on the dish, would you?" she says, pointing to the piece of peach on the ground. "Then wipe the floor. I don't wanna risk getting down there, or I may not get up again, ha!"

I do as she asks, and she carries the dish back to her desk and sits down in the swivel chair, stroking her chin.

"The scorpion's a glitch, that's all," says Dr. Pretorius quickly. She doesn't seem to care very much, and that upsets me. "The whole 3-D environment is based on the Surround-a-Room I created. The rain-forest game had these scorpions in it, and they've been carried over into this program, kinda by mistake. He's actually pretty harmless, I'd say. At least he was."

"*Was?*"

Dr. Pretorius sighs and sits back in her chair. "Listen. That scorpion had a tiny—and I mean *tiny*—bit of *very limited* artificial intelligence built into his code. The idea was that, as you played the game, he would learn your strengths and weaknesses as a player. But he seems to be getting smarter. He seems to be able to hide, for example, which was never the intention. The other avatars—that is, the other people— can see him. And so can you when you're in there, and we can see him on the screen—look."

On-screen, she brings up a view of the street and presses a button to play it. It's a recording from my helmet: everything that I saw is being played out in front of me. Dr. Pretorius is fast-forwarding through the video. There's the strangely deserted beach, the two ladies talking, the people outside the shop, me throwing the ball . . .

"That ball-throwing? Smart experiment, kid: just tell me first next time," she says.

Next time?

. . . and the reddish-black scorpion, huge and ugly. Dr. Pretorius points it out, behind a parked car. "See? He's hiding. That is *not* in the original code. That is artificial intelligence: AI-learned behavior. In the game, they could clone themselves. So far this one hasn't learned how to do that, and that is a good thing."

As we watch, the scorpion on the screen scuttles out from behind the car and comes toward me. Dr. Pretorius tuts and hits the space bar, making the picture freeze. "Pesky little critter. I'll get you eventually." Turning to us, she says, "It's just a question of going through the program and locating the rogue code. Time-consuming but entirely straightforward." Then she peers again at the piece of peach on the glass dish. "But there is something *much* more curious. . . ."

Dr. Pretorius looks over at me. "You OK? You've gone a little pale." She starts tapping the keyboard again. "The scorpion—the one I call Buster—seems to have learned to bridge the RL–VR gap, and that . . ." She catches the puzzled look on my face and pauses.

"The gap between real life—that's you, us, now—and virtual reality, where the scorpion exists. There's no way that Buster should be able to actually draw blood. But it seems as though he's learned how to interact with reality. Darn quickly too. As for *this*"—she pokes the peach with a long finger—"there is no way that this piece of peach you ate could become real, and be brought back to this world—to real life." She pokes it again. "But it has . . ."

She's still fiddling with the puked-up piece of peach, and

it's pretty gross. Her voice trails off and Ramzy prompts her. "What about it?"

It's almost as though she's talking to herself, and I have to strain to hear her. "I can't be certain, but the scorpion sting appears to have made this possible. Remarkable."

"Is that a good thing?" says Ramzy, and she stares at us both with her big pale eyes.

"No. It is *not* a good thing. It is potentially catastrophic. Unless I can eradicate the stray code, that darn scorpion's gonna wreck my whole experiment."

I look over at Ramzy. "Do you still want to have a turn?"

Before he can answer, Dr. Pretorius says, "No one's going back in there until I get this fixed. Understood?"

I don't need persuading. I'm still staring at the peach and wondering what she means.

Dr. Pretorius is back at her keyboard, tapping and scrolling, and then she brings up a screenshot of the shop window with the electronic calendar showing next week's date. She stares at it, a slow smile spreading across her face.

"Well, at least we know that part worked. We did it!" she says to herself. Then louder, "We did it!" She turns to me. She doesn't see that, behind her, Ramzy has taken out his phone and is silently recording the computer screen. His movements are quiet—he clearly doesn't want her to know what he's doing—and he slyly slips his phone back into his pocket as Dr. Pretorius turns back.

She glances at her watch. "We've taken too long already. I promise ya: we'll get this fixed. Right now, I've got a load of stuff to do and it's time for my evening swim. Let's go. I'll walk you out. And, kids? Thank you."

For a moment, she disappears into a little annex and leaves the door open. I can see in: there's a narrow single bed and a tiny bathroom. She emerges with her beach bag and closes the door behind her. She's caught me looking but doesn't seem to mind. She half shrugs.

"Even mad scientists have gotta sleep," she murmurs, adding—almost to herself—"ha!"

That evening, my headache gradually gets worse. Earlier in the day, I had been full of plans to hook up with Mr. Mash. I was going to check the webcam so at least I could *see* him. I was going to call the vicar, and maybe—if I asked nicely— he'd hold the phone next to Mr. Mash's ear while I watched on the webcam, and it would be the nearest thing I could get to actually being with him. I'd even practiced what I was going to say to him.

"*Hello, Mashie. It's me. Are you being a good boy?*" That sort of thing. It sounds silly, but it didn't *feel* silly.

Instead, I lie on my bed, panting. I hardly sleep, and my duvet cover is wet with sweat. It's only as I'm finally falling asleep that I remember that Ben could still be sick. I haven't even asked the vicar about him since Mum's memorial. *I'll ask him tomorrow,* I tell myself.

Chapter Twenty-Four

I have had headaches before. Everyone has had a headache. This is not just a headache, though: a throbbing or a tightening in my head. This is something else: an agony that starts at the back of my head and seems to extend in waves across the top and sides of my skull, meeting above my eyes where the pain intensifies.

If pain has a sound, then this is like a knife being scraped on a plate.

If pain has a color, then this manages—somehow—to be vivid acid-yellow (kind of like Dr. Pretorius's swimsuit, though that may be a coincidence).

And then the taste: a sour, metallic flavor on the back of my tongue, like rusty vinegar.

But above it all, worse than any of the other sensations, is the pain above my eyes, which has been getting worse and worse, and which makes me curl into a ball, clutching at my temples, moaning loudly.

I look at my phone and see that it's 8:00 a.m., so I must have fallen asleep at some point.

Dad will be in the workshop with Clem. Jessica's already at work (her second Saturday in a row). I am up in my room, writhing on my bed, when I call Dad, and I can barely speak. He and Clem both run back up the lane and burst into the house.

I hear him saying, "Georgie, Georgie? Are you OK?" but it sounds like he's shouting from miles away.

And Clem is saying, "Obviously, she's not—look at her! Call a doctor! Get an ambulance!"

And then I hear him on his phone to someone, saying, "She's having some sort of . . . I dunno, seizure. Oh my God! Georgie!"

As if from a long way away, there's a voice—a small voice—saying, "It's all right. It's all right. I think it's getting better." And I realize that it's my voice.

And it *is* getting better. The high-pitched, searing pain is diminishing, like a howling storm becomes a rain shower, then drizzle.

The lights that had been popping like fireworks behind my screwed-up eyes slowly stop; I take my balled fists away from the sides of my head. I lie on the floor of my bedroom, my face against the carpet, soaked in sweat, and start to cry. Dad holds me nervously, like I'm a wild animal, while

I sob at the memory of the pain, and with relief that it has passed.

Finally, after what seems like several minutes (but probably isn't), I take a deep breath, and a long, satisfying sniff, and sit upright.

And then I pass out and everything starts to unravel.

Chapter Twenty-Five

I come round in the ambulance. Dad is next to me, gripping my hand so hard that it almost hurts.

"Hi, my lovely," he says, and smiles with his mouth, but not his eyes, which are still wet.

There's a mask over my mouth that I pull aside to see if I can talk.

"How long have I been here? What time is it? Why am I here?"

"You passed out about ten minutes ago. The ambulance was pretty quick. We'll be arriving soon. Clem's riding up front. Jessica is meeting us there."

Jessica doesn't have far to go: the department where she works is part of the hospital.

One of the paramedics in the ambulance gently replaces the oxygen mask and says, "Shhh. We'll get you figured out."

· · ·

What happens next is a bit of a blur. There are doctors, nurses, blood tests, injections, a brain scan. Then ultrasound imaging, and Dad crying when he thinks I'm sleeping. Then, after a few hours, I'm sitting up in the hospital bed.

The headache has gone, to be replaced by a dull tingling, and even that seems to be diminishing.

Jessica and Dad are sitting at the side of my bed. A lady in a short white coat comes in. She is so soft-spoken that at times I strain to hear her, but she's just doing it to be nice. She has a tablet computer, and she wants some answers.

She introduces herself as Mimi. Her lapel badge says Dr. Mimi Chevapravat. She sits down next to me, opposite Jessica and Dad.

"Hi, Georgie," she says, and smiles warmly. "I'm the neurosurgical resident, and I've been looking at the tests we've done, and I'm glad to say that there seems to be no damage to your brain. We're not quite sure what happened, but we think it's a case of juvenile migraine. You should make a full recovery."

Well, that's good news. The only problem is the *what happened* bit. I'm struggling to remember myself.

"But," she continues, "I need to ask you some questions about your activities prior to the incident. This condition can often be triggered by bright lights, that sort of thing. Can you think of anything that might have set it off?"

I glance across at Dad. He looks so tired, and so worried, and I suddenly feel a wave of guilt wash over me.

Was this all my fault?

Inside my head is a mixture of everything: the Spanish City, a piece of peach, Dr. Pretorius, then Norman Two-Kids, and the vicar, and a bicycle helmet, and a box of oranges, and ugly Dudley the Staffie . . .

And none of it makes sense. It's as though all the pages of a book have been torn out and put back in the wrong order.

Didn't I? Didn't I what? Who said that?

"Georgie? Did you hear me?" It's Mimi again.

I don't know why, but I decide to just tell the truth. Maybe it's because I'm too tired to make anything up. Or maybe the secret's too big for me now. I mean, I'm just a kid.

I start slowly at first: meeting Dr. Pretorius on the beach that day; her invitation to see her studio; the dome inside the Spanish City with its vast floor with billions of ball bearings; the beach with the deck chair and the sand that felt real—I can remember that all right.

It begins to sound ridiculous as I say it. I catch glances between Jessica and Dad. I mean, I know it's all true—I saw it, I experienced it—although, when I try to remember bits, they sometimes dance away from me, like trying to catch clouds.

"This . . . Dr. Pretorius?" says Dad eventually. "Where does she live?"

I don't know. Did I ever know? Did I see her house? Does she live in the dome, in that little room I saw? Was that yesterday? I feel stupid and guilty and want to say sorry over and over.

"So a woman you have never met before, and you know nothing about, invites you and Ramzy Rahman to her, what . . . laboratory? In the Spanish City? And tells you to keep it secret? And you *do*?" Dad's voice is getting louder, and Jessica touches his arm: a sort of "calm down" gesture, which is nice of her, I guess.

The thing is, the more this interrogation goes on, the more I can see he has a point. A good one.

I'm not making much sense. *What were we thinking?*

There's more. I mention the Hawking II satellite and, most importantly, the bicycle helmet with its tiny electrical nodules inside and . . .

"Slow down, Georgie," says Mimi, putting her hand on my arm. "I'm interested in this . . . helmet?"

"A bicycle helmet, yes. A changed one," and I describe it in more detail.

"Modified, obviously," she says, shooting a glance at Dad, then addressing him rather than me. "This sounds like a sort of homemade TDCS."

"What's that?" says Dad, speaking for all of us, I think.

"Transcranial direct-current stimulation. It was popular with gamers a few years ago. Enhancing the gaming experience and so on. The early versions were pretty harmless: very low-level stimulation. There was one released for use in theme parks—the surround-something-or-other."

"The Surround-a-Room!" I exclaim. "I know! Dr. Pretorius invented it."

Mimi looks at me. "Is that what she told you, this, ah . . . this . . . Dr. Pretorius?" She doesn't exactly make finger quotes round "Dr. Pretorius" but her voice does.

I note the beginning of an uncomfortable feeling. Was Dr. Pretorius *lying* about that?

Mimi continues. "So, Georgie. You were saying that . . . erm"—she glances at her notes—"a satellite dish receiving a stream of ultra-high-definition live video signals from . . . ?"

"Hawking II. It's a military satellite." Even as I say it, it sounds ridiculous.

"*Yessss*," she drawls, and sucks the end of her pen. "And what happened next?"

"I . . . I can't remember. She has a . . . a quomp—a quantum computer called Little Girl—that calculates the probability of, like, everything, and creates a virtual model of what will happen. It's sort of a three-dimensional version of the future. I think." I pause to judge their reactions. Dad's brow is creased in puzzlement. I become more keen to tell them, but the harder I try to rearrange the scattered memories, the less sense I make. I want them to believe me, but I'm not even sure I believe myself.

"It's true!" I wail eventually. "I was there! The electronic calendar in the window of Norman Two-Kids's shop said the date a week from now."

As I say it, I realize it's no proof at all. In fact, it's probably the easiest thing in the world to fake a date on a virtual calendar.

The whole thing is crazy. Military satellites, ultra-high-definition video streams, quomps, and AI scorpions, and yet . . .

"Wait!" I say. "Look." I flip the bedsheet to one side. "This is where the giant scorpion got me!" I point to my leg, and there *is* a wound there. A little one. A tiny needle-prick that could be anything. There isn't even any blood, just a red dot.

Mimi hardly glances at it. "Hmph."

I had believed it all. I feel my chin wobbling but I stop it. Mimi gets up and clips her pen back into her pocket.

"Mr. and Mrs. Santos? May I have a word with you? In private?"

Jessica stands up. I want to say, *She's not Mrs. Santos. She's not my mum, you know,* but I don't have the energy. Mimi gives me a tight little smile and the three of them leave me there, wondering whether I've been the biggest fool ever.

Chapter Twenty-Six

They all troop back in a few minutes later and sit down in the same positions.

I have experienced, it would appear, a moderate to severe juvenile migraine resulting in temporary spontaneous confabulation as a result of exposure to unsafe and possibly untested TDCS.

"Of course you're not *lying*," says Mimi, although I don't like her tone of voice. It sounds like she means the opposite. "Confabulation is a medical term: you really believe these things are true."

I want to say "They *are* true!" but Mimi is still talking.

"This, Georgie, is *potentially* quite a serious matter." Her voice gets even quieter as if to emphasize the gravity of the situation. "Not medically, I mean. I'm referring rather to the incident that triggered your episode. With your parents' permission, I'll be asking the police to come and talk to you about your experiences at the Spanish City."

"Don't be scared," says Dad. "You've done nothing wrong. You've been careless, perhaps, but the real fault lies with this 'Dr. Pretorius.'" This time the finger quotes are real.

"Is she in trouble?" I ask.

"It's difficult to know," says Mimi. "The police will have a better idea whether there has been an actual crime. At the moment, my main concern is that no one else is forced to endure the pain you went through."

And even then I'm thinking, *I wasn't exactly forced,* but I say nothing.

Chapter Twenty-Seven

There's not much to do in a hospital. I have to stay in a little longer till they have the results of some tests or other.

My phone has been turned off so that I can rest, but when Jessica and Dad leave, and I'm alone in my room, I turn it on and see loads of messages—all from Ramzy. They start off normal, and I scroll through them quickly.

> Hi, Georgie—how are you? Hope you're feeling better.

> Hi, G—call me, msg me.

> You out of your coma yet, LOL. Just kidding. Pls reply!

> I tried to call you—is your phone off? I've got something to show you. Could be big!

> Yeah, sorry. Just got phone back. Going through msgs.

Then the messages stop. He hasn't sent one for hours. I call his number but it goes straight to voice mail. I stare at the phone, puzzled by Ramzy's sudden silence, and then I see I have an email waiting.

An email. From Ramzy. Who has never emailed me in his life.

You weren't picking up your phone so—SURPRISE!—here's an email. I'm grounded. Bummer. Phone confiscated, but not my laptop. Your dad called my dad and I'm guessing you told them all about Dr. P. Don't worry. I'd have done the same, I think.

Result—Big Shouty Drama.

I said we were just going round there to test a new 3D game. The "going into the future" bit sounded too weird. They'd have freaked out even more, and the level of freaking out here is already pretty freaking freaky.

Anyway, do you remember in the control room, when Dr. P was replaying some of the stuff recorded from your helmet? And she asked you to stand in front of Norman 2-Kids' calendar thingy? That was her proof.

Do you believe her? Well, here's a bit of

video I made while that was playing. I don't even know if Dr. P knew I was taking it. Check it out. Tell me what you notice. And I don't mean the calendar.

Ramzy

Before I get a chance to play it, though, Ramzy himself bursts into my room followed by a large woman in a long cloak and an angry face glaring out of her hijab. Aunty Nush.

"It's me," says Ramzy unnecessarily. "How are you?"

"Much better—thanks. I thought you were grounded?"

"I am. This is day release to visit the sick. Aunty Nush—this is Georgina."

If she smiles at me, I miss it, but her face changes a bit, like she's swallowing something unpleasant-tasting so maybe that is as near as Aunty Nush gets to a smile. She looks like she has forgotten how. She nods slowly a couple of times.

"Two buses to come here," says Ramzy. "Hope you appreciate it!"

"Yeah, but I'll be out soon. What's the rush?"

"Hang on." Ramzy turns to his aunty and takes her a chair, which creaks dangerously as she plonks herself down on it. They exchange some words in their language. Aunty Nush takes out her phone from the folds of her long cloak and Ramzy sits down next to me.

"Right. That's her sorted. She doesn't speak any English, so we're OK. So—what have you said?"

I tell Ramzy about Mimi's questions, and about the police being informed. Ramzy looks horrified and glances over at Aunty Nush. "The *police*?"

"I'm sorry. Dr. Pretorius could be in trouble. Thing is, Ramzy—I can't remember a lot of it. It's like the headache has fuzzied up my memory. But they reckon that the bicycle helmet injured my brain, and so she could be responsible. And they don't like the idea of some weirdo meeting kids on the beach and playing 3-D games, and—"

"But she wasn't . . . she's not . . . a *weirdo*," says Ramzy. "Is she?"

I really don't know the answer to that. I say, "Ramzy, do you think that was all faked? All that future stuff? My dad definitely does. And the doctors. I mean, what proof do we have?" I'm getting worried telling Ramzy about it, but he seems quite calm. He looks at Aunty Nush again, but she's absorbed in some game on her phone, glowering at it and stabbing at something with a forefinger.

"Georgie, man. Calm down. I had the very same thought, even as you were in the studio. I was behind Dr. P and she hardly spoke, but I did take a bit of video on my phone when you were standing in front of the shop window. I don't even think she noticed. I really think you should watch it, though."

The clip in Ramzy's email is still open on my laptop. I click on it, and as it plays, the memory begins to return, as though it's from a long, long time ago.

I'm standing in front of Norman Two-Kids's shop. There it is, the electronic calendar in the window. Is it proof that I'm in a computer-generated "future"? I'm beginning to doubt it.

"It's all just fake, Ramzy," I say, feeling dejected. "I mean—it's clever and everything, but I think we've been tricked. Why she would do that, I have no idea. I mean . . ."

"But, Georgie. Look closely. There's a way we can prove it. Really prove it." Ramzy is smirking a little now and teasing me with something he knows. "Look closer."

I drag the button back along to the start of the clip, and watch it again, noticing the giant scorpion hiding behind the car this time and it gives me a shiver. But I don't see anything odd about the calendar, and I say so.

"But look!" Ramzy can't keep the excitement out of his voice. "What's *next* to the calendar?"

"Erm . . . a Coca-Cola ad. A handwritten sign, which I can't make out, a video ad for the Geordie Jackpot lottery with the logo and whatnot, erm . . ."

"Yes! Yes! Describe the moving ad!"

"Can't you just tell me, Ramzy? OK . . . it's a bottle of champagne, and the label says *Is it you?* The cork pops out and there's stars and streamers and balls, and the words *This week's winning numbers,* and— Oh my Lord, Ramzy! Th-those balls!"

Ramzy is nodding slowly, a sly grin on his face.

I say, "They've got numbers on them. The numbers for the lottery draw. *Next week's* lottery draw!" I can't believe what I've just seen. Ramzy's eyes are shining with excitement.

"I've checked them. Those six numbers have not been selected in any of the draws in the last five years."

"Meaning?"

"Meaning that if Dr. Pretorius has faked the calendar by, I dunno, layering something on top of existing footage, then she's *also* gone to the huge trouble of changing the numbers on a moving advertisement next to it. Seems like a lot of effort."

I'm still trying to catch up. "So *if* the numbers of the next Geordie Jackpot match the ones here in this clip, then that will be proof that Dr. Pretorius's virtual future is real and not fake."

"Exactly. But you're missing one thing. We'll also be . . . what, Georgie?"

"I don't know, Ramzy!" I moan. "Stop being so mysterious!"

"Rich, Georgie! It's like a million pounds if you pick all six numbers!" He isn't quite shouting, but his excitement causes Aunty Nush to stop her phone game. She glares at him and snarls something I don't understand.

I swallow hard. I have never paid the Geordie Jackpot much attention.

All I know is this: if you buy a ticket, you can choose six numbers. Once every two weeks, a machine randomly picks six numbered balls. If the numbers on your ticket match the ones chosen by the machine, then you win.

Easy! Except I also know this: the chances of winning the big prize are incredibly tiny. But, if you knew *in advance* what the numbers were going to be, you could select those exact numbers on your ticket, and . . .

I must have been daydreaming because Ramzy nudges me and says, "Hey! You still with us?"

"Sorry, Ramzy, I'm just . . . a bit . . ."

"Pretty awesome, eh?"

That's one way of putting it.

Chapter Twenty-Eight

Shortly afterward, Ramzy leaves with Aunty Nush. (I think she even smiles at me: it's hard to tell. Her lips draw apart a bit, revealing broken, gappy teeth, and then her mouth closes over them again, like a sheet covering a corpse.)

Mimi has told me to rest. Relax. How on earth can I? My mind is racing with the possibility of winning a million pounds.

I look up the Geordie Jackpot and spend a good twenty minutes reading stories about people whose lives have been changed by a massive sum of money. Some of them, to be honest, are not happy stories.

Family breakups, arguments, divorce, drug problems, crime: some people, it seems, are not very good when it comes to large sums of money. Me? I'll be fine.

I let myself imagine what I would do. Split it with Ramzy? Definitely. Then I'll buy Dad a new workshop: he's always complaining that it's cold and needs up-to-date equipment.

About half an hour later, I'm still daydreaming of how I would spend the money when I hear voices outside my room, and the door opens.

"Hello, Georgina." It's Jessica. I'm allowed to go. *Discharged* is the word they use. "Your dad's had to go. Come with me," she says.

Ten minutes later, I'm following her through hospital corridors and across parking lots toward the building where she works. She's talking all the time—more, I think, than I remember her ever talking.

"The police will be calling this evening to interview you. Your dad has spoken to Ramzy's dad . . ." and so on. It's all very matter-of-fact, but then it usually is with Jessica.

I look at her bony back as she stalks ahead of me and I think—for the umpteenth time—how different she is from Dad. They met through Mum, indirectly. I think I said that already. It's hard to keep track, especially now my mind is a little fuzzy. Since Mum died, Dad has raised money every year for the local biobotics research unit. Two years ago, they invited Dad and Clem and me to the opening of a new part of the building. There's a big board with people's names carved on it, and Mum and Dad's are too:

ROBERTO AND CASSANDRA SANTOS

It was the only time I've ever seen Dad wear a tie. We were standing around, not knowing anyone, and a plain-looking lady with short, spiky hair came up to Dad and introduced herself.

"Hello," she said. "I'm Jessica Stone." She didn't bother to introduce herself to me or Clem.

There was something in the way that Dad looked at her that meant I knew. I know we can't really see the future, but I had a vivid mental picture of this Jessica Stone sitting on our sofa.

When we were going home after the ceremony in Dad's shiny old car, I said, "Dad, you know I don't want a step-mum," and he laughed but didn't say anything.

The biobotics lab at the hospital seems to be bigger than the time I was there with Dad and Clem. Outside, there's a new stack of trailers, two stories high, and definitely more people, all looking like they're in a hurry, clutching iPads and clipboards and speaking into their phones or earpieces as they walk.

"*No results yet . . . expected Tuesday . . .*"

"*Well, get on to it then—it's been a week already!*"

"*I've sent the samples twice. You can't have lost both of them, Tasha . . .*"

The main building is made of old red and orange bricks. Above the huge double doors is a sign:

THE EDWARD JENNER
DEPARTMENT OF BIOBOTICS

The sign looks old, with curly writing, but I know that it can't be because "biobotics" is a new science.

"Wait here," says Jessica. "I've got to clear you with security." Then, as an afterthought, "You feeling OK?" but she doesn't wait to see me nod in reply.

Inside the doors is a lobby with a high ceiling and a shiny stone floor the color of thick cream; in the middle of the floor is a plinth bearing a statue in whitish marble of a man wearing old-fashioned clothes and holding a small, naked boy on his lap. The boy looks like he's struggling, and the man is frowning in concentration: he's poking something into the boy's shoulder. I'm frowning too because I swear this statue wasn't here before.

"Simply marvelous, isn't it?" says a voice beside me, and I turn to see an elderly security guard in a dark uniform with a tie, staring in awe at the statue. He gently brushes the little boy's marble leg with the back of his hand.

"Hello, Jackson," I say, and he inclines his head.

"Charmed as always, Miss Santos. To what do I owe the considerable honor?"

I don't really want to get into why I've been to the hospital, so I just say, "Oh, just a checkup, you know?"

I guess being a hospital security guard means he knows not to be inquisitive about people's reasons for being there, and he nods slowly, and we turn our attention back to the statue.

"Is it new?" I ask. I didn't see it last time I visited, I'm sure of that.

Jackson chuckles. "Well, it's new to us, young lady. In fact, it's very old. Look."

He points to an engraved panel on the plinth, which says simply,

JENNER BY GIULIO MONTEVERDE

1878

"It's on permanent loan from Genoa, Italy. In honor of the work done by people like your stepmum."

Jessica is *not* my stepmum, I want to say, but Jackson is an old family friend so I let it go.

"What's he doing to the boy?" I ask.

"Giving him an injection. An inoculation. Immunizing him against . . ."

I know this from school. "Smallpox!"

"Very good."

"This must be the man that Jessica says saved so many people's lives."

He nods solemnly. "She's right. More than anyone else in history, they say, thanks to vaccinations."

Jessica approaches across the marble floor. "Sorry it took so long, Georgina. Security's a nightmare." She looks at Jackson. "Sorry, Jackson. You're an exception."

"You're exceptional yourself, Miss Stone. No offense taken."

"Come on," says Jessica to me. "Let's get you in. You're going to have to wait for a little bit before I can take you home."

I follow her through the lobby, down a long corridor into the new wing of the building. All along one wall are huge glass windows. On the other side is a laboratory like something from a movie. White-coated people with hairnets and face masks hurry between lab stations, with anxious expressions in their eyes. Rack upon rack of test tubes inch along a long conveyor belt, while articulated robot arms dip in and out of them.

It's transfixing to watch: like some sort of medical factory.

Then a shout goes up at the other end of the corridor. "There she is!"

Round a corner comes a small crowd of people in white lab coats, all of them hurrying toward us, their faces a mixture of fear, panic, and relief.

"Jessica! Where have you been?" says the lead one, a large man with a carefully sculpted beard.

Jessica seems flustered. "I . . . I've been here, I mean . . ." Her fingers go up to touch her ear. "I'm sorry. I have my earpiece turned off. *Earpiece on!* What's going on? This is my, erm . . . this is Georgina, by the way."

They all do the polite thing, and there are a few seconds of "Hi, Georgina, how are you?" but they don't mean it. As soon as they can, they turn their attention back to Jessica.

Beard Man: "It's a big one, Jess. I think we've at least identified where the CBE's coming from." He shows her his tablet. Jessica looks for a second and then says something that casts a chill into my heart.

"The church of St. Wulfran and All Saints?"

"It's an animal shelter," someone says.

St. Woof's.

The others nod and murmur.

"Looks like it. And it's already spread."

"This is *not* good."

Soon everyone is talking at once, and the crowd huddles together, squeezing me out, so I'm sort of on the margins of the group and it's pretty clear that everyone—Jessica included—has forgotten that I'm even there.

That's when I hear a shout from down the corridor: "No! Please, no!" Everyone turns to see a white-coated technician running toward them, clutching a phone to her ear. "I'll call you back!" she gasps, and then stops. I can see her face through the press of people, and I've never seen anyone look so distraught.

"It's here," she sobs. "It's confirmed. First human case, two others suspected . . ." Then her shoulders slump, her phone drops to the floor, and she covers her face with her hands.

The group of people I'm with gasp aloud, and Jessica mutters, "Oh no. Oh no, no, no . . . Please, God, no!"

The bearded man goes over to the crying woman, murmuring comforting words, and she whispers, "We tried . . . we tried so hard, and now everyone's going to . . ."

She cannot finish her words and starts weeping quietly. And then the group begins to move, gabbling as they hurry off back down the corridor, taking the sobbing woman with them. The panic in the atmosphere is so intense I can almost feel it on my skin.

And there I am, left alone, standing in the middle of the corridor.

Chapter Twenty-Nine

Jessica suddenly stops and looks back at me, as if seeing me for the first time.

"Can you get back on your own?" she says. "Take a taxi. Get Jackson to help you. And, Georgina—not a word. Not. A. Word." Her face is white with anxiety as she turns to leave. If part of me is feeling upset at being abandoned, the rest of me is so terrified that I feel like being sick.

Was that lady about to say, "Everyone's going to *die*?" Or was it something else?

I'm alone, blinking back tears, when I hear Jackson calling softly to me from the end of the corridor. He hasn't heard the commotion.

"Miss Santos! The kettle's on, and I have some Victoria sponge my wife baked. Would you care to join me?"

Not. A. Word.

The television is chattering in Jackson's little office while he makes tea and lays out the Victoria sponge on a china plate. I'm trying so hard to be polite while he chats amiably about how long he has till his retirement, and his wife's baking, and asking about Clem, but I can't get what has just happened out of my mind.

What had the lady in the white coat meant? We're all going to . . . what?

What had the man with the beard meant about St. Woof's?

"It's been a while, Georgie," Jackson was saying, "but it's always a pleasure to see you. Your mother would be pleased you've grown up so fit and healthy."

I force a smile. Jackson always says something nice about Mum when we meet: how clever she was, how well dressed, for example. Dad says he was very kind to me and Clem during that time I don't remember, when Mum was dying in a quarantine tent, surrounded by machines.

He sends us a Christmas card every year. It's always a Jesus-y one, never a Santa Claus one, and he writes a long message before signing his name.

Jackson has just started telling a story about Mum years ago when his radio crackles and I hear someone say, "Jackson: this is main reception. Would you check out a car parked in a reserved space in the south parking lot, please?"

"I'll be right back," says Jackson. "You stay here, and we'll figure you out a ride home, OK?"

I am barely listening because what is happening on the TV screen makes everything even worse.

Chapter Thirty

Look, if you're really sensitive about stuff, skip this bit. There are dead dogs in it.

The TV pictures show people wearing all-over protective suits, and face masks, and gloves. They're picking up dead dogs from the street and throwing them into the back of a truck. It doesn't look like this country, though.

REPORTER: *"Within days, all dogs in Britain may be banned from public spaces and from associating with other dogs. This is in response to the continued spread of the canine-borne Ebola disease. Several countries have already begun a program of humane killing of stray and pet dogs.*

"Earlier today, I spoke to the director of the National Centre for Disease Control, Ainsley Gill.

"Is there a risk that this disease will spread to humans?"

AINSLEY GILL: *"Well, at the moment, the risk seems small, but we're taking no chances. There have already been unconfirmed reports of human cases of CBE in China. Here in the UK, we are an island, which helps."*

REPORTER: *"All six of the UK cases are in the northeast of England. The dogs have been humanely destroyed. Researchers do not yet know the exact source of the outbreak. More on this story as it develops. This is Jamie Bates for News Now."*

I find I can hardly stand up. I stagger out of Jackson's hot office, a wave of fear washing over me.

I know more than the TV news. I know that the source of the outbreak had been traced to St. Woof's. I know there are now human cases in the UK.

And I know that I'm not supposed to know that.

How could that be?

There'll be a curfew. No dogs allowed outside.

How would that work?

In a daze, I shuffle past the statue of Edward Jenner toward the hazy sunshine. I barely hear Jackson behind me.

"Georgie! Miss Santos! You've forgotten your Victoria sponge!" I turn and he's standing there, a plate of cake in his hand, looking a little hurt.

"I . . . I'm sorry, Jackson, I have to go . . ." and I push through the double doors.

Somehow I make it to a waiting taxi. I clamber in and tell the driver my address, confirming the fare with my phone.

The little taxi screen in front of me shouts advertisements till I touch it to mute the volume.

I can still see the pictures, though. Trailers for films, ads for vacations, food, drinks . . . And, running under it all, a crawling message with the latest headlines:

Dog curfew "within days" says British government minister . . .

Northeast connection to CBE outbreak . . .

More CBE deaths in China . . .

USA—Canada border: "No Dogs" agreement . . .

German Chancellor: "This could be worse than the Black Death . . ."

I'm jolted out of my daze by the driver saying, "I didn't catch that, love. Do you want to change your destination?"

I have been muttering, "Mr. Mash, Mr. Mash, Mr. Mash," to myself, but the driver has given me an idea.

"Take me to St. Wulfran's church in Whitley Bay, please," I say.

Chapter Thirty-One

The taxi drops me at the end of the street, which has a police car parked across it and several officers in face masks preventing people from passing.

As I get closer, one holds up her hand to stop me. "Are you a resident?" she asks.

"N-no. I'm a volun—"

"Residents only, dear. If it's the park you're wanting, go round the back and up Clovelly Gardens."

"No. I don't need the park. It's the church. St. Woof's. I . . . I work there." It sounds a bit silly: I know as soon as I say it. Another police officer approaches, a man, and speaks to me through his face mask.

"Listen, love. I don't care if you're St. Wulfran 'imself. It's out of bounds for a reason, government orders. Now—"

"Can I at least speak to the vicar?"

The two of them stare at me, amazed—I think—at my nerve.

"No. You. Can't," says the man. "Now scram. This is an emergency."

I feel fear rising further inside me, and my voice gets higher in tone. *"What's going on?"*

"Check the news. Now I don't want to have to tell you again. Stand aside."

Behind me, a large van approaches the line of officers. Inside are several people in the same overalls I have seen before, all wearing face masks. The van is waved through, mounting the pavement to get past the police car that blocks the road.

I sit on a low wall and take out my phone to call St. Woof's. If I speak to the vicar directly, maybe I'll be able to find out what's going on.

"This is Reverend Maurice Cleghorn of St. Wulfran's Dog Shelter. I cannot take your call at the moment . . ."

I might have guessed.

"Eee, it's terrible, isn't it?"

I jump in fright at the voice. Sass Hennessey flicks her hair, sits down heavily next to me on the wall, and says again, *"Terrible."*

"What's happening?" I say. I have a fairly good idea, but I want to know how much Sass knows.

"It's that Dog Plague thingy, isn't it? All started here, they reckon. And it's going to get bad."

"How do you know?"

"Maurice told me."

There it is again. *Maurice.* Now I find I'm past caring. "You spoke to the vicar? How come?"

"I was there when the police and doctors arrived. They cleared us all out. Probably so we wouldn't see what they were doing."

I'm staring at Sass. She has a slightly smug look on her face. Like she knows something that I don't. She sees my puzzled look.

"You really have no clue, do you, Georgie? You do know what's going on in there, don't you?"

I can only shake my head dumbly. Is it my imagination or is Sass actually pleased to be telling me this? Perhaps she just enjoys being the one who knows and who can pass on information.

"All of the dogs . . ." and she draws a finger across her throat. I am horrified.

"They're cutting their throats?"

"No! You idiot. Of course not. 'Humane dispatch' they call it. Putting them down. Euthanasia. Lethal inj—"

"All right, all right, Sass. I get it." I'm breathing heavily. It's a few seconds before I can speak. "All of them?"

"Yup." This is when Sass fixes me with what I take to be a glare. "And all because *someone,* somewhere, ignored the cross-infection rules. Seems as though someone visited St. Woof's who was carrying the infection from China, and—"

"I . . . I'm sorry, Sass. I have to go." My head is swirling with thoughts, and I feel like throwing up.

I stagger away toward the seafront, and between the cars and the bikes, horns honking, and people yelling "Watch it!" till I'm on the path above the beach, looking down at a group of guys playing soccer, and people walking their dogs.

I'm gasping for breath, the air rasping in my throat as I suck in lungfuls.

Was it me?

I search my memory for the events of that day. The little Chinese girl . . . Dudley's soggy ball, which I took out of quarantine . . . Me handling it . . . then touching all the other dogs . . . my carelessness.

My carelessness!

And I think about the dogs in St. Woof's. Mr. Mash, of course, but also Sally-Ann and Ben and poor, ugly Dudley. Is it my fault?

I wipe a large tear away from my cheek and swallow hard and take a deep breath. One of those "that's the end of my panic" sighs when you think that it's all going to be a bit better. And then it hits me.

When I was in the dome, looking down at the beach a week from now. I knew something was different, but I hadn't been able to put my finger on it.

But now I think I know what it is.

Chapter Thirty-Two

I try to cast my mind back to the previous day in Dr. Pretorius's studio, which seems as though it was much longer ago. The book's pages are still jumbled up in my mind, and I'm trying to sort them out, but as soon as one is in place, the others seem to fly out and mix up again.

I crossed the road, didn't I?

I looked down at the beach.

Something was not right.

It was the people on the beach. With their dogs. Or rather the *lack* of people on the beach with their dogs. *That* was what was missing.

At that time of day, on that part of the beach, on a summer afternoon? There are normally *loads* of dogs. Half the beach is off-limits to dogs in the summer months anyway, so they're all crowded together on the other half: chasing balls, running in and out of the sea, shaking themselves dry, doing all of that fabulous doggy stuff that I love about them.

But in the future that I visited the dogs were gone.

I don't know how long I stand there, staring at the sand, the people, the dogs, the sea, my mind whirring with possibilities.

It must just have been a fault in the simulation, I tell myself. Perhaps it can't replicate that sort of thing? Perhaps Dr. Pretorius's computer program simply doesn't do animals. That makes sense, doesn't it? I'm desperate to convince myself, but I'm not doing a very good job of it.

I remember the giant scorpion—that is an animal. And something else as well: a conversation between some people I passed. What had they said?

"I says to 'im, you hide that dog if you dare . . ."

Who would hide a dog? And why?

What about the dog on the chain that's always barking? That hadn't been there. I have literally never passed that front garden and not seen the dog there.

A cold feeling comes over me, even though I'm sweating from running and the evening is warm. Did I really see the future? My mind is a storm of doubt and confusion and forgetfulness. It wasn't so long ago that I was pretty sure that Dr. Pretorius had tricked me and Ramzy—and now I'm doubting *that*.

Not only that, but it also seems as though it's my fault that Dog Plague broke out at St. Woof's, and it's already spreading.

And just when I think things can't get any worse, my phone buzzes in my pocket. Dad.

"Where are you? Are you OK?" He sounds agitated. "Jessica said you were on your way. She shouldn't have left you, really. I'd have come to collect you if—"

"I am. That is, I was. I got . . . delayed. It was . . . I'm fine, Dad. What's up?"

"Doesn't matter. Get back now. The police are here."

Oh, great.

Chapter Thirty-Three

I get off the FreeBike, leave it at the bottom of the lane, and walk up toward our house, panting from my pedaling and my mind swirling with anxiety. My headache has gone completely, but I feel as though my brain has been replaced with cotton wool, plus a cloud of worry and sadness about the dogs at St. Woof's.

I have to save Mr. Mash, that much I know. "Humane dispatch." I can't let that happen. I try to call Ramzy, but he doesn't pick up, and I remember he's probably still grounded.

There's a police car outside the house. Inside, Dad and two police officers, a man and a woman, are sitting at one end of the kitchen table, drinking tea and talking in low voices.

At the other end are Ramzy and his aunty Nush. She's giving him such a talking-to, in a low, furious voice. I can't understand what she's saying, but it sounds like one of those tellings-off that started half an hour ago and has continued nonstop. Her right forefinger is busy: when she's not wagging it under his nose, she's using it to jab him in the chest, making him wince. His head is bowed, and I feel so sorry for him.

I'm standing there for a few seconds, watching. No one has noticed me come in.

"Hello?" I say, and they all turn and look. I feel guilty already.

They're the same sort of questions—and I get the same sort of feelings—as at the hospital.

"How did you meet Dr. Pretorius?"

"What did she say to you?"

"What was this 3-D game?"

We answer truthfully, though I can tell that Ramzy now feels ashamed at having been deceived. The whole story just sounds ridiculous, and that's without mentioning the beach that had no dogs on it.

But Ramzy doesn't say anything about the video clip of the Geordie Jackpot numbers he took inside the studio. I don't understand why, but I don't bring it up, either.

I can only imagine that Ramzy, like me, still thinks—somewhere in the back of his mind—that it might all be real. I try to make eye contact with him—you know, to judge what he's thinking—but he keeps his eyes down all the time. Also Aunty Nush barely shifts her eyes off me. She watches me throughout the interview like I'm an escaped criminal who might attack her at any time. I'm sure she thinks I'm a bad influence on Ramzy. Two or three times, she shakes her head and says, "He good boy. Ramzy good boy."

I think, *If he's such a good boy, why are you being so horrible to him?*

"So tell me, Georgina, how would you get in touch with this Dr. Pretorius?" asks the woman officer. "Like, did you have a mobile number, or a messaging app, or ChAppster . . . ?"

Ramzy and I both shake our heads. "She never called us. We just . . . you know, met her. We arranged the next meeting, and turned up."

"And she didn't have your contact information?"

Again, we shake our heads.

The sheer craziness of our stories (which don't always match, thanks to my fuzzy memory) means that after about twenty minutes the officer who has done most of the questioning flips her notebook shut and turns off her bodycam. She speaks to Dad and to Aunty Nush.

"Thing is, Mr. Santos, Ms. Rahman, it's difficult to know whether or not a crime has been committed here. We have no record of a Dr. Emilia Pretorius in the area. The leasehold of the Spanish City dome is registered to a private limited company and there's insufficient evidence, on the basis of what we've been told today, to apply for a search warrant for the premises. We called round earlier: there's no one there, or at least no one answering."

Dad is not happy with this, I can tell. "But my daughter was hospitalized! And you're just going to let it go?"

The policewoman sighs. "Like I say, sir: no real evidence. One word against another, and juvenile migraine is not exactly uncommon. We would very much like to question this Dr. Pretorius, but we don't yet have grounds for an arrest or forced entry. We will definitely be keeping an eye out for her, but meanwhile my advice to you, Georgina, and to you, Ramzy, is to stay away from the Spanish City and, if you see this person again, report it to us. How's that?"

Ramzy and I nod, kind of relieved, but Dad's not giving up so easily. "How's that? Not very satisfactory is how it is, Officer. I've had—"

The policewoman interrupts. "I'm sorry, sir. It's not helped by the latest news. I don't know if you know, but all the security services in the country have had their leave canceled for the foreseeable future. This CBE—Dog Plague they're calling it—is proving to be very serious."

The other officer chips in: "I've had to cancel a week in Cornwall."

It all translates as: *I'm sorry, sir, but we have much more important things to be worried about than the fantasy of two kids and some games inventor who is probably harmless.*

182

As the police officers leave, Aunty Nush stands up. "Ramzy. He good boy," she says again.

The policewoman says, "I'm sure he is, ma'am."

After they've gone, Dad turns to us and says, "I guess you can consider yourselves pretty lucky that nothing worse happened."

I think he feels a bit uncomfortable. Aunty Nush, after all, is still in our kitchen, with a face like she's just licked a frog. Perhaps she didn't understand what was going on, although Ramzy translated.

Anyway, Dad can't really tell me off while Ramzy's there, and he can't tell Ramzy off, either, not while his aunt is there, so it's all a bit awkward.

Then Ramzy says, "We'd better go," and just as Aunty Nush is gathering up her cloak to step out the door, she looks at Dad and curls her lip.

"Ramzy good boy. She no."

She means me, obviously. And I'm thinking, *Well, thanks a lot, you meanie—that's got me into a lot of trouble!* Behind his aunty's back, Ramzy shrugs apologetically and then holds up his phone. He mouths the word *later* to me.

The door shuts, and I can hear Aunty Nush start in on Ramzy again as soon as they're walking away. Dad turns to me, arms folded. Then he says, "Blimey. Poor Ramzy!"

And I'm so relieved that I just step into his big arms and start sobbing, and he holds me tight. I'm crying for Dudley, and for Mr. Mash, and all the dogs that may die, and the people too, but it's not just that.

I'm crying for myself. I'm crying with guilt for what I've done. I'm crying because it's all my fault, and if I could go back and put it right I would, but I can't.

I don't know how long we're there, me and Dad, holding each other and me crying, but I don't hear Dad's phone ping. I just look up when I hear his voice.

"Aye aye," he says, reading a message. "Announcement on the TV at ten."

Behind him, Jessica has come through the door. "I thought there might be. Government statement." Then she adds, as an afterthought, "You OK, Georgina?"

Clem—who has been upstairs in the Teen Cave throughout all of this—is already in the front room with the TV on.

It is not the government, though. It's the king.

Chapter Thirty-Four

The television announcer says, "We now go live to Balmoral for a statement on the deepening CBE crisis by His Majesty the king." There's no music, no other introduction.

The king is in formal country clothes: tweed jacket, checked shirt, tie. He's seated at a desk in a grand, oak-paneled room. A window behind him shows Scottish hills. He looks serious, concern furrowing his brow, even before he's said anything.

STATEMENT BY HIS MAJESTY
THE KING

"I am speaking to you today from my home in Scotland. Even here in the Highlands it is impossible to escape the ghastly news of a disease spreading throughout the country with alarming speed.

"I have spoken today to both the prime

minister and the secretary of state for health, and they have informed me that the situation is very grave indeed. Without swift and decisive action, many thousands—maybe even many millions—of people may die.

"We may be facing a disease as deadly as the plagues of many hundreds of years ago. I say this not to alarm you, but to make clear the need for the measures that my government has announced. Without them, the survival of our families—indeed our nation itself—will be thrown into doubt.

"This is a situation that we cannot—and will not—tolerate.

"Canine-borne Ebola is, as you may already know, caused by a rapidly mutating virus, which even the very best doctors and scientists both here and in the rest of the world have so far failed to overcome.

"I am told that, in time, a remedy will be discovered, although that will certainly be too late to avoid some of the sadness and pain that await us.

"Only by acting now can we hope to prevail against this deadly disease.

"Accordingly, my government has this evening issued emergency instructions.

"With immediate effect, all dogs are to be kept indoors until further instructions are issued. That includes working dogs and assistance dogs as well as domestic pets.

"Dogs seen outside—and that includes private gardens and enclosed spaces—will be regarded as strays. Specialist police and army marksmen will, from tonight, be patrolling the streets of our cities and villages. They have been given orders to shoot such animals."

The king, at this point, swallows hard and closes his eyes for a moment.

"Gosh, he's going to cry," says Jessica, horrified.

"Don't be daft: he's the king," says Clem. I have to say, though, that he does look very upset. He goes on:

"As you may know, I am a lover of dogs myself. I know firsthand how difficult this will be, not only for you but also for your pets. They will not understand the absolute necessity of this temporary measure, but it is my sincere hope that you will, and that you will do your duty accordingly and comply with the law completely.

"The British are known worldwide as a nation of animal lovers. We are world leaders in protecting animals, which makes it all the more painful to have to announce these measures.

"I do hope that, wherever you are, you will join me in praying for a speedy conclusion to this challenge that we all face. I wish for resilience and fortitude in the struggle ahead.

"May God bless us all."

We sit in silence as the picture fades to black.

In the quiet, we hear a single gunshot.

"Maybe it was a car backfiring," says Dad. It's nice of him to try to make us feel better.

The chaos, however, is only just beginning.

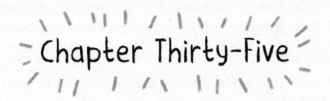

Chapter Thirty-Five

It starts with a series of late-night messages from Ramzy that begin as I'm lying in bed, thinking of the king nearly crying on TV.

Stray dogs will be shot, he said. That's bad enough. But Mr. Mash is in danger *now*.

Anyway, Ramzy's last message is simply:

Meet me by the tree. Midnight.

The tree. Mum's tree.

I throw back the duvet and look out my bedroom window. The moon is nearly full, making the fields a dark, inky green, and there is Mum's tree at the top of the slight hill. It's typical of Ramzy to pick such a spot to meet. It's exactly his idea of an adventure.

I view the situation differently. You see, there are some things that you just have to accept. Going to school, for example. You can complain about it, but you've still got to go. Rain on a school picnic is another.

Broccoli.

But leaving Mr. Mash to be put down doesn't fit into the category of "things you just have to accept."

So I get up and get dressed.

Chapter Thirty-Six

And that's why I find myself, shortly after midnight, standing in my rain boots in the poop composter behind St. Woof's, a handkerchief over my nose, but gagging nonetheless at the stink. Ramzy and I have hardly said a word all the way here: it's as if everything we're doing is just *understood*. I like him for that.

Leaving the house was easy. My bedroom's at the back, and there's a tree with a branch that I can reach from my window. We've even joked about it, Dad and I—he calls it the "fire escape."

I have a pair of long rubber gloves and swimming goggles in my jeans pocket, along with a handkerchief that I've soaked with some of Clem's aftershave "borrowed" from the bathroom cabinet.

Mum's tree was rustling loudly in the breeze when I got there. I half expected Ramzy to be hiding nearby just to scare me, and I was glad that he wasn't. It was all too serious for that. He just stepped out from behind the tree and said, "Hi."

"Did you get away OK?" I asked, and he shrugged as if to say, *Looks like it.*

"Aunty Nush all right?" In the moonlight, I got a flash of white as he rolled his eyes hard.

"She's a total pain," he said, "but thank God for headphones, eh?"

He's told me this before: Aunty Nush stays up late, watching TV shows, wearing headphones because they live in such a tiny flat. His dad is at home at the moment, and Ramzy says he's so tired that he sleeps most of the time, which only leaves his excitable little brothers.

"It's a risk I had to take," he said with a touch of bravado in his voice. We stood there for a moment by the rustling tree.

Eventually, I said, "Shall we do this then?"

Ramzy nodded and we turned to the path that leads out of the field. Behind us, the breeze shook the leaves even louder, as though it was wishing us on our way, and I smiled, despite my fear.

Too nervous to talk, we made our way in silence through the dark streets to the back wall of the churchyard.

There was a stretch of tape saying HEALTH RISK—DO NOT CROSS and we dodged under it. At the front of the church, a police car was parked on the street, with two officers inside, but that was it. We were pretty well concealed as we skirted the edge of the churchyard in the shadows and then—one by one—crept across the open lawn to the poop composter.

That was not, by the way, the original plan. No: the plan till two minutes ago was to climb in a window, or even just go in through the vestry side door, which I know is sometimes left open due to a really stiff lock. Thanks to the warm weather, the windows have been left open a lot. Except now all of the windows at ground level are locked, and the vestry door has a huge plastic tent covering it. So it wasn't much of a plan anyway, really.

"There's another way in," said Ramzy as we crouched under a big laurel bush, staring at the church. "But you're not gonna like it."

Which is how we ended up here.

The composter, about the size of a bathtub, is dug into the ground, about half a yard deep, and is covered with a heavy wooden lid made out of an old door. With the lid on, it doesn't smell so bad, especially as every few days some sort of chemical is sprinkled on all the poo to make it break down. But when Ramzy and I slide the lid off, the stench hits us like a punch in the throat.

Ramzy retches.

"Shhh," I say.

"I can't help it," he hisses. "Gimme the hanky." I untie it

from my face and hand it to him. He takes a grateful lungful of aftershave-scented cloth and hands it back. Silently, I put the rubber gloves on, retie the hankie round my mouth and nose, snap on the goggles, and finally tuck my jeans into the boots.

There's an infection risk that I'm *very* aware of. I have thought it through and decided that, so long as I take care, the danger is worth it.

Just below ground level is the chute that leads up into the old church. It's just wide enough for me to squeeze my shoulders in, but I'm going to have to kneel down in the muck.

Beneath my legs the poo oozes as I crouch down, and I have to fight the urge to be sick. I'm trying to breathe through my mouth, but I end up *tasting* the smell as well, and combined with Clem's cheap aftershave it seems to be causing a headache again, which is just another thing to scare me.

The chute isn't long, but there's a slight bend in the middle, and I have to push hard with my legs to propel myself upward. As I do so, my rubber-clad feet sink deeper into the composting poo, and I realize that I cannot get any farther.

"Ramzy?" I call as quietly as I can. I can lift my eyes upward and see where I'll be coming out. My voice travels up, too, and into the church. Ramzy hasn't heard.

Louder, I call, "Ramzy! I'm stuck," and above my head, it echoes round the church interior. A dog barks. "Shhhh!" I say.

"*Ramzy!*" I'm scared now, and scrabble some more with my feet.

The smell is truly overpowering and seems to have taken over my whole nose and throat.

"Help me!" I hear my words bounce off the stone walls inside the church: "*Help me . . . me . . . me!*" I hear a whine, which I'm sure is Mr. Mash. "I'm coming, Mashie!" I say, but I'm not going anywhere.

And then I feel Ramzy's hands on my legs. He has jumped into the poop pit and is shoving as hard as he can. Bit by bit, I find myself inching up the aluminum chute, till my head pops out the top, dislodging the square garbage can lid that covers it, and it clatters to the tiled floor, setting off a volley of barks.

At least they're still alive, I tell myself.

With my legs free of the muck below, I can use my feet to push myself the last bit, and seconds later I've heaved myself out and I'm standing in familiar surroundings. I try to take a breath of my favorite smell, but all I can smell is the poo on my clothes, boots . . . everything.

I had guessed that my arrival might set off some of the dogs, but I wasn't ready for just how many of them would wake up and start whining and barking. The noise grows as I tiptoe out of the vestry and up the aisle to Mr. Mash's pen and, in one swift movement, open his gate and go in.

"Mashie! I'm here," I whisper, and his tail starts its familiar full-bottom wag. "No, no, no tickling this time, Mashie. Come on, quickly."

I clip on his leash that hangs by the gate and bring him out, closing the gate behind me and heading straight back to the poop chute. I pass the quarantine section, where Dudley and Ben come to the front of their pens and watch us. Poor Sally-Ann's there as well now.

By now the barking has become a cacophony: all around me is a wall of yapping and I know I have to be quick; otherwise—

As I come round the corner into the storage room, the main lights flicker on in the church, flooding everything with a white glow, and I hear a man's voice—a policeman? I have no idea—shout, "Is anyone there?"

I can't wait. I lift up a startled Mr. Mash and hold him above the chute. He gives me an accusing look, but I have no choice. "Sorry!" I whisper as I drop him headfirst down the opening and he gives a startled little yelp as he descends.

I can hear heavy footsteps coming up the aisle, and I try not to panic. I have to get in there as fast as I can, so I just dive. Headfirst. Straight down the chute, and I land with my whole head and shoulders submerged in the stinking morass, right next to Mr. Mash and Ramzy. I haven't even got time to think about being disgusted; I just stand up in the half-composted poo and think to myself that I'm glad I kept my mouth shut. There's dog poo in my hair and in my ears and it is every bit as *totally disgusting* as you can imagine, but I'm just not thinking about that, as every bit of me is wondering how I'm going to go back and get my other dogs.

Ramzy stands next to me, fear written across his face; then suddenly he croaks, "Get down," and pulls me with him. As we crouch in the stinking slime, the beam of a flashlight slices round the corner and comes into the churchyard from the front, sweeping a bright circle of light across the grass.

"Who's there?" says a voice. "Identify yourself. This is the police."

As I feared.

Chapter Thirty-Seven

We crouch lower, our noses about a millimeter away from the poo.

The flashlight beam passes slowly over our heads. I'm holding my breath because of the smell, but I haven't got long left.

Then the beam comes back, even slower, and stops.

"Stand up, with your hands in the air."

I've heard it said that, at times of great stress, your thinking becomes clearer. At this moment, I know for certain that if we are caught, and arrested, or whatever it is that police do with kids, then Mr. Mash will be returned to St. Woof's and he'll die.

I am *not* going to let that happen.

I'm also very aware that the whole dogs thing is *my* obsession. Ramzy is coming along for the ride, but it's me who's driving the whole thing.

So it's not really a choice, is it? Yet it's Ramzy who makes the decision.

Out of the side of his mouth, he murmurs, "I'm gonna make a run for it, Georgie. He can't grab both of us, and that way you'll get away with Mashie."

At this exact moment—knee-deep in dog poo, a flashlight dazzling our eyes—I know that Ramzy is the most loyal friend I could ever have. In the darkness, he reaches toward me and squeezes my hand. It should have been a lovely moment, a real bonding, only something squishes between our palms as he does so.

The policeman says, "All right, climb out, very slowly. And no funny business."

We both stand up and start to clamber out of the pit.

"Oh my good God," says the policeman. The light is shining right at us, so I can't really see him, but he's standing about three yards away, aiming the flashlight beam first at Ramzy, then at me. Mr. Mash manages to jump out of the pit as well. The policeman's radio crackles and he talks into it.

"Two suspects, Sarge. Minors. And a dog. Round the back . . . and they're covered in, well . . . I hate to think, Sarge. Bring gloves."

I recognize his voice. It's the same policeman who told me to clear off from St. Woof's earlier. I'm scared that he'll recognize me.

He takes a couple of steps toward us. "Right," he says. "Who have we got here?" Without warning, Ramzy darts to the side and makes a run for it across the church lawn.

"Hey! You little . . . come back!" But he's too late, and realizes that if he chases Ramzy, then I'll run off and he might lose both of us. So instead—and completely against our expectations—he turns back to me and grabs me by both shoulders before I've even taken a step.

"*Euch.* What the . . . ?"

I am—as I think I've mentioned—absolutely covered in dog mess, and his grip slips at exactly the moment that Mr. Mash growls menacingly and advances toward him, showing his teeth. The policeman backs away.

"Call your dog off, love. That's an offense, that is."

"Mr. Mash," I start to say, but Mr. Mash isn't listening. Instead, he takes another step toward the policeman, his neck straining forward to the full length of the leash, and lets loose a volley of growls and barks.

I can see what's going to happen as the policeman backs away farther, and it takes just one final snarl from Mr. Mash for the policeman to stumble backward on the edge of the composting pit.

"Ah . . . ahhh . . . *noooo!*"

With flailing arms, he falls backward into the pit, landing awkwardly on his side, one hand plunged into the mire, his other scrabbling at the side of the pit.

It's our only chance. I turn and run as the policeman begins to climb out, but he's sliding around and toppling over. Mr. Mash is way ahead of me. "Stop!" echoes behind me.

I run and run, Ramzy joining us at the churchyard gate, and we keep running, through the new estate, down back lanes. All thought of the smell and the filth is banished by the single goal in my mind, which is to get as far away as possible.

And then we go down an alley between two houses and emerge at the top field by Mum's tree, and we can follow the hedge that runs down the side of the field with the cows. Eventually, I see our barn, and it's only when we're down there and have undone the padlock with the key that's hidden under a plant pot and are safely inside, drawing rasping breaths, that we speak our first words since we started running.

"Georgie . . . ," wheezes Ramzy.

"What?"

"You stink!"

We both start laughing, and carry on laughing like maniacs, even though it's two in the morning. I turn on the hose outside the dark barn and start the long process of getting us both, and Mr. Mash, clean.

I keep thinking of Mr. Mash snarling at the policeman and my bedroom wall poster:

Don't bite if a growl is enough.

Mr. Mash thinks the hosing down is great fun, and bites at the jet of water. I think, sadly, that it's the last fun he'll be having for a little while. He's going to have to stay very well hidden.

It's only then that I realize that he might, in fact, be sick. I was so focused on saving him from being put down, I didn't think about it. I say nothing to Ramzy, but just because Mashie wasn't in the quarantine section doesn't mean he hasn't already got the disease.

Well.

I'll just have to hope, won't I?

Chapter Thirty-Eight

I can't tell you everything that's been going on in the last few days. There's been just too much. We haven't heard any more "cars backfiring," though, which is a good thing.

Mainly, Ramzy and I have been living our days in fear of a police car approaching either of our houses. What we did was pretty serious, especially the running away from an officer bit. We both know that we'll be in big trouble. But we both also know that the police and practically everyone else who works in a uniform have got bigger things to worry about than a couple of kids in a pit of poo.

The day after our St. Woof's raid Ramzy messaged me.

> Pants and shoes drying out nicely under my bed though still a bit stinky. Aunty Nush & Dad suspect nothing. You? How's Mr. M?

I replied:

Mr. Mash is staying in the barn, completely undetected, so I take him food in my backpack. It's fairly easy to go down our lane toward the main road, and then double back just before the gate (I'm obscured by a big hedge), and so that's what I do.

I stay for about an hour, throwing a ball around the big barn, hiding in a pile of cardboard boxes till Mashie finds me, wagging his whole bottom with delight, and then I just sit there, scratching his tummy and trying not to think of the other dogs I had to leave behind.

I wonder if he misses his friends. I wonder whether the awful thing that I cannot even write about has happened at St. Woof's yet. I wonder what the poor vicar makes of everything. It all seems so unnecessary, putting them down. Mr. Mash seems fine.

Sitting there, in the dusty barn, among the old rusty car doors, and a long exhaust pipe and other car junk, I jump a little when my phone buzzes with an incoming message. It's the vicar: he says he'll be coming round tonight.

I leave the little window in the barn open to let in some

fresh air because Mr. Mash has just let one go; then I close the door, promising to come and see him again soon. It's not much of a life for him, but it is at least a life.

Dad has the radio on in the workshop, and for the first time I can remember it's tuned to a news station. No classic rock, which is Dad's usual favorite, just Bad News: endless updates on the spread of CBE.

"A'right, dear?" he says when I walk in. I think he's lost weight. He's pretty big, my dad, but his face looks thinner. "What you been up to?"

I shrug in response. "Oh, you know—this 'n' that." He doesn't appear to mind. Everyone's in a strange mood, it seems. Dad sits on the side ledge of the campervan. He bites into a sandwich and offers me one. He shakes his head at the radio.

"It's getting worse," he says with his mouth full, although I already know because I've heard the latest update, which announced that two people have now died in the UK, and other cases are suspected. This makes me nervous, in case Mr. Mash *is* sick. But if he is, he isn't showing any signs of it. There are also now countless dogs dead from the virus, and several more have been shot overnight.

"They were all strays," says Dad, trying to comfort me. This at least means that the dogs' owners are not upset, but it doesn't stop me from feeling sad for the dogs.

Later that evening, Clem and I are on the sofa, watching the television. It is like we're in some sort of a daze.

Round and around it goes: the same pictures from China, from France, from Canada, from everywhere. The same reporters cropping up, standing in front of hospitals or government buildings, or landmarks like the Statue of Liberty, and saying pretty much the same thing.

> "... the United States government has announced that the country's reserve military force, the National Guard, has been put on full alert ..."

> "... further cases of people falling victim to the deadly CBE virus have been reported in Mexico City, the Mexican government said today ..."

> "... President Batushansky reacted aggressively to the massing of troops on his country's border, and expressed his wish that the CBE crisis would not damage the ongoing peace process between the two nations ..."

I nearly jump off the sofa when I hear the doorbell. It's the vicar from St. Woof's, and I don't think I have ever seen a grown-up so changed in appearance.

Where once there was a pink-faced, healthy-looking man with a sparkle in his eyes and a friendly—even goofy—smile, there is now a shell. His shoulders sag, his face is an odd grayish color, and he looks as though he hasn't slept in days.

I'm terrified he's going to say something about Mr. Mash. Ramzy and I might be feeling very pleased with ourselves for having dodged the police—but there's still a dog missing from St. Woof's, and the police will have told the vicar all about the previous night.

"H-hello, Vicar," I say, and he gives me a tight smile. *Oh no, he knows,* I think. *He's going to tell Dad.*

Dad is coming up the path behind him.

"Maurice!" he calls. "I saw you go past. Come on in. Mind, it's a bad business this, eh? I'm so sorry about your dogs."

"I can't stay, Rob," he says, his voice cracking with fatigue, or emotion, or both. "I wanted to give something to Georgie."

He fumbles in his pocket and pulls out a dog's collar, which he dumps in my hands. "It's OK," he says. "It's been sterilized."

I hold it up. The little round disc attached to the collar says DUDLEY and I grip it in my palm.

"Poor old Dudley," says the vicar.

"Was . . . was he . . . ?" I can't even say it but the vicar knows.

"He didn't suffer one bit," he says, shaking his head. "And you can take comfort that the last weeks of his life were made better by you and your wee friend."

I nodded. "Have they all . . . ?"

The vicar swallowed. "Yes, Georgie. It was the vet's instructions. The risk was too great. They have all been put down."

I hear Dad gasp. "What about Mr. Mash?" he asks.

That, I think, *should have been my reaction. Isn't it suspicious that I'm not more upset about Mr. Mash?*

"Yes—what about Mr. Mash?" I say quickly. It sounds unbelievable but Dad hasn't noticed.

"Well," says the vicar. He's taking his time, choosing his words carefully. "As I think Georgie already knows . . ."

He's looking at me steadily. "Mr. Mash was, ah . . . *rehomed* very recently. Two young people arrived with the intention of giving him a good home."

All I can do is nod. Dad nods too and says, "That's good."

"I just hope they know what they're doing," he concludes. "And that they don't put Mr. Mash at any further risk. *Or themselves,*" he adds with extra weight. "It has been a devilish few days. The health authorities seem convinced that the British outbreak began with us at St. Woof's. A breach of the sanitary regulations would be all that was needed to set it off."

I turn away and run upstairs.

I collapse on my bed, letting Dudley's collar fall from my hand onto the bedroom floor, and I just stare at the ceiling, unable to feel anything.

Still, nobody knows that the whole thing is my fault.

Chapter Thirty-Nine

I wake up a little later to feel someone running their fingers through my tousled hair, which is very strange. I can smell the strong soap that Jessica uses at work on her hands, and when I open my eyes, she's staring out my window. She's never done anything like this before.

Perhaps she thinks I'm still asleep. I hear her say, "I'm sorry, Georgie. I'm so sorry," over and over again.

Georgie. Jessica never calls me Georgie.

I open my eyes and murmur, "Why? Why are you sorry?"

She stiffens a little in surprise and pulls her hand away from my head. There's a long silence. And I mean a *loooong* silence. I lie on my side and stare at the moon through my window. I hadn't even closed the curtains, and it splashes my bedroom with shadows. A gray-blue light falls on the dogs on my duvet cover, and the puppy calendar that I get in my stocking every Christmas. "Jessica?" I say eventually. I hear her take a deep breath.

I don't turn round to look at her; I don't want to make eye contact. She says the quietest, "Sorry." I'm not even sure what she's sorry for, but I say nothing.

We stay like that for a moment; then she says, "It's going to be tough. The next few weeks, months, years even. It's going to be tougher than any of us have ever known, and I'm sorry I've not been able to do the one thing that I'm supposed to do."

"What do you mean?" I turn my head to look at her. The pale light creates deep lines on her face and forehead. She honestly looks about twenty years older.

"Find the cure. I know it's not just me but—"

"It's not your fault, Jessica. None of this is your fault. It's . . ."

I stop myself from saying, "It's mine."

Jessica sighs. "It's not yours, either."

She's wrong there. Dead wrong. But I can't tell her. Instead, I'll just have to put it right.

At that moment, that *instant*, an idea begins to form in my head.

I can hear the familiar music of the ten o'clock news from the TV downstairs, but I don't feel like listening to any more stories about dogs being shot, and people dying, and reporters being gloomy.

I roll back over and close my eyes, as if I'm going to sleep.

A moment later, Jessica gets up from my bed and leaves the room. My eyes are wide open, and my brain is fizzing with the thought of what I have to do.

But I might never have done it if my phone had not pinged beneath my pillow at that moment, with an incoming message.

Chapter Forty

It's a very short message.

READ THIS.

There's a link to a Web page, which I click on.

MYSTERY OF THE
BILLIONAIRE RECLUSE

by our Norway reporter, Nils Oskarssen

---

*With enough money, they say,
you can be who you like.*

OSLO: Dr. Erika Pettarssen—the inventor of the global social-media platform, ChAppster—certainly has enough money: more than enough to disappear completely from public life. Where she is, however, is unknown, leading to the belief that she may have changed her identity in order to hide.

Her $1.2 billion fortune makes her one of only 5,000 billionaires in the world, although her whereabouts seem to be an unfathomable mystery.

Until 2012, the successful games and app designer—regarded by many in the industry as a genius—lived alone on a small, private island in the Oslofjord between Norway and Sweden. She had no close family, and few friends. Neighbors—and there weren't many—said she swam frequently in the chilly sea. They described her as "intensely private."

Her groundbreaking work on 3-D virtual-reality installations such as Disney's Surround-a-Room had already made her wealthy. But it was her ownership of the social-media app ChAppster that saw her riches rocket when she sold the company five years ago.

DANGEROUS EXPERIMENTS

Since then, her island mansion has stood empty, and Dr. Erika Pettarssen has disappeared.

In a rare interview with the *Oslo Times* in 2005, Dr. Pettarssen hinted at her future.

"I have plans I want to work on. One day, I may just take off, you know? I have an idea—a model, if you will—that could, well, change the whole future, ha ha. There are possibilities arising with 3-D modeling, and quantum computing, that are hugely exciting." She added, "I work best on my own, without commercial pressures."

Born in England to a Norwegian father and a South African mother, the young Erika Pettarssen moved to the USA as a young child and grew up first in Ohio and then Florida. She was an outstanding student and gained a scholarship to the California Institute of Technology.

A doctorate from Harvard followed, and a career in academia beckoned. A young Bill Gates, the founder of Microsoft, was a student, and she liked to joke, "I taught that Bill everything he knows!"

Then came a move to Norway during the tech boom of the early twenty-first century.

Shortly before her disappearance, she launched the Erika Pettarssen Foundation, a charitable organization providing scholarships for underprivileged students from Africa. The foundation runs independently and says it has "no contact" with its founder.

Oslo Police Department issued a statement saying, "We do not know where Dr. Erika Pettarssen is, but why should we? Unless she breaks the law, this is not a police concern."

The article is accompanied by a grainy color photograph of a woman who may—or may not—be Dr. Pretorius. She is black and slim, but the woman in the photo is wearing sunglasses and a baseball cap, and appears to have short, cropped hair. A second photograph shows a large, low house surrounded by big lawns—the kind of photo taken from a helicopter or drone.

I read the page again, and then again. I check the source: it is definitely the website of the newspaper. I check the newspaper: it is real and "reputable." This is all basic stuff from our Online Education lessons, but it has never seemed important till now.

You still there?

Then Ramzy's face pops up wanting to LiveTalk. I turn his volume down low.

"Told you it was important. What do you think?"

"Is it her?" I whisper. "Where'd you find it? How?"

There's a pause, and then we have the *strangest* conversation, which goes like this:

Ramzy says, "What do you mean?"

"What do you mean, what do I mean? I mean—how did you find that article?"

"But you know—you were there. When I found that envelope in Dr. Pretorius's room."

"What envelope? What room? Stop it, Ramzy."

"Georgie? Are you messing with me? The envelope with the name on it that I said I'd check out. Georgie!"

And I have a horrible feeling that a chunk of my memory—a tiny chunk—has been wiped out. Ramzy is so insistent that I have to believe him. It's happened two or three times in the last few days. Yesterday I said to Dad, "Will you pass me the . . . the . . . the, erm . . . tsk, the . . . butter!"

We just laughed but he did give me a funny look. And the day before I walked past the barn and was on the street before I remembered that I had a bagful of dog food for Mr. Mash and had to turn back.

Lying in bed, talking to Ramzy, I have this sensation in my stomach that this might keep happening, and I know exactly why: I have damaged my brain. Meanwhile, Ramzy is still on LiveTalk.

". . . I think it's probably her but I'm not certain."

I force myself back into the conversation. "She has the same initials," I say, "and we know Dr. Pretorius likes swimming."

Ramzy lets the silence hang till I admit, "That's not proof, is it?"

"We could just ask her?" Ramzy says, as if it's the most normal thing in the world. *"Excuse me, Dr. Pretorius, are you secretly the billionaire recluse, Dr. Erika Pettarssen?"*

"Don't be silly," I say—but it's a typical Ramzy idea. No social filter, you see. He would totally do it.

I'm only half concentrating on what he's saying, though, because the article is echoing in my mind, joining with the thought I had after Jessica was in my room. Can I do it? Can *we* do it? Ramzy keeps talking for a bit. I hardly even remember to say good night.

Afterward, I lie in bed, my arm dangling over the edge, and in my imagination I feel the comforting rasp of Mr. Mash's rough tongue on the back of my hand.

To be honest, I don't really sleep. I don't think I've slept a full night for ages. Instead, I wriggle and turn and sweat, and have bad dreams that I can't even remember. I wake up with a dry mouth and a damp, cold duvet sticking to me again.

Dr. Pettarssen's words from the article echo in my mind. *Change the whole future.*

My wild idea turns over and over in my head.

Chapter Forty-One

The next day I'm up at seven to go and check on Mr. Mash in the barn.

It's one of those summer days that's hot even before the day has really started. When I come downstairs, Jessica and Dad are both up already, and things have worsened over-night.

"Shush," says Jessica, holding up her hand. She's listening to the radio.

". . . the government announced at midnight. Unless a cure is found within a week, all international travel will be suspended. Furthermore, in an attempt to slow down the spread of the illness to humans, a cull of every dog in the country would begin.

"Veterinarians have already begun a limited program of euthanasia in some dog shelters close

to the center of the outbreak. This would be ex-
tended nationwide if—"

Jessica switches off the radio angrily.

"I can't stand it anymore! It's as if we're being *blamed*! We are trying. We are working our hardest . . ." The rest of her sentence is lost as Dad puts his arms round her and she buries her face in his shoulder.

I do feel sorry for Jessica. She's not my favorite person in the world, but if anyone knows it's not her fault, then it's me.

The words of the woman on the radio ring in my ears as I walk down the lane to the barn.

A cull of every dog in the country would begin.

A cull. A mass killing.

Unless a cure is found within a week.

A WEEK! That means we don't have long, and I have no idea if the thing that was spinning round and round in my head as I twisted in my hot duvet is even going to work.

I cheer up a little bit when I see Mr. Mash. Being cooped up does not suit him, though: it doesn't suit any dog.

Mr. Mash wags his tail hard when I go in and rolls over on his back for a tummy tickle.

"It's for your own good, Mashie," I explain to him again and again. I throw the ball for him around the barn, but it's no fun for a dog like him, who wants to run and run on the beach, biting at the waves as if they're attacking him.

"He's looking better," says a boy standing in the doorway of the barn.

I look up, startled. I know the voice. It is familiar.

He's wearing a face mask and thin latex gloves. "Aunty Nush," he says by way of explanation, and I nod my understanding. It's Ramzy, of course. How could I . . . ? What . . . is happening to me?

"Come, Mashie," I say. I loop a bit of old string through his collar and tie the other end to the handle of an old car door. Mr. Mash settles down, with a sigh.

Is that it? he seems to say to me. *Some pal you are.*

"You do know, though, the disease isn't airborne?" I say to Ramzy, indicating his face mask. I don't dare tell him that I forgot his name just now. It's way too strange. "You can't get it by breathing. You have to—"

"I know," he says, pulling it down over his chin to free up his mouth. "But do you want to argue with my aunty Nush? Go ahead: I'll bring the popcorn."

"Anyway, I thought you were grounded?"

"I am. But some things are more important than getting told off."

I think about what could be worse than getting told off by the terrifying Aunty Nush and can't really come up with anything. But then Ramzy is braver than me.

He sits on an old oil drum, his feet not quite touching the floor, and says, "So? You want to talk to me about what's

221

going on with you? I can tell when you're working on something."

"Huh?" I say.

"Last night on the phone, you went all distant. What are you planning?"

Well, I'm going to have to tell him my plan at some point.

So I do, although "plan" is an exaggeration. It's more of an idea, and he helps me figure it out as we go. Soon we have something resembling an actual plan.

Ramzy calls it "adventurous," and I agree. Although better descriptions would be: reckless. Stupid. Unworkable:

1. We test whether or not Dr. Pretorius's dome really did take me a week into the future by checking the lottery numbers in the draw tomorrow. If they match, then we know it was real. As a bonus, we also buy a lottery ticket, which will make us millionaires. Yay to that, at least.

2. If it turns out that what happens in the dome really *is* the future, or at least a very accurate prediction of it, then we use it to go a whole year into the future and bring back the cure for CBE.

"What could possibly go wrong?" says Ramzy with an uncertain grin.

But the middle-of-the-night idea is looking a lot less solid in the harsh light of day.

"And exactly how," I ask, thinking aloud, "are we going to 'bring back' the cure?"

"I don't know," he says. "It'll be written down, right? Like a formula."

"Sure," I say, rolling my eyes. "So I just go to the future and ask someone for the recipe for an incredibly complex antiviral drug and then memorize it. Simple."

He frowns and bites his bottom lip with his rabbit teeth.

"And there's worse," I say as a thought hits me. "What if we can only get hold of . . . like . . . some actual medicine? Not a formula. A vial, or a syringe, or whatever. How would we get it back to *now* so that it can be, you know, examined and reproduced?"

Ramzy thinks. Then he smiles. "But that's obvious! You swallow it!"

"Ramzy, have you gone completely nuts? There's no way I can just—"

"You can! Remember the peach? You swallowed a lump of peach and it came back *inside you*! It was the scorpion sting that—how did she say it?—'breached the RL–VR gap' or something. You're the only one who can do it, Georgie! It'll be in a little glass tube that you can swallow whole—you know: like medicines always are." There's a pause and then he adds, "Probably."

I take a deep breath. "It won't work, Ramzy. We don't know if Dr. Pretorius is even there in the dome, and, well . . ."

"Well, what?"

I sit down next to Mr. Mash and scratch his ears and I tell Ramzy about my memory blanks. How things are just disappearing. How I couldn't remember who he was five minutes ago.

He listens, then says, "That's not good, Georgie."

"I know. I can't do it again. I mean, that headache, and the memory thing . . ."

We sit in silence for a while. Mr. Mash is still panting from the ball-throwing. He must be getting unfit. Eventually, Ramzy says, "Can I show you something? In town?" And he's halfway to the barn door before I can reply.

For the last two days, I haven't been away from home. What I see next changes everything.

Chapter Forty-Two

In the space of two days, the whole town has become completely different.

People don't come to Whitley Bay on vacation anymore—not like they do to the more famous resorts, like Blackpool, or Brighton, or Bournemouth. ("Whitley Bay's a resort," Dad says. "The last!" It's one of his favorite jokes, which tells you more about my dad than it does about Whitley Bay.) Still, on sunny, summer days, the area usually has a buzz about it. The RV park is busy, there are lines outside Bill's Fish Bar in Culvercot, and a mini fairground appears on the Links, the wide stretch of grass overlooking the beach, with a ghost train and other rides, and fortune-tellers who can see your future.

Today, though . . .

After the announcement by the king, everything has changed. There's hardly anyone about.

We stand by the railing overlooking the beach. "See?"

Ramzy says. "No dogs—just like in the 3-D game version. Why would it show that if it wasn't true?"

Ramzy has again yanked the face mask under his chin because he says it's making him sweat. Of the few people who are out on the streets, about half are wearing face masks and latex gloves.

"Check this out," he says, pointing at a notice tied to a lamppost.

The letters are in black and white against a blood-red background, and there's a picture of a dog looking menacing.

CBE—THE RISKS

"Dog Plague" poses a
significant risk to humans.

Until further notice, all dogs seen
outdoors will be regarded as strays
and may be shot.

Report stray dogs by calling
this number:

0800 777 4445

Do not approach a stray dog
under any circumstances.

By order of HM Government

We walk past the Spanish City—the cafes are closed with their shutters up—and continue up the road past our school and on to Norman Two-Kids's shop, where Norman stands outside, arms folded, as if daring anyone to come in and buy something. Everything is there: the electronic calendar, the poster announcing the numbers for the previous Geordie Jackpot.

The last time I saw Norman, I was throwing his fruit around the street. He glares at me, and I have to remind myself that the incident with the oranges is not due to happen for a few days yet, so he has no particular reason to give me the evil eye. It's just how he looks at all kids.

Thinking about the oranges makes me feel a bit dizzy. Of course, I'm not *actually* going to go back to Norman Two-Kids's shop and throw his fruit around the street. So when did it happen? Will it happen at all? And what if I don't do it?

Is it possible to damage the future?

I'm daydreaming. Ramzy is saying something.

". . . come on. I've got the money."

Norman Two-Kids sucks in his belly to let us get past and then follows us into the shop to make sure we don't steal anything.

Ramzy is all grinning confidence. He swaggers up to the Jackpot desk, where you pick out a piece of card and fill in your numbers with the little blunt pencil that hangs from a string. About the only sound in the shop is the whir-ring of small cameras above us—another of Norman's anti-theft measures.

Ramzy presents his card, along with a two-pound coin, to a scowling Norman, who is supposed to shove the card in his machine and give Ramzy the official ticket.

"Whassat?" he rasps. He too has on a face mask and gloves.

"I'd like a Geordie Jackpot ticket, please, sir!" says Ramzy.

Sir! I'm nervous, but there's something about this that makes me want to laugh. I bite my cheek to stop myself from giggling.

"You makin' fun of me? How old you?"

"Erm . . . erm . . ." Ramzy is trying to think of the right answer.

"I am waitin'. What year you born in, huh?" And before Ramzy can answer, Norman says, "You not sixteen, right? You gotta be sixteen to buy Jackpot ticket. Why not you pull-ing my other leg, huh? He's got jingly bells on it."

It's "jingly bells" that does it. I just snort with laughter, and Norman turns his wrath on me.

"Oh, you fink is funny ha ha, little missy, huh? Come in here, makin' fun out of poor Sanjiv, right? When we all gonna die soon from Dog Plague, huh? See how funny you fink I am then, eh? When you lyin' dead, you not gonna be laughin' ha ha ha then, right? Go on! Get lost and come back when you sixteen, if you make it." He starts to come round from behind the counter, and we bolt out the door and down the street.

When we're a safe distance, we look back and he has taken up his position again, glaring at us and guarding his doorway against potential customers.

I start to laugh. "Geez, Ramz! There's our answer! We'll just have to check the numbers without having a ticket. No million quid for us!" I chuckle some more.

Then I notice Ramzy isn't joining in. Instead, he's pale and looking at me with a disappointed expression, his eyes narrow slits. We stop walking. "Erm . . . you OK, Ramz?" I've never seen him look so defeated, so . . . *small.* It really seems as though he has shrunk and his eyes are shining as though he's blinking away tears.

"I don't believe I'm hearing this. 'No million quid for us!' you say, like it's nothing. Well, it might be nothing to you, Georgie Santos, in your converted farmhouse, with your rich dad, and—"

"Hey, he's not *rich*, Ramzy. He's—"

"When was the last time you were told you couldn't even take a bus 'cause there was no money? Do you live in a tiny, damp flat, and go to bed hungry so your little brothers can eat more? Do you—"

"Ramzy, I'm sorry. You never said!"

"Of *course* I never said. What am I gonna say? 'Hi, I'm Ramzy the poor kid—can I have some money?' Look at me: I'm the kid who has to wear his school uniform on no-uniform day 'cause I don't have the charity money. Back home? Back home, we had plenty of money. My dad was a government engineer. Now he's a delivery driver when he can get the work, and he's gonna lose *that* job soon because some stupid drone can do it."

"I know, Ramzy."

"You know nothing, Georgie. You're just like the rest. Everything's in front of you but you can't see it. And so I get the chance to win a million pounds snatched from me, and you're like, 'Hey ho, never mind!' *Never mind?*" He flings up his arms in disgust and stalks off.

"Wait!" I say, but he doesn't, so I run after him. "What about your aunty Nush? She can buy a ticket."

"Oh right, that's really gonna happen, isn't it?" Ramzy's tone has become bitter and sarcastic. "So far as Aunty Nush is concerned, buying a Geordie Jackpot ticket would send her straight to hell for gambling. I'd probably get to go as well, just for asking her, and as an added punishment for writing all over my school shirt, which was due to be handed down to my little brother. Not a chance."

"Your dad?"

"He's not as hardcore as Aunty Nush, but . . . no way. He's not back till the weekend, anyway. Besides—what about *your dad?*" He shouts these last words over his shoulder as he strides off furiously.

I knew he'd ask that. Thing is, given Dad's attitude to our adventures in the dome, I can't imagine he would agree to it. I mean, I'd basically be asking him to buy me a Jackpot ticket because I saw the numbers when I visited the future in Dr. Pretorius's lab, and that is *not* going to go down well.

Ramzy is staring out to sea, his hands gripping the rusty iron railing. I can see his shoulders shaking because he's crying, and my first thought is to go over and comfort him, but then I think of the Wisdom of the Dogs poster.

If someone is having a bad day, be silent,
sit near, and nuzzle them gently.

However bad a day Ramzy is having, I know he would not want me to nuzzle him gently. But I can do the rest. I sit on the next bench over and say nothing.

Eventually, he comes and sits next to me. We watch the circling seagulls.

We've got to get a lottery ticket somehow. But how?

And then I have an idea.

Chapter Forty-Three

"Let me get this straight," Clem says. "If I buy you a Jackpot ticket with your money, then I get to keep half of anything we win?" He's lying on his back under the campervan, and I'm actually having this conversation with his feet.

"That's right," I say. "Just sign here."

Ramzy has written this "contract." He copied something he saw on the Internet, added words like "herewith" and "notwithstanding" and printed it off in a fancy font. He was quick, but he still didn't want me coming up to his apartment, so I waited outside, quite happy not to risk bumping into Aunty Nush.

To whom it maye concern

I, the undersinged, heretofore do solemly swear to give half of my winnings to Mr. Ramzy Rahman in the event of that I am winning the Geordie Jackpot herewith.

Being of sound mind notwithstanding.

By the power invested in me, in the event that I do not win anything, then I do not owe Ramzy Rahman nothing at all.

Singed this _ _ _ _ _ _ _ day of _ _ _ _ _ _ _ _ _ _ _ _ in the year of our Lord 20_ _ _ _ _ _ _

_ _

Clem wriggles out from under the van to look at Ramzy's contract. He pushes his glasses up his nose and curls his lip doubtfully.

"And this is all because you reckon you saw the numbers when you played that weirdo's stupid game? I thought we'd established that that was a load of old nonsense?"

"Listen, Clem, I know it doesn't sound likely. But, well . . . with all the chaos going on outside, it's a bit of hope, eh? And if the numbers are right, everyone wins. If they're not, then no one loses. And we'll give you the money to buy the ticket."

I have to say it sounds good. Clem takes his phone from out of his overalls pocket. "We can do it right here," he says. "I can download the Geordie Jackpot app and buy a ticket online. You got your money, Ramzy?"

"No!" I say. "It has to be a ticket. An actual ticket."

"Why?"

"Because it was bought from Norman Two-Kids's shop. I . . . I saw him talking about it. When I, erm . . . visited the future. Doing it differently will, erm . . ." Of course, I don't actually know what doing it differently would do.

Clem snorts. "What? Punch a hole in the space–time continuum?" He waves his hands in the air and adopts a scared voice. "*Oh, help me, Doctor, the TARDIS is about to blow up!* You're mental, the two of you, you know that? Now, if you wanna be useful, start rubbing the rust off that bumper over there. Otherwise, get lost. I'm busy." He puts his phone back in his pocket and turns back to the campervan.

"Clement, please listen," says Ramzy, using Clem's full name for added emphasis. It sounds weird but it gets his attention. "Have a look at this."

Ramzy takes out his own phone, which has the clip of me outside Norman Two-Kids's shop recorded in Dr. Pretorius's control room.

Clem looks at it carefully and frowns in appreciation. "This," he says, as if he knows what he's talking about, "looks like very superior 3-D CGI. And you were in it? Impressive." Then he says, "Hang on." He looks closely at the screen of Ramzy's phone. "I know who that is." He points to one of the people who were talking to Norman Two-Kids. "That's Anna Hennessey. She was in my class. She's doing an internship as a journalist at the *Evening Chronicle* this summer. We can settle this right away."

Anna Hennessey. Sass's older sister.

Clem taps in a number on his own phone and holds it to his ear.

Speaking into the phone, Clem's voice drops about an octave. It's hilarious. It sounds as though he has a cold, but it seems that this is his "talking to girls" voice.

"*Hiii!* Anna. Yeah! Clem here . . . Clement Santos? From school . . . yeah, that one . . . Look, I've got a silly question, and don't take this the wrong way . . . No, no, no, not that. Listen . . . At any point in your work experience have you spoken to the guy who runs the corner shop on Marine Drive? Or . . . or . . . or been asked by anyone to *pretend* to interview him . . . ? [*LONG PAUSE*] Erm, no . . . no reason, it's just [*Clem hasn't thought this bit through, and he's struggling*] . . . I spoke to him today and, erm . . . he said he'd done an interview with the *Chronicle* and I thought it might have been you, that's all."

The relief in Clem's voice at having thought up that lie is obvious. He's even forgotten his deep voice.

"No? You sure? No, of course I don't think you're lying! I just wanted to be . . . Yeah. Yeah. Thanks, Anna . . . By the way, if you're not doing anyth— No. Sure. No. Bye." He ends the call.

I raise my eyebrows at him.

"Nice girl," he says.

Imitating his deep voice, I say, *"Very nice!"* and he shakes his head in irritation.

"She's never been near Norman Two-Kids's shop. So I have no idea how this was done," he said, pointing to Ramzy's phone. "It's one thing to create lifelike avatars, AI bots, and so on, but this is, like, *real* people."

For a moment, none of us says anything. Then Clem says, "It's obviously just someone who really looks like her." But he doesn't sound convinced.

He reads over Ramzy's contract again.

"Got a pen?" he asks.

Chapter Forty-Four

Half an hour later, the three of us have come out of Norman Two-Kids's shop again and Clem is clutching a Jackpot ticket bearing the numbers I saw in Dr. Pretorius's studio.

"Just for the record," Clem says, "I think this is nonsense. I've no idea how that recording was done, but it's still impossible."

Ramzy's cheeky grin has returned. "So why'd you do it, then?"

Clem looks up and down the deserted street and shrugs. In the distance, a police siren yowls.

"I guess . . . it is good to hope for something. It seems like everything's going wrong. In less than a week, everything's been turned on its head."

The siren gets louder as it comes down the street, and when it passes, we see that it isn't a police car but an ambulance heading to the seafront. We're walking in the same direction, and a hundred yards later, we see it parked outside one of the cafes at the front of the Spanish City. A small crowd is gathering, and we watch from a distance as two paramedics get out of the back with a stretcher and a box of equipment and dash inside. We hear people talking, some of the voices muffled by face masks.

". . . just collapsed, poor thing . . ."

"Eee . . . I hope it's not that dog thing . . . I'm terrified . . ."

A few moments later, the small crowd parts, and the paramedics reappear, pushing someone on a wheeled stretcher. One of them is carrying a yellow canvas beach bag, and I know straightaway. The huge ball of white hair poking out from under the red stretcher blanket confirms it.

I push my way through to the front and cry out, "Dr. Pretorius!" but her eyes are shut. One of the paramedics is holding up a bag of something (a drip? I don't know the terms) and a tube leads from it to Dr. Pretorius's thin brown arm lying on top of the blanket. She has one of those oxygen masks over her nose and mouth.

"Out the way, dear, out the way," says one. "Comin' through . . ."

Ramzy elbows his way to the front and walks straight up to the paramedic. "Is she dead?" he asks.

The paramedic doesn't look at him. "No, son. Heart attack. Prob'ly gonna be OK."

Seconds later, the rear doors of the ambulance slam shut.

The siren wails and the vehicle moves off the wide pedestrian area and onto the road, heading north.

With the drama over, the people who were watching drift away, leaving me, Ramzy, and Clem standing in the open entrance to the Spanish City complex. The amusement arcade is empty, its gaming machines blinking and bleeping at no one; I see Sass Hennessey's mum staring out the window of the Polly Donkin Tea Rooms.

"So that was her?" says Clem. "The weirdo with the time machine?" His tone is mocking, and—having just seen her carted off in an ambulance—pretty insensitive if you ask me.

"It's *not* a time machine, Clem. It's multisensory virtual reality."

He's unimpressed. "Whatever."

A voice speaks up behind us. "That was your friend, wasn't it, Georgie?" It's Sass's mum.

I don't know what to say except, "Yeah."

"Mad as anything, y'know. You wanna be careful. I've told Saskia and Anna they're to have nothing at all to do wi' her." She purses her lips disapprovingly.

"What happened?" asks Ramzy.

"Well, I didn't see exactly," says Sass's mum, but she seems pleased to be asked and smooths down her little white waitress's apron. "But I heard her calling, 'Help me!' Well, it's a good thing it's quiet, or I wouldn'a heard her. When I got there, she'd passed out on the floor in a puddle. At first, I thought she'd . . . Well, turned out to be seawater 'cause she was all wet from her swim. And so I called the ambulance and stayed with her till they came. She wasn't makin' any sense, mind." She turns her head to look into the cafe. "I've got a customer. But mark my words: she's an odd duck, that one. The last thing she said before she passed out was something about *scorpions*."

"What about scorpions?" I say, a bit too eagerly, because Sass's mum gives me a funny look.

"Just that. 'Stop the scorpions' or summin' like that. Like I say, mad as." She taps her temple with her forefinger; then she hurries off.

"Come on," says Ramzy. "Let's have a look."

"A look?" says Clem. "What for?" He isn't used to Ramzy's sudden bursts of enthusiasm the way I am. He really does think that we're just stupid kids: it's written all over his face.

"Clues. Obviously!" says Ramzy as if Clem is the stupid one.

At the back of the passageway between the tea rooms and the amusement halls is the door that leads to the dome. The cleaners obviously don't come this far very often because the floor is littered with candy wrappers and wooden Popsicle sticks, and more recent debris like the empty packages with medical labels used by the paramedics.

Clem is impatient. "Does this actually matter? I mean . . . what difference . . ."

"If she was coming in, she would have her key out. And if she collapsed with it in her hand . . ." Ramzy starts kicking aside some of the litter, and after only a few seconds, stoops to pick up a key.

Clem at least has the good grace to look impressed when Ramzy turns the key in the lock and opens the door.

Chapter Forty-Five

I know I'm showing off, but when I say "Studio lights!" and they come on in the dome, I am *so pleased* to hear a little gasp come from Clem's direction.

We stand at the edge of the wide circle filled with ball bearings. The pin lights in the black ceiling glow like stars.

As I show it off to Clem, it's almost as though this massive dome, and everything that goes with it, is mine. It's not often, I don't think, that an eleven-year-old gets to impress her sixteen-year-old brother, and Clem is definitely impressed. He hunkers down to pick up some ball bearings and lets them trickle through his fingers.

"It's still switched on!" calls Ramzy from behind us. He's in the control room, and there we see it all: the huge computer screens, the colored keyboard, Little Girl the quomp with her blinking lights—everything. My heart is thumping.

At the end of the long desk is the bicycle helmet with the bumps all over the inside.

This was my plan, and it is going better than I could have ever hoped! The only thing missing is Dr. Pretorius.

All that's left to do is:

1. Put the helmet on, making sure it's tight.

2. Align the satellite receiver on the roof outside with the satellite Hawking II at the exact time the satellite passes over.

3. At the same time, launch the program that creates the 3-D game, and . . .

4. Make the quomp analyze the likely future.

5. Input the coordinates for where I want the studio projection to place me.

6. Link up my helmet to the whole computer simulation.

7. Travel to the future and bring back the cure. Somehow.

Ta-da!

I slump down on Dr. Pretorius's swivel chair. Of course, I have no idea how to do *any* of that. Especially the bits that only Dr. Pretorius knows how to do, like aligning the satellite and setting up the computer and, well, pretty much all of it.

I explain this to Clem, who comes over all big-brothery again.

"You didn't seriously think all that was possible, did you? I mean—that was your *plan*?"

I'm angry at myself more than at him, but I reply, "Have you got a better one? One that doesn't involve tinkering around with old engines? I mean, that's what *you're* good at, isn't it? Well, it doesn't help us here, does it? If you think—"

Ramzy interrupts. "Hey, hey, come on," he says. "We just need to wait till Dr. Pretorius gets back."

"And what if she doesn't come back?" I say.

"They said it was a heart attack, right? I'm sure she'll, um, get better."

"Right. And how long will that take?" I say.

He turns his mouth down and shrugs. "No idea. But it's our only hope. We could try to launch all the software and everything ourselves, but we'd probably wreck it."

He's right, of course.

There's nothing we can do but wait. And by then it might be too late.

Chapter Forty-Six

It's a strange feeling being there, in Dr. Pretorius's control room, without Dr. Pretorius. I've always kind of been on my best behavior. You know: not poking around too much in case I'm on the receiving end of a sharp word or a slapped hand for touching something I shouldn't . . .

And now, well, Clem is wandering around, up and down the old restaurant kitchen, going, "Wow!" and so on, poking at things and staring at the screens, which are showing different MSVR environments. It looks as though Dr. Pretorius was in the middle of working on something when she took her swimming break and left everything running, but there's still no way I could launch the program properly.

Then Ramzy says, "Look at this!" and beckons me over. On the bench, next to the sink, is a wallet, which he flips open with one finger. There are bank cards inside, and he eases one out, still not picking up the wallet.

The name embossed on the card says:

Ramzy and I look at each other. "The missing billionaire," says Ramzy. "Hiding in plain sight."

Clem, meanwhile, has left the control room and I can hear his feet clattering on the metal staircase to the storage area. Ramzy and I follow him and reach the top of the stairs to hear him say a drawn-out *"Whoooa!"* of amazement.

In the middle of the concrete floor is the uncovered copter-drone, with a bucket seat attached, all ten arms bearing a pole with a rotor blade.

"Check *this* out," says Clem, walking round it in exactly the way he looks at old cars on the street. He crouches down and places his palm beneath one of the drone's arms. He lifts the whole thing effortlessly. He gives a low whistle.

"Three-D-printed graphene," he says. "Super light and ten times stronger than steel." He sees that I'm impressed by his knowledge and gives a shy half-shrug. "They're making car parts out of it now. But this . . ." He shakes his head in admiration; then he points at a series of tiny square panels running down every arm. "Solar-powered too. This could fly forever." He stands up again, hand on hips. "Forget about your dome. *This* is the future right here!"

"Do you believe us now?" I ask. "I mean, she's a genius, right?"

He just smiles and says, "Maybe. But we can't just hang out here until she gets back from the hospital. *If* she gets back."

I sigh. He's right, of course, but we're not a happy trio as we let ourselves out of the dome and trudge back along the seafront. Without Dr. Pretorius to operate the FutureDome (which is how I now think of it), there's no hope of enacting our plan—even if it *could* work.

The beach is still empty, except for a few kids playing in the sand. Away in the distance, a dog—too far away to make out the type—plays in the shallow waves like Mr. Mash likes to do, and it seems so normal that I smile. Perhaps it's my scrambled brain, but I have momentarily forgotten that lone dogs will be shot.

And then, moments later, when we've turned off the seafront toward Ramzy's street, there's the sharp crack of a single gunshot.

We all flinch but none of us says a thing.

Chapter Forty-Seven

The three of us continue past the turnoff to Ramzy's street, slouching along in silence.

Dad calls Clem to check on the progress of the campervan and Clem has to lie, saying he's been working hard, and adding words like "fuel tank welding" and "drive shaft" and "split axle," none of which mean a thing to me.

"I've got to get back," Clem says, picking up his pace. "Dad wants to do a test drive this evening. He's got a buyer coming next week and the whole thing's still a death trap."

He turns off toward the workshop, leaving me and Ramzy to do the quick double-back along the hedge to the barn. I don't think Clem sees me.

This thing with the Jackpot ticket, and then with Dr. Pretorius and the ambulance and the dome, and finally the gunshot that nobody mentioned . . . it has all brought Clem and me closer than we've been in months, but I'm still not ready to tell him that I'm secretly keeping Mr. Mash in the barn.

The smell hits me even before I open the barn door. An unmistakable reek of dog poo and vomited blood that I smelt before at St. Woof's, but this is much, *much* worse. I gag and hold my nose as I rush inside, leaving Ramzy at the door. Mr. Mash is lying on his side in a pool of blood and puke, and I know immediately that my worst fears have been realized.

"Mr. Mash! Mashie! No, no, no!" I cry, and—without thinking—I rush forward and kneel down in the mess to cradle his head. He wags his tail weakly but cannot get to his feet.

Then behind me I hear, "Georgie! What are you doing? Get away from him *now!*" Clem is yelling at me, horrified, with Ramzy beside him, both of their faces creased with fear.

The stupidity of what I have done strikes me instantly. Handling a dog with a deadly infection? I leap up as though electrocuted and back away from Mr. Mash, who struggles up from the floor. "NO! No, Mashie—stay away," I sob. "I'm sorry, stay away. Stay!"

I'm not thinking straight and move my hand to my mouth to stifle a sob, only to have it whacked away, hard, with a broom handle, wielded by my brother.

"*Owww!*"

Clem is beside me, speaking so quietly and calmly that it terrifies me. "Go to the tap outside, Georgie. Go *now*. Do *not* touch anything. Do not touch your mouth or your eyes or anything, do you understand? Take off all your clothes and rinse everything off. *What are you waiting for?*"

My face crumples and—I'm sorry—I start crying. "Don't wipe your eyes!" shouts Clem. *"Move!"*

He is furious and scared, and I'm rooted to the spot with fear, both for myself and for Mr. Mash. I start to take my top off, but Clem yells, "Stop! There's blood on your top that could get in your eyes. Stay still."

He pulls on a thick pair of rubber mechanic's gloves and, grabbing a pair of garden shears from the wall, comes toward me. He sees me looking at Ramzy, who is still in the doorway. He pauses for a second. I think he realizes that—even in a life-or-death situation—I'm hesitating about getting undressed in front of my friend.

"Ramzy—go up to the house. The back door's open. Grab some towels from the bathroom and some clothes from Georgie's room. Quick!" Ramzy runs off, while Clem cuts me out of my clothes. I turn my back to him, but somehow being naked in front of my brother is OK—probably because I have bigger things to worry about.

"Have you any cuts on your hands?" asks Clem. I examine my hands under the running water from the hose. There are none. "Your knees, where you knelt down?"

There are none there either. I begin to feel my panic receding a little. There's a five-liter container of disinfectant behind the barn door, and I slosh half of it over me, pouring it on top of my head and making sure it covers every bit of me.

"Does it sting anywhere?" asks Clem. I shake my head.

"Good—that means you've got no cuts or anywhere the virus could get in. That stuff hurts like heck if you get it on a cut. I think, Georgie, you're OK."

I start to sob with relief, and just let Clem hold me. Out of the corner of my eye, I see Ramzy coming back down the lane, his eyes furiously studying the ground so as not to embarrass me, which is nice of him.

"I'm sorry, Georgie. It's all I could find. It was hanging on the back of your door."

I'm cowering behind the barn door, and from the other side he hands me my fluffy spaniel onesie with the floppy ears and a tail.

I zip myself into the spaniel suit (matching slippers too—*thanks, Ramz*), while Ramzy and Clem use a brush and the rest of the disinfectant to clear up the bloody mess that Mr. Mash has produced. He watches them work, his head resting on his front paws.

He seems to say, *I'm sorry about the mess, boys. I didn't mean it. I don't feel very well, you see.*

Then the three of us sit on the grass verge outside the barn. Clem has made a bonfire with my clothes (including my favorite jeans) doused in gas and they flame and smolder in a rusty iron firepit.

We don't speak for ages, until at last I say: "He's going to die, isn't he? Mashie? It's Dog Plague, isn't it?"

Clem sighs. He puts his arm round me and squeezes. He says nothing: a nothing that means yes. I knew it was coming, but—strangely—it doesn't make me cry again.

Instead, I swallow hard and look up the lane and beyond our house to the evening-blue sky and Mum's tree bent over the horizon.

Chapter Forty-Eight

We're all in it now. Me, Ramzy, Clem.

I have a dying dog in the barn. And once again—guess what?—it's *all my fault.*

For the next three days, it's all I can think about. I can't tell Dad because that would involve the whole breaking-into-St.-Woof's story, and who knows where *that* would end? And I'm certainly not going to suddenly open up to Jessica.

Nope. This is another secret I'm going to have to hold in.

And all the time the clock is ticking down to the day the government will start culling all dogs. We want to stop listening to the news on the radio or the television. I've turned off any notifications on my phone that would tell me what is happening. Because if it's good news I'll hear straightaway. If it's bad news, I don't want to know.

I spend most of the time in the warm barn, watching poor Mr. Mash shivering, stroking his ears with my thick gloves on. He doesn't understand why he can't lick me like he used to. He doesn't understand why I have to keep him in the barn and hold on to his collar tightly when I come near him to stop him jumping up.

He doesn't understand that he's dying, and perhaps that's a good thing.

He drinks a lot of water, and he pees a lot, but he's been getting weaker and unable to get up to have a pee, so in the mornings when I come to see him he's lying where the pee has soaked into the barn floor, and it stinks, and I start to cry again as I clean him up. I can't remember the last time he wagged his tail.

He doesn't even fart anymore. I never thought I'd miss his smelly gas, but I do.

I've hardly seen Dad. Jessica is still working crazy hours; Dad's spending most of his time out in his pickup truck, visiting other campervan owners, buying spare parts. They're piling up in the workshop, and I'm terrified he's soon going to try to store some of them in the barn. I have taken the precaution of keeping the padlock key in my pocket instead of leaving it under the pot.

And as for Clem? He thinks I should just confess everything and get the vet to come and give Mr. Mash "the injection."

We're standing in the workshop when Clem says that, for perhaps the hundredth time, and I flip.

"You mean kill him, don't you?" I shout. "Don't you get it? That's why I rescued him in the first place!"

Clem doesn't really do shouting. He puts down his wrench and leans back against the workbench, shaking his head.

"It didn't do any good, though, did it, Georgie? All the other dogs at St. Woof's—they're all asleep now in dog heaven, while poor Mr. Mash is puking and peeing and pooing where he lies, while we have to watch him. It's cruel, Georgie."

There's nothing I can say. He's right, of course. I know what I have to do. We stand in silence while the news plays on the radio.

> ". . . experts say that a cure for the devastating Dog Plague currently sweeping the world remains elusive, and fears are mounting that any discovery will come too late to save millions of pet dogs.
>
> "Meanwhile, more human cases of the disease have been confirmed . . ."

I can't stop myself. It's as if I've been taken over by another Georgie, as I snatch the little speaker unit from the workbench and smash it on the floor.

"Stop it! Stop it! *Stop it!*" I scream, and stamp on the little box with my rain boot. Clem knows better than to intervene.

He just turns away, back to the campervan, while I run out of the workshop and down the field to the barn and I burst open the door to Mr. Mash's enclosure.

He's lying there, and he wags his tail weakly as I run to him, forgetting all the rules, and I gather him in my arms, burying my nose in the back of his ears, desperately trying to locate his unique doggy smell but getting only disinfectant. I hold him, sobbing into his fur and saying, "I'm sorry, I'm sorry," over and over.

I don't know how long I'm there. Eventually, I move away and sit with my back against the barn's wooden wall and take out my phone. I swallow hard and scroll down my contacts to: REV. MAURICE CLEGHORN.

I rehearse in my head what I will say to the vicar.

I'm sorry, Vicar . . .

I know that you already know it was me and Ramzy that night . . .

I need the vet to come out to our barn . . .

She needs to . . .

I just can't say it, even in my head. My thumb hovers over the vicar's name. Perhaps if I just click and start the conversation, then it'll figure itself out?

I rest my head against the wooden wall to think it through. I have been sleeping so badly lately that I find my eyelids drooping closed.

.   .   .

When I wake a bit later, the shadows in the barn are longer and my neck is stiff from my odd position propped up against the wall.

It's my phone that has woken me. It buzzes on the dusty floor.

> Coming over to see Mr. M.

I start to type a reply, but before I've finished it, I hear the wooden door rattle open and Ramzy is crouching next to me.

"Hello. You look awful."

"Thanks, Ramz. I needed that."

"Even Mashie looks better than you."

"Hey, that's a bit much."

I look across at Mr. Mash who, for the first time in days, has sat up.

I get to my feet slowly. "Mashie?"

His tail thumps on the ground; then he's on all four legs, straining at the string that holds him back. It's more movement than he has made in days.

It's not a recovery. It can't be a recovery. I remind myself that he has a fatal illness.

But . . . can I dare to hope?

I message Clem and he comes straight over and stands, arms folded across his chest. He scratches his patchy beard, staring at Mr. Mash the way I've seen him staring at an engine as it ticks over. Clem never fell in love with Mr. Mash the way I did, but that's not to say he doesn't care.

Eventually, he says, "I'm no vet, but he definitely looks better."

It's not just my imagination, then. "How?" I say. "I mean—CBE: it's incurable."

He shrugs. "No idea. Don't get your hopes up, Georgie. He's probably not going to recover. But you never know. Perhaps Mr. Mash here . . ."

"What?"

Clem stares at Mr. Mash, who is still standing, his tail wagging.

"Well . . . ," says Clem. "Maybe he's resistant to the virus for some reason. I mean, he's probably not. But I dunno . . . his immune system or something might . . ." He trails off and shrugs.

"Is that even possible?" Ramzy says.

Clem is still looking thoughtful, and he shakes his head. "I doubt it. But I mean . . . what if he does hold the key? Deep in his blood or his cells or his DNA or whatever. Maybe our Mashie could . . . I dunno . . . ?"

Another voice adds: "Save the world? Even if it's true, it's too late."

All three of us swing round to see Jessica outlined in the doorway. I can tell she's been watching us for a while.

"Kitchen," she says. "Now."

Chapter Forty-Nine

Everyone knows now. We sit around the kitchen table: me, Jessica, Dad, Clem, and Ramzy. In the middle of the table is yet another chunk of engine—Dad's pickup truck this time, which has been acting up. On top of that is a long, narrow test tube, like a pencil, filled with Mr. Mash's blood that Jessica has just extracted with a syringe.

We've told Dad everything about stealing Mr. Mash.

If I was expecting a huge telling-off, and grounding, and allowance-canceling, and calls to Ramzy's dad, and the vicar, and the police, and all of that, well . . . it just didn't happen.

(In fact, I could swear that Dad was smirking when I told him about the policeman falling into the poo pit. He was trying not to, and was turning pink with the effort till Jessica kicked him under the table. I think. Jessica certainly wasn't smiling, but then that isn't new.)

I point at the glass tube of blood on the table. "Now it can all end. Can't it?"

Jessica sighs. She's got her patient and slow voice on,

like a teacher. "Listen, Georgina. This is all new—all new to everyone. Even if it turns out that Mr. Mash *has* recovered from CBE—which is very unlikely, impossible even—then . . ."

"We know he has!" I say. "You saw him!"

"It's far too early to say. He may be having a period of remission, when the symptoms diminish temporarily." She looks pensive. "Though I haven't heard of that happening." She shakes her head. "Anyway. It does *not* mean he's cured. We don't even know for certain that he *had* CBE. He was never tested. It could be . . . I don't know, something similar."

"Something *similar*?" I get up from the table so quickly that I knock the chair backward. "It was exactly the same! Everything!"

"Well, it's a shame I didn't see it," Jessica says drily. "It's a shame there are no witnesses. But . . ." She trails off and then picks up the test tube, holding it to the light.

"But *what*?"

She breathes in through her nose and puts the test tube down. "There is something. It's only a theory at the moment, but it's something I've been working on. You see—until now, there has simply been no way that you can extract the relevant T-cell anti-pathogen from blood *with* immunity and re-create it to make a cure, but if Mr. Mash has recovered, then . . ."

And she's off, her face becoming more animated than

I've ever seen it as she tells us what might—possibly—be the route to a cure. To be honest, I don't understand a word and am relieved when, after about half a minute, she ends with: "It's a theory. We've never been able to test it until now, and it'll take months anyway, but, well . . . we're desperate."

"Months?" says Ramzy, who till now has been pretty quiet.

Jessica nods sadly. "It's possible that Mr. Mash's mixed-breed DNA holds the secret. So many dogs these days are highly bred to be perfect examples of their type. But we have no idea what dogs there are in Mashie's DNA makeup. If it's not exactly unique, it could at least be very unusual. But without proof that he definitely had CBE, I'm going to have to do this on my own. It's going to take time, and I'm going to have to pull in some favors from the nanotech people, and—"

"How long?"

Jessica sucks her teeth. "Three months? Four? You have to first grow a culture of pathogens, and apply the . . ."

She's off again. I feel as though my stomach has dropped to the floor. "Too late then. Like you said."

She looks out the kitchen window for a long time before answering.

"Too late for the dogs. And too late for lots of people. But it *will* save some of us. I mean, if my theory is correct. Four months, max, and there'll be a cure. I hope."

"How many will die before that?" says Ramzy.

She doesn't answer.

Dad gets up from the table and switches on the kettle for another cup of tea. "If only, Georgie!" he says in a fake, jolly tone. "If only that mad old lady with her future thing-amajig had been real, eh? We could see how this would all pan out, eh?"

Yeah. If only . . .

Chapter Fifty

It's ten to eight, and Ramzy, Clem, and I are walking quickly up the top field, with Ramzy checking the time every thirty seconds so that he's back by the stroke of eight, avoiding the wrath of Aunty Nush.

We've reached Mum's tree, and we're about to split up: Ramzy to face whatever ghastly fate Aunty Nush might have awaiting him, me to check on Mr. Mash, and Clem to do yet more work on his stupid campervan.

Clem says, "Have you two forgotten what day it is today?" and I shrug as Ramzy checks his phone yet again.

"Yep. It's the day I meet my certain death at the hands of Aunty Nush. I was meant to be home hours ago."

From his pocket, a smirking Clem pulls a yellow piece of folded paper, and Ramzy and I gasp in unison. I can't believe I forgot about it. Only . . . there have been a few other things to distract us.

"The Geordie Jackpot draw is at eight," Clem says, taking

out his phone. "We may as well find out if we're going to be millionaires or not."

Ramzy's already on his phone, speaking to his aunty. I've no idea what he's saying. Well, I do actually: you can tell just from the tone.

"I know, Aunty, I know. I'm sorry, I'm sorry. I'm with Georgie and we lost track of time. I'll put her dad on . . ."

Ramzy hands the phone to Clem, whispering, "Be your dad. Say you'll bring me home soon. She won't understand anyway."

Clem is startled, but rises to the challenge and puts on his deep voice again. "Ah, hello, Mrs. Rahman, Rob Santos here. Ramzy is quite safe and I'll certainly bring him home soon. My deepest apologies for the inconvenience. Good evening."

It sounds *nothing* like Dad, but Ramzy has the phone back now, and whether or not it's saved him a punishment, at least it's bought him some extra time. Clem, meanwhile, has already connected to the Geordie Jackpot site.

It's an odd place, I guess, to discover if you're going to become a millionaire or not: we sit on a raised grass mound beneath the tree in the sticky evening heat, peering at Clem's phone screen. A huge, circular spinning basket is tossing around fifty numbered balls.

There's tense music playing underneath the announcer, who is off-screen. He has a warm, Geordie voice.

"Good luck, everyone! This is the draw for the Geordie Jackpot for July the twenty-seventh. Stand by for the first number."

Clem holds the ticket next to his phone so we can check the numbers, although I realize at that point that I've memorized them: 5–22–23–40–44–49.

The music continues: *dum-dum-dum-dum-dum*—a relentless, tense beat.

And then the machine spits out a numbered ball, which falls down a chute and is tumbling too fast to make out the number till it comes to a standstill, at which point the announcer says, "And the first number tonight is . . . *number forty!*"

I can't bear to hear the rest. I just know that they'll match. Breathing quickly, I get up and walk round Mum's tree a few times. I can still hear the announcer. Clem is clenching his fist and going, "*Yesss!*" Ramzy is silent and open-mouthed.

"*Number twenty-two!*"

"*Number forty-nine!*"

I actually feel sick. Not at the prospect of winning so much money. Well, not *just* at the prospect of winning so much money. But because of the promise I've made to myself if it turns out that Dr. Pretorius was telling the truth.

I've been putting it out of my mind (without much success, I should add) but now it's becoming real.

"*Number five!*"

"Oh my God," moans Clem.

"*Number forty-four!*"

That is when I sink to my knees. My legs simply won't hold me up as I wait for the number that I know will be next.

"*And finally . . . number twenty-three! And that concludes . . .*"

I don't hear the rest. There's a ringing in my ears, and I am dimly aware that Ramzy and Clem are on their feet, clutching each other and spinning around, cheering and whooping, and then I'm joining in, although my mind is miles away.

Because I have to do this. I just have to.

"Stop!" I shout. But they don't. The whooping continues till I scream again: "*Stop it!*"

"Jeez, Georgie, what's up? Why are you crying?" says Clem as he lets go of Ramzy.

I take a deep, shaky breath, and eventually I say, "Do you know how to drive, Clem?"

"Eh? What? Erm . . . yeah. Sort of."

"Will that campervan of yours work?"

"No. I mean, yes: he'll, well . . . he'll start. He'll go. But he's not legally roadworthy. Why? What's this about? We're rich, Georgie! Why are you . . . We've got hardly any gas, and the catalytic converter's not properly insulated, so the whole thing's a fire hazard, but . . . but . . . why? We've got a million pounds to claim!"

I am aware, on some deep, inexplicable level, that I'm

making a decision that will change my life. That will change everything.

"I know. I know. But what's the point of money if everyone ends up dying? Hang on." I lean my back against the knobbly bark of the tree, trying to calm my breathing, trying—unsuccessfully—to stop my heart from thumping. I look up through the leaves at the patches of blue sky peeking through. I can hear little bits of the song from *Chitty Chitty Bang Bang* that always makes me think of Mum:

> *Someone to tend to, be a friend to.*
> *I have you two!*

It's not spooky or anything—I know it's just in my imagination—and it makes me smile. My hammering heart has quieted down.

I think of what Jessica said.

Four months, max, and there'll be a cure.

Four months is too long to wait—too many people will die. But if we can go four months into the future? Or longer? A year, to be on the safe side?

I look round the tree, where Clem and Ramzy have been waiting for me, and my mind is made up.

"Hey, you two," I say, echoing the words of the song. "The million pounds is going to have to wait. Because, Clement

Santos and Ramzy Rahman, we're going to bust Dr. Pretorius out of the hospital!"

Ramzy knows there's more to it. He has a little puzzled smile when he says, "And . . . ?"

"And what do you think? We're going to save the world!"

PART THREE

Chapter Fifty-One

In the workshop, we lower the campervan down off its mechanical lift and push it, back end first, out of the workshop.

"Dad's gonna kill me," Clem keeps muttering, and checking his watch because Dad said he'd join him in the workshop in half an hour. "Where's the keys, the keys?" he whines, emptying the contents of his overalls onto the dashboard of the camper till he finds the keys at the bottom of his pocket and tries to start the engine.

The engine goes *click-click-click,* and even I know that means the battery is dead.

"Right," says Clem. "Jump-start it is."

A "jump-start" is different from using a key and involves Ramzy and me pushing the van to get it going, then running alongside the vehicle as it trundles downhill, steered by Clem, till the motor starts. When it chugs to life, Ramzy shouts, "Yay!" and we both vault into the open side of the van as it kangaroos down the lane and onto the road.

I look back and my heart melts. Framed by the open window of the barn, poor Mr. Mash is straining on the end of his string, desperate to join our adventure. I give him a little wave and blow him a kiss. Ramzy sees me and I'm embarrassed for a second, but he just smiles.

"We're doing it for him, and all the dogs," he says—and he's right.

"This is ridiculous!" shouts Clem over the noise of the campervan's engine, which is rattling and spluttering, like an old man clearing his throat right in your ear. "Whoa!" He swerves to avoid a cyclist, who swears at him.

We stand out on the road, that's for certain. Pretty much the only other vehicles are a handful of cars. Ours is the only one making such a noise. I'm sure you can hear us as far as Blyth. As well as the ancient engine, there's a whole bunch of Clem's tools rolling around the metal floor: screwdrivers, wrenches, and a hacksaw. It's a din.

"So!" yells Clem. "Tell me again your idea, Georgie. I'm not sure I quite grasped its sheer insanity the first time you dazzled me with it— *Whooaa, you idiot!*"

(Hard swerve again.)

The idea—crazy or not—is the only one we have. The original plan was to wait till the results of the Geordie Jackpot either confirmed that:

a) Dr. Pretorius's FutureDome was for real, or

b) it was just a mad scientist's loopy fantasy.

If it turned out to be real, we would then use the dome to go to the future and bring back the cure. Assuming Jessica has found one—which I'm trying not to think about too much. *Where will we get it from? Not sure. A test tube? I don't know.* I figure I'll work that one out when I get there.

And now—thanks to the Geordie Jackpot result—we know that the FutureDome works.

As my Wisdom of the Dogs poster says:

If what you want is buried, dig and dig until you find it.

There's just one problem: we don't know how to operate the FutureDome on our own. But if we can get to the hospital and persuade Dr. Pretorius to come back with us to her studio, we can get the programs up and running. If she can't leave the hospital, at least she could give us instructions.

Maybe.

There's another problem, but I'm trying not to think about it. My brain, the headaches, my memory. It was bad enough last time . . .

"Can't we just take a taxi?" shouts Ramzy, interrupting my scattered thoughts. Clem shakes his head. He's *totally* on board with this now. It's as if the Jackpot win has triggered something inside him, and he's completely enthusiastic—even a bit crazed.

"Taxis won't take a patient from the hospital without authorization. And we *definitely* won't have authorization. Oops, look natural—police car ahead!"

The police car, painted red and marked ARMED POLICE, is parked on the Links, and my stomach flips over, thinking of the dog I saw before. They don't even glance in our direction. Even if they did, I tell myself, they'd just see a campervan with a young man at the wheel. On any other day, the smoke and exhaust fumes billowing out of the back end—breaking probably every single "clean air" law—might have attracted their attention, but not today.

"How do you know which hospital she's at?" Ramzy asks. He seems to be trying to find fault with the revised plan, but I can hardly blame him: *risky* doesn't even begin to cover it.

"I don't. But the ambulance went north from the Spanish City. If it was going to Cramlington or to the Royal Victoria or any of the others, it would have gone south to join the coast road." I sound more confident than I feel.

"Are you sure?"

"*No, Ramzy!* I'm very far from sure. But what's *your* suggestion?"

"This is our only hope, anyway, Ramzy!" shouts Clem from the front seat. "There's not enough gas to go anywhere else. I threw it all on the bonfire when we burned Georgie's clothes."

This is new information to me. "How far *can* we go?" I ask as I look over Clem's shoulder. The fuel gauge needle is stuck on the red warning section.

"I had a liter and a bit. This old thing, in this state, does about thirty-five miles to the gallon. But I've no idea how that converts."

We're silent for a bit; then Ramzy pipes up. "About nine miles."

Clem swings round to look at him, then back at the road. "How'd you do that?"

Ramzy shrugs. "I'm good at math."

Nine miles. That will get us to the hospital and back. Just. Already I can see the signs for North Tyneside General Hospital, and a few minutes later the large sandy-brown building set off the main road.

"How long will it take to get her?" asks Clem as he draws to a shuddering halt by the open entrance to the parking lot. He keeps the engine running.

"It could be ages. I don't even know where in the hospital she is."

"That's a problem, then. You see, I can't stop the engine. The battery charges from the motion of the engine, but it was totally dead. There's not enough charge in it yet, so if

277

I turn the engine off, we won't get it started again. I'll need to wait here with my engine ticking over. People don't like that—especially not in hospitals. You know—pollution and all that."

"Can you drive round the roads?"

"Yeah, but it's using up gas and we don't have much."

"We'll have to risk it," says Ramzy. "Drive up and down the road outside. We'll message you when we're one minute from the entrance. Come by and get us."

"Is it gonna work?" says Clem. We all look at one another, none of us wanting to say, *"No, it's a ridiculous idea."*

Perhaps it's the tension, I don't know, but we all end up laughing as Ramzy and I get out.

"Good luck!" says Clem, pulling away.

We're going to need it.

Chapter Fifty-Two

Just by the entrance to the parking lot is a flower bed crammed with large, tall flowers that I don't know the name of but that I can snap off pretty easily. Ramzy picks some too till we have a bunch: the sort of bunch you'd take when you visit a sick person in the hospital.

It's nine p.m. and eerily quiet. Above the swishing of cars on the road, the only other sound is the noisy spluttering of the campervan as Clem accelerates away up the street. Ramzy and I both take a deep breath.

"Stealing an old lady from hospital, Ramzy? Is that adventure enough for you?" I ask.

He seems to consider it, biting his bottom lip, eventually saying, "Yeah. We mustn't mess up, though."

"Good advice, thanks," I say, but I don't think he gets my sarcasm.

I lead the way up the long driveway toward the large glass doors of the hospital entrance.

"Remember, Georgie. Cool heads. No one suspects kids. We just behave as if we're meant to be here. Think about the Famous Five. What would they do?"

"Well, I don't think the kids in an Enid Blyton story would be sneaking into a hospital with stolen flowers to rescue a mad scientist, for one thing. BUT if they did, I think they would be cool and super polite."

Ramzy lifts his chin and pulls back his shoulders. "Then that's how we are! So . . . after you, Sergeant Santos."

"Why, thank you, Private Rahman."

Our jokiness is an act: in fact, my heart is pounding even harder than it was by the tree earlier. The glass doors hiss open as we approach. Inside, the reception area is smaller than I'd expected, and therefore we could be spotted much more easily. A small group of four or five people are clustered round the front desk, which is good. The receptionist may not notice us.

A large sign on the wall gives a guide to all the different departments, like this:

X-rays and Radiology—Wright Annex (straight ahead)

Natal and Neonatal—Renwick Wing (G)

Oncology—Stables Wing (1st floor)

It's a long list. Ramzy and I stand to the side, trying not to look obvious, searching for the one we want.

Geriatric Services and Ward—(G)

There's an arrow pointing through the double doors ahead of us. Ramzy rearranges the flowers he's clutching to make them look a bit tidier, and I can see that his hands are trembling, making the leaves on the stolen bouquet shake. The receptionist is still busy with the group of people surrounding her desk.

"Ready?" I say, and Ramzy takes a deep breath and nods at exactly the moment I hear the other set of doors open behind us and a deep voice say, "Well, what a surprise! It's Miss Georgina Santos, as I live and breathe!"

I turn to see Jackson, the security guard, grinning his head off in the middle of the lobby.

This is *not* a good start.

Chapter Fifty-Three

"J-Jackson!" I stammer, and force a smile. "Hi!"

"Well, hello to you, Miss Santos. And who's your friend?" Jackson strides toward us, beaming.

"Th-this is Ramzy. Ramzy Rahman."

Ramzy smiles and raises his hand in greeting, flashing me a panicked glance at the same time. I half expect him to do his "Ramzy Rahman, *sah!*" salute, but he doesn't. Nerves, I guess, but I'm relieved.

"Hello, Ramzy. The name's Jackson. I'm an old friend of Georgie's family." He thrusts out his huge hand, and Ramzy shakes it.

From somewhere inside Ramzy come the words, "How do you do?" which delights Jackson. He straightens his back and puts his head on one side.

"*How do you do?*" he repeats. "Very well, thank you, my friend. And what brings you here?"

OK, so here's a tip if you're ever thinking of sneaking in

anywhere, like a hospital, say. *Have a story planned.* Make sure you know what you're going to say if you're challenged. Rehearse it. Check it for flaws. That way, you won't do what I do, which is to say, "Erm . . . ah, we're . . . erm . . . ah . . ."

That doesn't sound good. Jackson's eyes narrow a bit and he glances down at the flowers. He must know that they're stolen and I find myself flushing with shame. He turns his head to me during my pathetic stumbling. It's Ramzy who digs us out. Smooth as you like, he says, "It's my great-grandmother. She suffered a stroke, and we've come to visit her. She . . . she may not have long left."

He's faking but he is brilliant. He even makes his voice choke on the last bit, like he's really upset. Jackson is taken in completely.

"Do you know where she is, young man?" he says softly.

"She . . . she's on the geriatric ward." (*Sniff.*)

Jackson looks up at the big clock on the wall. "Well," he says, shaking his head, "strictly speaking, we're outside of visiting hours at the moment. But you know what? Seeing as it's you, I think we can make an exception. Follow me."

He goes purposefully through the double doors, and then through another door marked AUTHORIZED PERSON-NEL ONLY, and swipes his security tag on the panel, which beeps and allows us through to a scruffy service corridor that smells of school lunches.

"It's quite a walk to the ward where your great-grandmother is," says Jackson. "This is much quicker. Evening, Philomena!" he says to a lady pushing a cleaning cart.

After several turns and one long corridor, we come to another double door and go through it. Before us is a sign saying DEPARTMENT OF GERIATRICS.

"Thank you so much, Jackson," says Ramzy, all polite. "We'll be fine now."

"Fine? No way! I'm going to make sure you get to see your great-grandma. Leave it to me."

"No, no, really . . . it's fine!"

Jackson's not taking no for an answer and is already talking at the nurses' station.

". . . outside of visiting hours. But they're very good friends of mine, and I was hoping you'd make an exception."

A tired-looking young nurse looks at us over the top of his glasses and purses his lips. "Name?" he says.

"I'm Georgina Santos and this is . . ."

"No. I need the name of the patient you're visiting," says the nurse, looking back at his computer screen. Beside us, Jackson is smiling with pride at his success in getting us in.

"Pretorius," I say.

At the same time, Ramzy says, "Pettarssen."

The nurse looks up sharply.

"Pettarssen-Pretorius. It's, erm . . . hyphenated," I say.

The nurse is peering back at the computer screen. I can't see what he's looking at, but from the expression on his face I can guess what he's about to say next.

"We don't have anyone on the ward with tha—"

He is interrupted by a loud American voice. "Yes, you do! It's a family nickname! Hi, kids—thanks for comin' to see me!" Dr. Emilia Pretorius is scooting toward us in a wheelchair, dressed in men's striped pajamas and a dressing gown, her white hair as round as ever. She takes the flowers. "Are those for me? Swell! Put 'em in water for me, would you, Jesmond?"

She places them on the counter in front of the nurse, who starts to say, "I don't think—"

Whatever it is that he doesn't think, Dr. Pretorius isn't interested, and talks to us instead. "Come on, kids, let's go to the room at the end. Did you bring some of them cookies from your ma? How's old Philip gettin' along without me? Did you feed the cat?"

It's all made up—but it works. Her whirlwind of energy leaves Jesmond the nurse and Jackson standing bewildered as Dr. Pretorius wheels herself off in the direction of the ward's empty TV lounge. There are about eight other beds in the ward, all occupied by very old people who are either asleep or gaping silently in confused wonder as we pass. Ramzy remembers to turn and smile at Jackson, and then he scuttles to catch up with Dr. Pretorius, who is now mentioning her made-up son-in-law. "What a fine gentleman . . ."

The second the door to the lounge is closed, Dr. Pretorius switches character.

"What the Sam Hill is going on?" Her cool eyes are blazing with curiosity over her spectacles, which have slipped to the end of her nose. "I figure you kids aren't stupid, so there must be a good reason, but you're gonna tell me it now, aren't you? Who was that security guard?"

"That was Jackson. He's a friend of my, erm . . . my dad's girlfriend. Dr. Pretorius, what's wrong? Why exactly are you in the hospital?"

"Ah, don't worry about me." She waves her hand dismissively. "Minor heart attack. Easily treated these days. But it's part of what's gonna take me soon enough anyhow, if I don't get there first. I told you that. The way things are goin' we're all gonna die of Dog Plague anyways. So what brings you here? Can't bear life without me? Ha!"

And so I tell her, as quickly as I can, that we want to break her out of the hospital, go to the dome, and travel to the future in order to get the cure for Dog Plague and save the world. Even as I say it, it sounds ridiculous and I find myself trailing off and glancing nervously at the door. There's a long silence.

"That's the craziest thing I've ever heard," says Dr. Pretorius, shaking her head solemnly.

Another long pause.

"I *love* it!"

Chapter Fifty-Four

"This is exactly why I invented the darn thing!" Dr. Pretorius continues. "You kids are geniuses! So—any ideas how we're gonna blow this joint?" Her eyes are darting everywhere, as if she's hoping to see a sign saying ESCAPE ROUTE—THIS WAY.

Ramzy and I look at each other and then at Dr. Pretorius, who has forced herself out of her wheelchair with a walking stick and is standing at the big windows that reach the floor. Ramzy speaks first, in a voice that sounds like an apology.

"Well," he starts, "we thought we were doing pretty well to get here with a vehicle, and—"

"You got wheels? Swell! What now? I tell you one thing: wheelin' me past that Nurse Jesmond ain't gonna happen without him noticing. He's got a streak of mean, I tell ya. Then you gotta *looong* walk to the exit, and your friend Jackson ain't gonna help none either."

I look out the big window, across the parking lot to the road in the distance. The summer sky is darkening. "Is that the main road out there? The one Clem is on?" I ask no one in particular, and no one answers. I take out my phone and call him.

"Clem. Drive past the hospital and tell us if you see flashing lights in a ground-floor window."

Ramzy is by the light switch and hits it repeatedly to turn it on and off. "Keep going, Ramzy. Clem, can you see it? Well, drive faster . . . OK, OK, sorry . . . Can you see it now? Great! Pull up and honk your horn when you're there. This is your one-minute warning."

There's an agonizing wait of a few minutes while Clem gets into position. Then we hear it: a long, rasping *paaaarp-paaaarp* of the campervan's old horn coming across the parking lot and through the thick glass windows. Meanwhile, Dr. Pretorius has struggled into a pair of jeans and a sweater from her yellow bag, and thrown her beach robe over her shoulders. She's still barefoot and, exhausted by the effort of getting back into her wheelchair, gives in to a violent bout of coughing.

There's a curtain to push aside to access the handle to the outside door—and that's when we all see it. A notice on the glass that has been hidden.

THIS DOOR IS ALARMED
OPEN ONLY IN THE CASE OF AN EMERGENCY

We stop. We look at one another again; then Dr. Pretorius says, "Well, if this ain't an emergency, I don't know what is. Besides, what are they gonna do? We're leaving a hospital, not robbing a bank! Ha! We'll be long gone before anything happens."

"But, Dr. Pretorius, what if . . ." I begin, but her hand is already on the handle.

"Too darn late!" With a hard tug, she yanks the handle down and pushes the door wide open. She flops back down in the wheelchair as the alarm starts screaming a rhythmic *whoop-whoop-whoop.*

"Let's go!" she yells. We help push the wheelchair over the ledge, and she's off at full speed, which turns out to be only a brisk walking pace. "Faster!" she cries. "Push me! Yeehaw!"

Ramzy and I each take one of the wheelchair handle and tip the chair back on to its big rear wheels, causing Dr. Pretorius to yelp in surprise. Then we run with it as fast as we can, across the lawn, down over the curb, onto the pavement of the parking lot, in between parked cars, while the alarm wails in our ears. We hear behind us: "Hey!"

Jackson is standing in the doorway, and beside him is Jesmond. Now Jackson's pretty old, and he won't be able to catch us. But Jesmond? He's lean and tall and young and he's already started to sprint across the lawn.

Jesmond is gaining on us, definitely. After all, two kids and an old lady in a wheelchair are no match for a lithe young man who is practically leaping over the cars in his enthusiasm to stop us.

Ahead is the campervan, pulled up at the side of the road, its side door open. Also ahead, in front of the campervan, is a low wall. It's only about twenty inches high, but it stands between us and our goal. There are only ten yards between the wall and the van, but it might as well be an ocean.

There's no way we can get Dr. Pretorius and her wheelchair over that wall.

It's all over before it's even begun.

Chapter Fifty-Five

We are twenty yards from the wall, and Jesmond the nurse is about the same distance behind us when we see movement inside the van. A large figure in luminous green running gear emerges from the side door, loping toward the wall and shouting, "Lift her over!"

Sass Hennessey?

A second later, she's standing on the wall as we stumble to a halt. We can't look back, but I can hear Jesmond's footsteps getting closer. He's only a few paces from us when Sass reaches down and, with an almighty lunge, grabs the wheels of the chair. As she pulls up, Ramzy and I push, and the whole thing—the wheelchair with a squealing Dr. Pretorius in it—is over the wall, and Sass is pushing it to the open-sided van.

Ramzy's over the wall and I've just about made it when I feel a strong hand on my arm and a vicious pull back.

"Not so fast," says Jesmond, spinning me round to face

him. His white-blond hair is stuck to his forehead and he's panting hard. "What . . . what the hell are . . . are you doing?" he gasps, not lessening his grip, even though I'm wriggling.

I don't get a chance to answer, as I see him looking over my shoulder with genuine fear in his eyes. I hear a terrible scream and turn my head to see Sass, crimson in the face, running from the van toward us, emitting a war cry and circling Dr. Pretorius's walking stick around her head like a helicopter blade.

"Aaaaaaaaarrrgghhh!"

Nurse Jesmond doesn't say anything. He just emits a little squeak and lets go of my arm as the full force of Sass's bulk hurtles toward him.

I take my chance and run as Sass lowers the walking stick and utters a gentle, "Sorry." Then she turns to catch up to us, leaving Jesmond gawping in astonishment.

The campervan is already moving off and I'm the last to jump in, just behind Sass, and pull the door closed behind me.

I have now, officially, no idea what's going on. I stare at Sass Hennessey, who is sitting hunched on the flat floor of the van, hanging on to Dr. Pretorius's wheelchair to stop it rolling around inside. Dr. Pretorius is muttering, "Are there no brakes on this cockamamie thing?"

I eventually say, simply, "Saskia?"

"I was just . . . just on an evening run," she pants, still red in the face from her demented charge at the nurse, "when your brother's car stalled at the lights at the end of the road."

Clem looks at us in the rearview mirror and shouts back over the roar of the engine. "I needed a jump-start, so I asked Sass!"

"Yeah. And I figured he could give me a lift home in return. Good job I was hanging on: I think he tried to drive off without me!"

I think that that is exactly what Clem did, but I keep the thought to myself. Instead, I say to Sass, "But . . . but why? Why do all *that*?"

She looks at me levelly, or as levelly as is possible in the rocking campervan. She says something that sounds like, "Friends help friends, eh?" but I can't be hearing properly over the rattling.

This much is pretty clear, though: a campervan containing Clem, Sass Hennessey, me, Ramzy, and Dr. Pretorius (in a wheelchair) is belching exhaust fumes and puffing back along the road toward Whitley Bay seafront, on our way to saving the world.

It is not going to be easy, though.

I scramble over the others to claim a place on the front bench seat next to Clem. We have just driven past the car labeled ARMED POLICE that we saw before, and that's when I see a gray, brown, and white shape dodging a car and lolloping slowly over the grassy hill that leads down to the beach. I scream and Clem flinches.

For a moment—just long enough for me to be absolutely certain it's him—Mr. Mash pauses at the top of a dune before disappearing from view. At the same time, the police-car door opens, and an officer in body armor gets out, watches to see where Mr. Mash is going, then goes quickly to the rear of the vehicle and opens the trunk.

He's going to try shooting my dog.

"Look!" I shout. "It's Mr. Mash. He's in trouble. Turn left, turn left, Clem, now!"

"I can't," he says. "There's no road!"

He's right, of course—there is no road to turn left onto. I know, though, that Mr. Mash's life is at stake, and I'm not going to ignore it. Leaning over, I grab the steering wheel and pull it sharply, causing the van to lurch violently to the left. There's a screech of brakes behind us, a honking of horns, a crunch of steel, and a tinkling of glass as cars collide.

Beneath us is a clanking metal sound: the impact of mounting the pavement has caused something to come loose from the campervan, and then we're off the road, up the pavement, and driving on the grass.

"There goes the exhaust!" shouts Clem. The engine is even noisier than before.

I've opened the side door of the van and am out while it's still moving, running over the low hill and shouting, "Mashie! Mashie!"

At the same time, by the police car, the officer has taken a rifle out of the trunk and is screwing the barrel into the stock.

Chapter Fifty-Six

"Stop! Stop! Don't shoot!" I'm yelling, but I'm not sure I can be heard over the cacophony of car horns behind me and the coughing of the campervan's engine. I glance back: we've created quite a mess, and there's a long backup of cars.

I'm running over the top of the dune now, and there, ahead of me on the beach, is Mr. Mash, ambling down to the water's edge, casting a long shadow across the sand in the setting sun. On the ridge to my left, the policeman has raised the rifle to his shoulder.

Surely he won't fire from there? I'm not much good at estimating distances, but it's pretty much the length of the lane up to our house. A hundred yards? More? No one could shoot a dog from that far away . . .

Could they?

I do the only thing possible. Desperately, I alter my course so that I'm directly between the policeman and Mr. Mash. "Don't shoot!" I'm screaming and, at the same time, "Mr. Mash!"

The silly, deaf thing turns round at last and starts trotting toward me. I don't dare turn my head back to look at the shooter. I just run as fast as I can through the soft sand to Mr. Mash and then I fall on him and gather him in my arms, before turning and looking back up the beach.

The marksman has lowered his weapon. I can't see his face, but he's standing with his arms by his sides, and I know the immediate danger has passed. Now all I have to do is get back to the campervan.

I see it all happening as I stagger back up the beach with Mr. Mash in my arms, licking my face. I don't dare put him down in case he runs off again, freaked out by all the panic around him. The policeman with the gun walks back to his vehicle, replaces the weapon in the trunk, and gets in the car, then slowly drives round to the campervan, whose engine is still chugging loudly.

Both of the officers get out of the car. One goes to the driver's side of the campervan and talks to Clem through the open window. I hear him say, "Is this your vehicle, son?"

The other waits for me to approach, beckoning me with his upturned palm, a very impatient expression on his face. I stop a couple yards away, head bowed, Mr. Mash still in my arms.

"You, young lady, are very, very lucky," he begins.

I hear the other one saying to Clem, "Turn the engine

off and get out of the vehicle, son." When Clem switches off the engine of the campervan, everything is suddenly quieter, and in the silence I begin to realize how crazy this whole escapade is.

"Well, well, well, laddie. Where do we start?" the policeman says to Clem. "How about dangerous driving? I think we've probably got an unroadworthy vehicle here an' all . . ."

It's all going on at once. Over by the road, only two cars seem to have been damaged and have pulled onto the side of the road. The traffic is moving again. The policeman who was talking to me has finished his lecture ("stupid risk . . . breaking the law . . . control your dog . . .") and has told me to get back in the van with Mr. Mash. The full cull hasn't started yet—only strays are being shot—but he must have thought that Mr. Mash was one till I came along. Sass is where I left her, but she's crying quietly, and Dr. Pretorius has a face like a thundercloud: dark and brooding.

Clem has been taken to the police car, where he's being frisked by the other officer, and . . . Ramzy? Where on earth is Ramzy?

As I climb into the van through the side door, he appears from behind the van and hops back in. The police officers haven't even seen him.

"Where have you been?" I whisper, but he shakes his head to shut me up, keeping his hands deep in his pockets.

"You all," says the officer who was armed. "Stay right here." He swishes the sliding side door shut with a clunk, and we're silent for a few moments, apart from Sass's soft whimpering, which is really annoying.

But I can hardly blame her. There is a sadness rising in my throat: the sort of sadness that turns into a lump, then into a sob, and, if I'm not careful, soon I'll be crying along with Sass and I do *not* want that. Instead, I stick my face into Mr. Mash's neck fur and try not to be mad at him for escaping.

I stopped him from being shot. That's good. But it has stopped us from getting to the dome, and that is very, very bad.

We stay like that for several seconds, Mr. Mash and I, till I'm aware of a movement in the front of the van, and the noise of Dr. Pretorius coughing violently.

When she's finished, she takes a long, wheezing breath and says, "I guess I'm the only one who knows how to drive this bus. Outta the way—make room for a dying woman." And, with that, she heaves her spindly frame over the bench seat, panting hard, till she's sitting behind the steering wheel. Her hand pauses over the dangling key. "We got one chance, gang. One chance at this. If this battery isn't charged by now, we're toast!"

"But . . . but . . ." I don't even know what I'm going to

object to, and she is definitely not taking any notice anyway. The policemen haven't noticed her in the driver's seat yet, but they will soon.

"But what, kid?" she growls without even turning round. "Give up? I don't think so. Besides . . ."

She turns the key. The engine wheezes, splutters . . . and . . .

Vrooom! It bursts into life.

". . . we gotta job to finish. And it may be the last thing I ever do! Ha ha ha *haaa!*"

Chapter Fifty-Seven

Through the window I see the horrified faces of the police officers as they realize what's going on, and the massive grin on Clem's face. He raises his handcuffed wrists in salute and says, "Yaaaay!" as the van, with its unlikely collection of passengers, bumps off across the grass, over the pavement, past the angry drivers of the two cars that collided, and joins the thin line of traffic headed to Whitley Bay. Behind us, the police car's siren whoops angrily.

"The police!" I shout. "They'll catch us easily. What are . . ."

But Dr. Pretorius is shaking her head, making her hair bobble furiously. "No, they won't, thanks to our buddy Mr. Rahman and his screwdriver."

Ramzy is smiling shyly. Behind us, I can see the police officers outside their car, examining its rear wheels. The car had gone a short distance, then stopped.

From his pocket, Ramzy pulls a short, sharpened screwdriver that had been rolling around on the floor of the van.

"I did it before, back home. I was only six. They'd send the littlest kids out to stab the tires on the rebel soldiers' trucks. If they caught you, they'd beat you. So we became good at not being caught."

I stare at Ramzy in disbelief. "You never told me about that!"

He shrugs. "You never asked."

We have about a half mile left till we get to the Spanish City. Dr. Pretorius is gunning the engine hard, passing cars where she can, and a foul smell is filling the inside of the van.

"Oh, Mashie!" I protest. "Not now!"

He looks at me with his big eyes as if to say, *Not me. Not this time!*

"Open the windows, folks!" shouts Dr. Pretorius between coughs. "That's gas fumes and an overheating cat converter. You don't wanna breathe much of this."

As I open the sliding window, I glance over at Ramzy, and he's chuckling to himself, actually laughing.

"What's so funny?" I snap. He doesn't seem to be taking this seriously at all. He shakes his head in wonder.

"Look!" he shouts, pointing at us all. "One, two, three, four of us. And a dog. On an adventure. We're the Famous Five!"

"Ramzy! Have you any idea how serious this is? This is not some . . ."

But I stop because, at the exact moment that the dome of the Spanish City appears, creamy white in the distance, the engine splutters, shudders, and dies. My words fade with the sound of the motor. Gradually and agonizingly, the van rolls to a halt in the middle of the road, causing our second traffic jam in about ten minutes. Again the car horns sound in protest.

We're a hundred yards away, maybe a little more.

"Oh hell," moans Dr. Pretorius. "Did no one think of puttin' gas in this darned thing?"

Chapter Fifty-Eight

As we tumble out into the fresh air, the campervan's interior is filling with smoke and there's an acrid smell of electrical burning coming from the dashboard.

We look ahead. There are people on the footpath between us and the Spanish City—walking up and down, chatting, carrying shopping bags, and talking on their phones. No dogs, of course. But it's not exactly a clear route for a wheelchair.

Dr. Pretorius turns back to look at Sass. "You! Can you do your . . . your thing again? Clear those people out of the way?"

Sass nods. "Move aside!" she shouts as she runs ahead of us like a steamroller, and the people milling around the front of the Spanish City melt away in terror as she approaches.

I don't stop to think about what a weird picture we must make. Sass—in her bright lime-green running gear, windmilling her arms and yelling at people—is followed by Dr.

Pretorius in her wheelchair, along with me, clutching a baffled-looking mutt, and Ramzy, as we push everyone along as fast as we can.

I hear someone say, "Get that dog indoors!"

Above us in the twilight sky, a police drone is flashing blue and squawking: "STOP! THIS IS A POLICE COMMAND. STOP!" But it's coming too fast and trying to swoop low, and as we run through the Spanish City's entrance, it smashes into the wall above us, chunks of metal and carbon fiber raining down onto the pavement behind us. Back where we left it, the campervan is now smoking badly from under the hood, and a few flames are licking up the sides.

"Can somebody just explain to me what's going on?" says Sass, her blond hair in disarray and sticking to her face. She's bewildered, and her head is swiveling between us all.

Ramzy says, "Later, Sass. Right now, we need your help." I don't know *why* we need her but I decide to trust Ramzy.

From around her shoulders, Dr. Pretorius pulls off her woollen beach robe and gives it to Sass. "Put this on, honey."

Inside the precinct, the Polly Donkin Tea Rooms and the amusement arcade are shuttered up for the night. No one follows us as we head toward the back of the echoey mall. Ramzy still has the key, and Dr. Pretorius sees this but says nothing. I think she understands what has happened.

Minutes later, we're through the back door that leads

to the storage area and up to the dome. "Lock it behind us, Ramzy," says Dr. Pretorius. "We do *not* wanna be interrupted. Now—who's gonna carry me upstairs?"

And now I know why we need Sass. She and Ramzy carry Dr. Pretorius easily up the metal staircase, followed by Mr. Mash. I go ahead and bring the doc's wheeled desk chair from the control room and meet them when they get to the top. When Dr. Pretorius is in the chair, she's convulsed by a violent coughing fit. She coughs and coughs, thumping the arm of the chair. When she's finished, she's gasping with the effort.

She wheezes, "All righty. If I've got the timing right, Hawking II is already in position. We've already lost time." She points at Sass. "You in the green: go back downstairs and make sure the back doors to the storage bay are secure, with the steel bar in position. It's heavy but I reckon you can lift it."

Sass's eyes light up, and without another word, she leaves the control room. Suddenly it's as if everybody knows what to do. I've strapped the helmet on tight, squeezing the catch on the chinstrap into place and shoving the earpieces in. My fingers are trembling, and I'm trying not to think of the headache I suffered last time, but I can't stop the fear completely.

If I have any doubt about what I'm about to do, it's dispelled when I look down at Mr. Mash, exhausted by the excitement and lying on his side in the control room, panting. I look around, and just for a moment—a few seconds—the room is quiet. I can't see Ramzy, and Dr. Pretorius has stopped her frenzied key-bashing and is scrolling carefully through some text on a screen.

I crouch down and take Mr. Mash's head in my hands, and in the quiet, my damaged memory brings back the dogs I loved at St. Woof's: Sally-Ann, and Ben, and . . . and . . . and the ugly one whose collar disc is on my bedside table. I swallow hard. Now is not the time to get all emotional.

"Thanks for getting better, Mashie!" I whisper. "Your blood might be our only hope." He turns his head to give my hand a lick.

Lick, germs, viruses . . . I just don't care anymore. I'm just hoping—assuming—that Mr. Mash is better. If he isn't, then this whole venture may be a waste of time. This has to work.

I stand in the doorway to the studio. Dr. Pretorius has been bashing away at the keyboard for minutes now; the screens and consoles are lighting up and flashing, warning sounds are beeping, and at last she turns to me with a fiery light in her old eyes.

"You sure about this?" she asks, and I nod. I'm about to go through the door when there's a movement from the corner of the annex. Ramzy's standing there with another helmet strapped to his head.

"If you thought I'd let you do this alone, you don't understand the spirit of adventure!" he declares in a grand voice. I know the whole idea of Ramzy coming along probably increases the danger, but it feels like the opposite.

He says, "Fire me up, Dr. P—we're going in!"

"No, Ramzy—it's too dangerous! Think of the headache you'll get," I say.

"Ach—what's a headache, man, when you're saving the world? Besides, it'll take two of us to fight the scorpion."

I hadn't even thought of the scorpion.

Thanks, Ramzy. Thanks a million.

And, with that, he grabs my hand and together we shuffle to the center of the ball-bearing floor as the door locks shut behind us and we're plunged into total darkness.

I can already feel the tingling in my scalp.

PART FOUR

Chapter Fifty-Nine

In my ear, Dr. Pretorius coughs and says, "Coordinates set to place you outside the hospital at midday, exactly one year from now. Got that? From here on in, you're on your own. Ramzy—the addition of your prefrontal cortex waves is an unknown quantity. We're sailin' in uncharted waters, my friends. Excuse me," and there's another burst of coughing.

Then, as before, the shapes begin to appear in front of me—only this time they're accompanied by Ramzy going, "Whoa! Awesome! Hey, look at you!"

I turn to face him, and he looks the same, more or less. Up close, some of the edges of his body, at the shoulders, for example, are a little pixelated. But it's Ramzy: he's in the same dirty Real Madrid top and school shorts; he's wearing a bicycle helmet. I look beyond him, and the world is coming into focus. Trees form before my eyes, the road, the grass verges, the hospital building.

"Take a sniff, guys. You'll notice I've fixed the smell thing," says Dr. Pretorius. Then she coughs again. "Oh, and . . . by the way . . . the, ah . . . the scorpion. Li'l ol' Buster. He may have, kinda, ah . . ."

I stop marveling and feel a chill come over me. *Why is she being so hesitant?* "What is it?" I say.

"With me in the hospital, the whole program has been left running unchecked for the last three days. The artificial intelligence has probably had some effect on the scorpion that may not be altogether . . . desirable, but then again it may be totally fine and dandy. Just, you know—keep an eye out."

I can't swallow. Not only am I as scared as heck, but there's something not right.

"Are you sure the date is right?" I say through the microphone. "There's . . . I dunno . . ."

Dr. Pretorius replies, "Accordin' to this, Georgie, it's dead right. Midday on July twenty-seventh one year from now. What's wrong? The video feed to the control room is down: I can't see anything."

"Can't you see what I see? It's empty. There are hardly any cars."

Ramzy looks around. "You're right. There's nobody about. It's really quiet."

A tide of litter is banked up along the little wall, and the grass on the verges is higher than my ankles. The flower beds where we picked flowers only an hour or so ago are choked with weeds. I sniff: there's an unclean smell everywhere, like old trash bags.

But it's when I turn to look at the hospital building that I gasp in shock. A chain-link fence three or four yards high, topped with vicious razor wire, has been erected all along the perimeter. The parking lot is empty apart from one or two dirty-looking cars and some green army vehicles. The main entrance has been converted into a military checkpoint, with uniformed soldiers guarding a large metal gate and carrying big guns across their chests.

We're on the other side of the road, and no one has noticed us yet.

"Can they see us?" asks Ramzy.

I think back to my encounter with Norman Two-Kids. "Oh yes," I say. "While we're in the program, they're as real as us. But I don't think we should make ourselves conspicuous."

"But what's happening? Why all the soldiers? I don't like this, Georgie."

"Me neither. Dr. Pretorius? We can't get in. Can you see the fence?"

Dr. Pretorius clears her throat and rasps, "I can see bits of it now. It's pretty low-resolution, but yeah: soldiers, barbed wire. Seems to me that the hospital's become a military zone, as would be expected if a disease gets out of control.

Faced with a plague, people are gonna get pretty angry, and desperate, and so . . ." She breaks off to cough, and by this stage I'm getting very scared.

"And so," she continues, "be real careful."

"But how do we get into the hospital? That's where the cure will be. There's soldiers and guns and everything. And a huge fence."

"Like I say, don't take risks," says Dr. Pretorius. "So long as you're in there, they're as real as you are."

"This is too weird," says Ramzy, shaking his head, but I've had an idea.

"Follow me," I say. "And act natural."

"Yup. As natural as two kids in a 3-D virtual future with bicycle helmets on *can* act," he says, but he follows me anyway, up the road, past more of the hospital, till we're looking at the big old building that houses the Edward Jenner Department of Biobotics. There are no soldiers here, although the wire fence looks just as solid. There are some stacked-up metal crates and oil drums that could offer some cover for what I'm about to try.

"Dr. Pretorius, what would happen if we just ran at the fence, full tilt?" I ask. I'm forming an idea, but I have no clue if it'll work.

"Well, ordinarily, when you touch something, the MSVR tricks your brain into believing you've touched it. So the fence would feel real."

"But it's an illusion, right? There's nothing *actually* stopping us. The fence isn't really there. So, if we ran at it, what could stop us?"

Ramzy pipes up: "Remember the deck chair I threw at the scorpion on the first day! It went straight through it!"

"I don't recommend it, kiddo. This is totally untested."

"The *whole thing* is totally untested," I say. "In fact, we're testing it right now. And, right now, we have no choice. Come on, Ramzy. *Now!*"

Chapter Sixty

It's desperation. I have come this far, and I'm not going to let an imaginary fence—however realistic—stand in my way. I look up the road for cars; there are none and I grab Ramzy's wrist and we run at the fence.

"Head down, eyes shut!" I yell, and at the moment we've crossed the road and are about to hit the fence, I feel Ramzy's wrist twist free of my grip.

"No!" he shouts, but I'm going too fast to stop myself and as I hit the wire fence, I feel a shock go through my whole body like a million cans of fizzy drink being opened inside me at once. I feel myself hit the hard ground and I scream out in pain at the shock and the impact, but . . .

I know the fence didn't stop me. I kept moving when I should have been stopped in my tracks.

I can't focus my vision and there's a ringing in my ears, but I sit up, look back, and there's Ramzy on the other side of the fence.

My heart is thudding in my chest, and there's a pain behind my eyes, but I've made it! I start to laugh. "Come on, Ramzy: you can do it too. It hurts but it's OK!"

"I can't," he says. "There's something wrong with my helmet. Everything keeps going black, like I'm back in the dome."

"Just do it!" I urge.

He bites his lip and nods, taking a step back to build his run-up. Then there's a voice. "Hey, you! What are you doing? Who are you talking to?"

I look around, and there's a soldier approaching on my side of the wire, holding a big black rifle across his chest. He's talking to Ramzy and hasn't seen me. I slink behind an oil drum and crouch down.

"This is a protected government facility," says the soldier. "Just what on earth are you doing?"

"J-just looking," says Ramzy.

"Just *looking*? What is there to see, son?"

"Erm . . . nothing."

"Dead right. Nothing. So get lost. Go on—off with you."

I can hear Ramzy's footsteps retreating, then a distant shout. "Good luck, Georgie!"

"Less of your cheek!" shouts the soldier. "Keep going, son. Don't stop till you get home!" I hear the soldier talking to someone in his headset. "Some kid on the perimeter fence, sir . . . Nah, fence intact, no threat . . . Righto, sir . . ."

He goes back the way he came, and I wait a few minutes before I whisper, "Dr. Pretorius? Can you hear me?"

Nothing.

A bit louder now: "Dr. Pretorius? Ramzy?" I wiggle my earpieces but nothing happens. I can still hear the noises around me, but nothing from Dr. Pretorius or Ramzy.

A wave of fear passes through me, and I tell myself, *It's OK. You're still in the dome studio.*

But without proper communication, it's impossible to *feel* certain. I tell myself to relax, to stay calm. That Dr. Pretorius will be working on a solution. It's just a slight technical glitch caused when I went through the fence and . . . *something* happened.

But I also know that I'm on my own. On my own in the future, surrounded by armed soldiers and running out of time.

Chapter Sixty-One

Now, ordinarily, when you're in trouble, it's a relief to see someone you recognize. But that is *not* what I feel when I look across at the Edward Jenner building and see a woman walking toward the entrance.

I swallow hard. Shortish, with angular limbs and spiky hair.

Jessica.

And following her is a boy . . . no, a girl. A girl I recognize.

Me.

Chapter Sixty-Two

OK. Screech of brakes. Freeze-frame.

Stop! I mean, *really* stop.

Of all the things I am not expecting, this doesn't even get on the list because it's impossible even to *think* of.

I hunker down behind the oil drum again, my breath coming in rapid little pants.

It can't be, I tell myself. *This is ridiculous.*

Cautiously, I peep round the oil drum. The two of them have stopped a few yards from the door to the Jenner building. They're too far away for me to hear what they're saying, but it is definitely, *definitely* Jessica.

Jessica and . . . ?

Honestly, I hardly dare look at the figure next to her. But when I dare to peep again, there's no mistaking her. I mean me. Same short, curly hair. Is she taller? Maybe a bit, but we're a year ahead, don't forget, and—as Dad said—I'm due a growth spurt. Favorite checked shirt. Jeans? They're new. I like them. New shoes too. Smart shoulder bag, the one I got from Clem, slung across her chest . . .

Hang on, I tell myself. *This is not a fashion show.* I guess I'm just blown away by seeing myself, and I'm trying to drink in every detail. They're standing by the entrance, talking. Soon they'll go in and I will have lost my chance, so . . .

I work out a route that will get me to the entrance without being very noticeable. On the lawn, with its back to the wire fence, is a low outbuilding that will provide some cover, but at *some* point I need to get access to the inside of the Jenner building, and what I do there is something I haven't yet worked out.

At the Jenner building door, two armed soldiers have just checked the security pass around the neck of a man in a white lab coat who has gone in. Jessica follows him, leaving me—Other Me—standing outside beside a low wall.

Other Me has a pass around her neck, too, but she doesn't go in. Instead, she pulls some earphones out of her jeans pocket. She puts them in her ears, touches her smartwatch (*Cool!* I think. *Must have got that for my birthday . . .*), and sits down on the wall, bobbing her head to the music.

Exactly like I do.

I have an idea. It's bold but it's *got* to work. It's going to involve meeting myself, and I know I don't have long.

Half crouching, half running, I get up from behind the

oil drum and scuttle the twenty or so yards across the lawn to the outbuilding, where I press myself against the side. I expect to hear "Hey you! Halt!" at any time, but no one has seen me. It's good cover: I cannot be seen by the soldiers standing in the doorway, and I'm within hissing distance of Other Me.

"Pssst!" I say. *"Pssst! Hey! Georgie!"*

Chapter Sixty-Three

I'm suddenly reminded of Dad.

"*Will you take those damn things out of your ears?*" he often yells. "*I've been speaking to you for the last two minutes and you haven't heard a single word!*"

Now I know exactly how he feels.

My hissed attempt to get Other Me's attention hasn't worked at all. Peeping round the corner, I can see her mouthing the words of a song. I'm thinking of throwing something, a pebble maybe, when my phone buzzes with an incoming message.

I look down and see that it's Ramzy. This is when—if they aren't already strange enough—things get even stranger.

Even as I'm tapping my screen to answer him, I'm trying to work out what's going on.

1. I'm in a three-dimensional re-creation of my world
    a year from now, inside a huge, dome-shaped

studio in Whitley Bay, in which the hospital up the road is surrounded by wire fencing and soldiers.

2. So is Ramzy, although he's on the other side of a virtual wire fence.

3. This world also contains a three-dimensional re-creation of me, Georgie Santos, who is about five yards away, listening to music on some steps.

4. Ramzy is calling me on my phone, which we are supposed to have switched off, but in the panic, we have both forgotten to do.

I know. I'm finding it hard to get my own head around it.

"Ramzy? Where are you?" I'm half whispering. "I've lost contact with Dr. Pretorius."

"Me too. I'm scared, Georgie. I'm going to take off my helmet."

"No—don't do that, Ramzy, it's dangerous. Ramzy!" I shout the last word, and hear no more.

"*Ramzy!*" I shout again.

"Who are you talking to?" The voice comes from behind me, and I immediately know who it is. Slowly, I turn round.

Can we just pause for a second—because I think this might be the weirdest thing that has ever happened to any-one ever.

It's not like looking in a mirror. Not at all. A mirror image does exactly what you do. Other Me doesn't.

I gasp. She doesn't.

I say, "Oh my God." She doesn't.

You see, *I* know that Other Me is me. She doesn't know that. I think she just thinks I'm someone who looks very like her.

She looks me up and down. She must recognize my favorite red top, with the star on the front? The jeans that have worn through at the knees, with an ancient ink stain on the thigh? My dark, curly hair that's exactly the same as hers? My light brown eyes?

She does that blinky thing that I do: two or three rapid blinks when I'm surprised.

Other Me says: "Who, erm . . ." I think she's going to ask me who I am, but she doesn't. "Who were you talking to just then?"

"Ramzy."

"How?" I hold up my phone.

"You can't be," she says, shaking her head.

"Why not?"

"Because Ramzy's dead."

Chapter Sixty-Four

Other Me looks at me carefully while I take in this information.

She checks over both shoulders. We cannot be seen. There's a few seconds during which we just stare at each other, till Other Me starts to nod slowly, the way you would when suddenly everything makes sense.

She breaks the silence by saying, "It's OK. I know who you are. I've been expecting you. Kind of."

I say nothing. It's just so strange, hearing me talk but not forming the words myself. But she is probably as astonished as I am. Then she says, "You're in the dome right now, aren't you?"

"Yes."

She puffs out her cheeks (like I do) and says, "Wow." Then she reaches out and touches my face, gently running her fingers over my cheek, then my hair, saying, "Wow!" again and smiling.

"Does that mean you're not . . . real?" I ask, and she smiles. I've got a nice smile, I think.

"I'm real, all right. This is all real, although I wish it wasn't. I knew you were coming. That is, I hoped you would."

I frown at her in puzzlement.

Other Me flicks her eyes from side to side to check if anyone's coming; then she says, "You nearly didn't come at all." Still I say nothing.

She continues: "That time, in the lane, when we . . . when you decided to take the campervan, to get Clem to help, to spring Dr. Pretorius from the hospital . . . you nearly didn't do it."

Is this a statement or a question? She's right, of course: we very nearly didn't do it. It was scary, risky, unworkable. It really *very nearly* never happened.

Other Me goes on, her voice becoming sad: "But you *did* do it, right? I mean, you went through with it. Took the campervan, busted Dr. Pretorius out, went to the dome. You must have."

"Um," I say. "Yeah. It wasn't easy, but yeah." I think about it, picturing the moment when we were about to go ahead with the plan. "If I hadn't remembered Mum's song, I don't think I'd have had the nerve."

She's looking at me blankly. "What?"

"Mum's song," I say. "*Someone to tend to, be a friend to . . .*

329

I thought about it, and it . . . gave me the courage, I guess. To do it."

She nods sadly. "Well, I didn't think of that, and I *didn't* do it. I had the chance to change everything, to take the risk, to put it all right, but I was scared and I messed it up and . . . well, you've seen." She looks about at the razor wire and I see her swallow hard. "You see, you changed your world. I didn't, and this is the result." She waves her hand to indicate the barbed wire, the checkpoints, the awfulness of what the world has become.

"Wh-what happened?"

"What do you think? It was exactly as we feared. Worse, in fact. Dog Plague. CBE. It took millions. Young people, old people, all the dogs, and worst of all . . ." Other Me trails off, staring at the sky. Her chin wobbles as she tries to form a word beginning with R.

"Ramzy?" I say, and she nods and looks down. "How? I mean . . ."

Other Me sighs deeply and doesn't look up. "Because I chickened out. Instead of taking the plunge, breaking out Dr. Pretorius . . . I just . . . got too scared. That's why all the soldiers are here. It went crazy. Riots, people looting hospitals, people stealing medicines. Millions and millions of people died. It's been horrible, Georgie. And all because I was cowardly." A tear rolls down her cheek and she brushes it away.

"Cautious, I think."

"No. No! Sometimes you have to do the risky thing. And I didn't. Do you remember that poster on our bedroom wall?"

"The Wisdom of the Dogs?"

"If what you want is buried . . ."

We say the last bit together: *"Dig and dig until you find it."*

Other Me says simply, "I stopped digging too soon."

I let this sink in. On the other side of the wire fence, an army truck trundles past.

"Why are you here today?" I ask. "At the hospital?"

"I knew what our plan was. I wondered: if I didn't carry out the plan, maybe *you* would. I've thought of nothing else for the last year. It's been driving me nuts. And in case you're wondering, this is just as weird for me as it is for you. For me. And you. You know what I mean." She chuckles, and it sounds so like me that I laugh, too, and she laughs at me laughing, and within seconds we're both howling, and that turns to crying, and I don't know what I'm crying about.

"Mr. Mash?" I say, and Other Me shakes her head and I breathe in sharply.

"We had his blood sample, though," she says. "That was a smart move. It's going to help us."

"Dr. Pretorius?"

"She died in the hospital. Another heart attack. All her stuff was scrapped. No one knew what it was and, to be honest, everyone had other concerns. Georgie?" Other Me turns to me, wiping away tears, but more form in their place. "You've got to do this. You've *got* to. However strange this whole setup is, you've got to stop this. I can get you the cure. You can take it back to . . . to . . . the past, I guess?"

"Georgie! There you are!"

We both turn round, shocked. Jessica looks first at Other Me and then at me. Then two things happen at once. The alarm on my phone starts to go *ping pong, ping pong,* warning me that my time in the dome is about to come to an abrupt end.

And Jessica? She looks at me, then at Other Me, then at me again, her eyes narrowed to slits from curiosity.

"Oh my G—"

Chapter Sixty-Five

"God!" Jessica's exclamation is still ringing in my ears when everything goes black, and I fall to my knees with the familiar severe headache that I experienced before. I scrabble with my fingers for the helmet's release catch.

In my head, behind my eyes, it's as though there's a firework display going on: flashes and bursts of color accompany every stab of pain, and I'm gasping for breath. Somewhere, miles away, I can hear a voice.

I look up. I'm back in the dome, back in my own time.

"Georgie? Georgie?" It's Ramzy, but in the total darkness of the dome studio I cannot see him. As my head clears, I know that he's not miles away, but only a few yards.

"Where are you, Ramzy? You OK?"

"Yeah. Headache from hell, but yeah. I've been stuck. While the floor's active, I can't get across it: my feet stay in the same position when I walk."

"I know. It does that. But now it's stopped, I think."

The flashlight from Ramzy's phone suddenly pierces the darkness. It swoops round the vast circle above us and comes to rest on my face, and I screw up my eyes. I feel like I'm being interrogated, especially when Ramzy says, "Did you get it?"

That is when the full force of everything comes rushing over me, like a shower of shame. I shake my head but cannot say the word *no*. With the light in my eyes, I can't see Ramzy's reaction, but it's nice of him not to say what I would say, which is, "Why on earth not?"

We cross the floor to the edge of the circle, using the light's beam to find the entrance to the annex. Together, we heave the door open and the sight that greets us makes us both gasp.

At the end of the room, propped up against the wall, lies Dr. Pretorius. Beside her is Mr. Mash, his nose nudging her hand. At first I think she's dead, but her eyes flicker open. She licks her lips with a dry tongue and croaks, "Hi, kiddos." And the effort makes her eyes shut again.

"Dr. Pretorius!" I say, rushing over to her. "Are you all right?"

"Yeah. Dandy," she says without reopening her eyes. "Just, you know, I had a sort of repeat minor myocardial infarction. That's a heart attack." The effort of talking is making her breaths shallow and frequent. "Still . . . actually . . . having one."

334

"We've got to get you to the hospital," says Ramzy, and he takes out his phone to make the call.

We're both startled by the force of her command.

"*No! No, no, no.* Give me an aspirin. Over there . . . in the drawer."

I give her the pill and she chews on it, glugging some water from a bottle on the desk. She blinks hard, and finally her eyes settle on me.

"I'm sorry I lost contact with you in there. I just blacked out. I only came round thanks to your darn mutt lickin' my face. Gee, he stinks." She takes another effortful breath. "I don't know how long I've got left, but we've got to stay here and finish this. If I go to the hospital, it'll be days, weeks. Perhaps, you know . . . forever."

I say, "But if you don't go to the hospital, you'll die!"

Dr. Pretorius's face contorts in a spasm of pain and she sucks a long breath through her teeth. She's panting as she talks.

"We're all gonna die, kid. And a whole lot of us much sooner than we should if we don't do this. It's ninety minutes till the satellite passes over again. We gotta wait here, 'cause out there there's a bunch of angry, worried folks. Are you gonna go back in and finish the job?"

Do I have a choice? I don't have a choice. I've seen what will happen if I don't go back. Lots of people will die.

Ramzy will die.

It's the Wisdom of the Dogs. I've got to keep digging.

As if in response, my phone buzzes and it's Dad calling. I let it buzz while I think what to do, and after a few seconds I click to decline the call. I just don't know what to say at the moment. Instead, I bury my face in Mr. Mash's fur, take a deep sniff of his doggy smell, and I have to try really hard not to cry. Crying is not needed right now.

We all look up when there's a thumping on the control-room door.

"Let me in! Let me in!"

Chapter Sixty-Six

It's a blond girl in an electric-green Lycra one-piece. I don't remember her name till Ramzy says it.

"Sass!"

Then it comes flooding back. I had completely forgotten she was downstairs. I had forgotten who she was. It's the brain thing again, although I say nothing.

"They're banging on the big door downstairs!" she says, hands flapping in panic. "It's really loud."

"Yeah—that's the wolf-head knocker," says Ramzy.

"Well, I wanna go home now," she says. "I went out without my phone. Me mam's gonna go nuts!" And at that moment, all of Sass's bullying bluster has evaporated. It's suddenly as though she's half the size, and her eyes are scared and blinking back tears. "I don't understand any of this," she says. "I'm scared and I just wanna go home."

Dr. Pretorius doesn't even look at her when she growls, "Sorry, honeybunch. You ain't goin' *nowhere*."

Chapter Sixty-Seven

Think about it: we're not going to get away with this for long.

1. Outside—in what I am now thinking of as the "normal" world—it's ten o'clock.

2. There's a badly damaged VW campervan smoldering on the seafront.

3. Clem has been arrested and probably taken to Whitley Bay police station, where Dad will have been informed and all sorts of trouble will be kicking off.

4. Ramzy, for his part, has been missing from home for hours. He has turned off his phone. Heaven only knows what Aunty Nush will be thinking. She'll have told his dad, and—according to Ramzy—his dad will be back soon.

"We're gonna have to do something," says Ramzy. "I mean, Aunty Nush is a nightmare, but she'll be worried sick and I feel bad about that."

"Will she call the police?" I say. My head is beginning to ache now, and I know it's going to get worse.

"Nah. Because, one, she's terrified of the police. She remembers what they were like back home. Two, she can't speak English, so what's she gonna say? And three . . ." He cocks his head and listens. "I think they already know we're here." As he says this, there's the *whoop* of a siren from outside.

I'm already typing a message to Dad.

> Hi. You're prob worried and I'm sorry. I'm safe and so is Ramzy. Mr. M is with us. I hope that by the morning this will all have been worthwhile. Pls trust me. I love you, Georgie

I press *send* and turn off my phone.

"Dr. Pretorius. How many entrances are there to the dome?"

Dr. Pretorius swallows hard and takes another sip of water. "There's the back door to the main bit of the Spanish City: the one we came through before. Did you lock it?"

"Yes, definitely. But it won't hold forever, will it?"

"It won't hold for five minutes against a half-decent locksmith. The back double doors are much more secure. They're locked with steel bars across them. Did you do that?" she says to Sass.

Sass nods. She's terrified, and I feel a bit sorry for her. "Will anyone get in?" she asks in a small voice.

Dr. Pretorius coughs and grimaces with the pain. "Sure they will. If they think you're at risk. If they think I'm harming you, if they think you're in danger of harming yourself. Sorry to break it to you, but they've got every reason to try to force entry. You're kids, for Pete's sake."

She's right, of course. Somewhere in the last few hours, I'd kind of forgotten that.

"Shush!" says Ramzy, holding up his hand.

There's a *thump, thump, thump* coming from downstairs. Someone is trying to get through the back door from the Spanish City.

Chapter Sixty-Eight

Ramzy and I have snuck down the metal steps that link the loading bay to the dome's control room. The thumping on the door to the Spanish City continues, along with shouts. It's a Geordie woman's voice, both stern and friendly at the same time.

"Ramzy! Georgie! This is the police. Open the door! You're not in any trouble. We can open this lock without you if we have to, so please open up."

I'm absolutely terrified. Ramzy, though, is loving it. With a finger on his lips, he tiptoes over to a pile of old builders' debris left over from the conversion of the dome and starts looking for something. I don't know what, but I can't help thinking back to that time we spoke to the builder as we walked past ages ago.

And then, without warning, everything is blank like this:

And then it's not again. I'm blinking hard. During the blank time, everything was white, and I heard nothing, and now it's OK again. I don't know how long it lasted. No one has moved, at least not much.

"Ramzy?" I say. But I don't know what to ask him. I look over at him, and he still has his finger on his lips to say *shhhh*.

"Hey, Georgie," says the policewoman. "I can hear you. Open the door now, dear."

Ramzy's struggling back with a metal cylinder the size of a fire extinguisher, with a nozzle attached. Liquid Weld. He comes close enough to speak into my ear.

"You know this stuff? Hardens on contact with air. Should take care of that door." He looks at me, carefully. "You OK?"

I'm not, but I nod. The last thing we need to deal with now is my brain melting.

We stand on the other side of the door from the police-woman, and I hear her say, "It's no use. Either they can't hear us, or they're deliberately ignorin' us. We could bash it in."

Another voice says, "It's a metal door, Sarge. We'll have to get the enforcer. Or a locksmith."

"The nearest locksmith is in North Shields. Go get the enforcer."

I've no idea what an enforcer is, but it's obviously something that can open a door.

Meanwhile, Ramzy's reading the instructions on the cylinder, which look to me to be a long list of WARNINGS and HAZARDS and stuff in red letters.

"Do you have any safety goggles?" he whispers, but doesn't wait for my answer. "Stand back," he says, and I don't need to be asked twice. Seconds later, a whitish stream is pulsing out of the nozzle. Where it hits the floor, it hardens into a gray metallic lump.

Ramzy aims the stream at the door. Up the line where the door connects with the wall, covering the hinges; across the top and down the side with the locks and handle and into the keyholes.

"Can you hear that, Sarge? There's someone . . . Listen."

For good measure, Ramzy finishes off with a thick deposit between the floor and the door, emptying the cylinder; then he steps back to inspect his handiwork. The whole door is sealed to the wall, and the voices on the other side are more muffled.

"Dunno what that is. But there's definitely someone there. Ramzy! Georgie! Saskia!"

We don't wait. Seconds later, we're back up the stairs to the control room, slamming the door shut behind us.

In the few minutes we've been away, Sass has helped Dr. Pretorius to get into her large swivel desk chair, and Dr. Pretorius is fiddling with Ramzy's bicycle helmet. It really seems as though every movement of her fingers is a huge effort.

"What do we do now?" says Ramzy.

Dr. Pretorius clears her throat noisily. "You can help me escape all of this when we're done. Under the tarp in the loading bay. I just hope it still works."

"The copter-drone?" breathes Ramzy with awe.

"I know you've been dying to know. Do you reckon you can carry me down?"

Sass nods.

"Yeah," says Ramzy. "But what about before that? Are we . . . trying again?"

"We don't have a choice," I say. "I'm going back in."

They all look at me.

I'm crouched down, stroking Mr. Mash's ears, which are standing up and alert: Mashie knows something big is going on, but he's smart enough not to get in the way. I look up and shift myself to a comfortable seated position, ready to tell them what happened when I met myself in the future.

"You have to listen to me now," I say, "because I'm not even sure I believe this myself."

I start to tell them everything, about the soldiers and the empty parking lot, but I keep forgetting bits. Plus, I'm not going to mention Ramzy being dead in the future, because he's looking at me with his big eyes, and it's just too weird. So everything's a bit garbled.

Poor Sass is looking at me, then at Dr. Pretorius, and then at Ramzy in turn, with this look of pure bafflement on her face. She doesn't say a word and appears terrified at what she's ended up in.

"Look," I say in the end, "it's simple. If I don't go back, millions of people are going to die."

There's silence. Then suddenly Dr. Pretorius turns. She's staring at one of the screens broadcasting a television channel. A reporter is standing outside the Spanish City with a microphone.

Chapter Sixty-Nine

". . . Thanks, James. We're coming live from the scene in Whitley Bay where police have surrounded the entertainment complex known as the Spanish City following reports of the kidnapping of three children by an as yet unidentified adult female.

"The children, who are not being named at this stage, were part of a high-speed chase along the seafront in the burning vehicle you can see behind me."

"High-speed chase? It wasn't that fast," says Ramzy. He has found some stale bread and cheese and is chewing between glugs of water.

"Shush!"

"A few moments ago, police made an unsuccessful attempt to gain access to the

part of the complex where the children are
being held, and efforts to contact the alleged
kidnapper have so far been unsuccessful. I am
joined now by the father of one of the children."

"Oh my God!" says Ramzy. "Dad!"

Mr. Rahman is unshaven and exhausted-looking, his bald head beaded with sweat. Beside him, Aunty Nush is twisting the fabric of her headscarf round her fingers.

The reporter doesn't even get a chance to ask a question before Ramzy's dad leans into the microphone and shouts, "Ramzy! We're comin' to get you!"

Ramzy's on his feet, yelling at the TV. "No, Dad!" Then he says something else in a different language. On the screen, the reporter has pointed the microphone at Aunty Nush, who says pretty much the only thing I have ever heard her say.

"Ramzy good boy! He good boy," and then she wipes her eyes.

Ramzy shouts back at the TV, "I *am* a good boy, Aunty! I am! You'll see!" Poor Ramzy: he looks close to tears.

The reporter turns his attention back to Mr. Rahman. "The police have said you may need to be patient. What do you say to that?"

He's not able to reply because Aunty Nush interrupts him with a long stream of words. Mr. Rahman replies just

as loudly, and the only thing I can hear him say is "*Na-nush,
na-nush, na, na.*" They're having an argument on TV.

"What are they saying?" I ask Ramzy, who looks horrified.

"*Na, Nush.* It means, 'No, Nush.' She said . . . she said . . ."
Ramzy's shaking his head in disbelief.

"What did she say?" I'm almost shouting with frustration.

"Well, after she told Dad he was a useless piece of erm . . .
waste, she said she's going to use his truck to break in, and if
he tries to stop her she'll kill him with her bare hands." He
says it quietly, and he sounds almost admiring as he gazes at
the TV. Under his breath he says, "Wow, Aunty Nush!"

The newsreader on TV is commenting on what he sees:
"*Extraordinary scenes at Whitley Bay where the father of one of
the children allegedly being held in the Spanish City entertainment complex is on the scene . . .*"

Dr. Pretorius has been hitting keys like crazy during all of
this. Her energy has returned along with a sense of purpose
that's infectious.

"You're gonna have to go in *now*, kid. Hawking II has just
come into position. I can't fix the communications channel,
and Ramzy's helmet is completely trashed, so you're on your
own in there."

Ramzy looks at me. "Can you do it?" he asks.

There's a pause. I can't even speak I'm so scared.

"Well," he says, "if anyone can, it's you." He smiles, then

gives me an awkward hug, which is a first for me and Ramzy. "It's been an adventure," he says.

I breathe in deeply through my nose and lift my head. It seems to help me to speak again. "How long have we got till your aunty's back?" I ask Ramzy. He chews his lip in thought.

"Nine or ten minutes? Dad parks the tractor unit on the street if he's just done a long run. So she'll go home, get his keys, and drive back . . ."

"Can she drive?"

Ramzy gives me a withering look. "She drove an armored personnel carrier in the war, so she can drive the front end of a truck."

I believe him. Ramzy's aunty Nush is turning out to be more than just the scary woman I thought.

"Lock the door, you in the green," croaks Dr. Pretorius, indicating Sass and then pointing at the door to the control room. "It'll hold for a few more minutes. Georgie, get that helmet on and go!" She's not even looking at us as she breathlessly barks commands, but thumping the keyboard and watching figures and lights scroll up and illuminate on the screens.

"Go, go, go! I'm sending you back exactly where you left off, OK?"

At that moment, I'm surprised to feel that I don't really have a choice. This is just something that I have to do, like it or not, and I find myself strapping on the helmet and pushing open the heavy door to the studio. To my horror, Mr. Mash squeezes past me and straight onto the strange ball-bearing floor beneath the dome. He manages a few paces and then stops, baffled at the unusual sensation beneath his paws.

"No!" I cry. "Come back! Mashie! Come back!" But he won't move. Instead, he sits down on the floor, lifts his ears, and cocks his head as if to say, *I'm coming with you—like it or not.*

"Mashie, Mashie," I plead as I shuffle through the ball bearings myself. "Come on!"

The last thing I hear is Dr. Pretorius saying, "Ain't no time. Leave him alone. You haven't got long before Ramzy's old gal makes her breakthrough."

The studio door slams behind me with a *thunk* and it's pitch-black. I feel the floor begin its quivering motion, which makes Mr. Mash whimper again. I can't tell where he is. Can he even walk on it now?

"Mashie?" I call gently.

Then the band above my eyes glows blue; it gets a bit lighter as the shapes become sharper, and I'm back where I was ninety minutes ago.

Jessica is still openmouthed in astonishment.

Other Me looks just like me.

And I've got less than ten minutes left to save the world.

Chapter Seventy

Standing by the entrance to the Jenner building, Jessica looks first at me, then at Other Me. She blinks hard and then says, "You . . . you disappeared for a second just then. Are you . . . are you a ghost or something? I don't understand. What's going on?"

Just for a second.

This future thing is weird.

Her gaze flicks between me and Other Me. But for all the urgency that's crowding in on me, I feel my brain clearing and I'm thinking straight again.

"No, I'm not a ghost. But . . . I know it's weird. It's weird for us all. Listen, Jessica—this Georgie will explain. Right now, I need to get to your lab and get a sample of the CBE medicine—the cure."

Jessica looks at me blankly.

"The cure," I repeat. "It does exist, doesn't it?"

Please don't say no.

"Yes, of course it does," snaps Jessica. "Only it's . . . it's highly classified. The formula is protected by—"

"I don't need the formula," I say, thinking of when I swallowed the piece of peach. "I just need . . . a vial or something. Preferably quite small?"

"Well, we have that, in the lab," says Jessica, "but I don't see how—"

"Let me worry about that," I say, and it comes out sounding much more confident than I feel inside.

She shakes her head. "It doesn't matter. You can't just walk in and help yourself to the drugs in the lab. It wouldn't be . . ."

Dammit, I should have rehearsed this. Jessica's whole expression is dumbstruck, and I can't blame her.

"The cure! I need the cure. For CBE. Dog Plague!" I'm desperate. No one is moving—they're both just staring at me. *"Now!"*

"Look here, young lady," says Jessica. "I have no idea at all just what on earth is going on. But if you think for one minute that—"

"Mum!" says Other Me at last. "Mum! Just this once, you've got to believe me. You know all that stuff with Dr. Pretorius, and the dome, and everything? Last year?"

Jessica narrows her eyes in response. "How could I forget?" she says drily.

"It was *true.* You have to believe me. Believe us!"

At that moment, I feel a cold, wet nose against my hand, and look down to see Mr. Mash. Here. In the future. Goodness knows what he can actually *see*—nothing, probably, because for him the dome is in total darkness, and everything I can see is generated by my bicycle helmet, and he isn't wearing one. But he can smell me, and he licks my hand.

Other Me has sunk to her knees, tears streaming down her face now. "Oh, Mashie!" she wails as he approaches her and lets her scratch his ears. Jessica is just shaking her head in utter disbelief.

"Th-that's Mr. Mash?" she croaks. "But he . . . he's . . ."

"*Now* do you believe me?" says Other Me through her sobs. "I'll explain it more later. Right now, we haven't got long—am I right, er . . . Georgie?"

"What? Eh?" Everything's so strange, and everything is coming at me at once, so that my head feels like it's buffering the overload of information, including that Other Me and Jessica seem to have a different relationship to the one *I* have with her. And now Other Me is asking me a question.

I look at my phone. "Nine minutes." And then I look over Other Me's shoulder and my stomach freezes. Marching across the lawn toward us are four . . . no, five, six . . . loads of them . . .

Giant scorpions, heading straight for us, with the biggest—Buster—in the lead.

"Oh no," I murmur. "They're back."

Other Me turns round and her face freezes in pure terror.

"Oh no, oh no, oh no! I've had nightmares about them for months."

"What the *heck* are they?" Jessica gasps.

"Giant multisensory VR scorpions," I say, and I can anticipate her next question. "Yes, they attack. They can see you, and they're super smart. Can you distract them?"

"Can they hurt us?" says Other Me.

"I don't know, but they can definitely hurt me. Remember outside the shop when Buster stung me? They're smarter now, and they've cloned themselves."

They're getting closer. Other Me turns to Jessica. "Mum, if you ever, *ever* needed to trust me, it's right now. Do what Georgie says. It's time for me to be as brave as her." She turns to face the scorpions. "Hey, you big bullies! Come and get me!"

And with that she starts walking toward them. I try to protest, to say, "Georgie, stop!" but the words freeze in my mouth. Because it's working. The scorpions stop and turn slightly, their attention distracted by Other Me.

"What is she *doing*?" shrieks Jessica.

"We have eight minutes. Come with me *now*!" I grab Jessica by the wrist and drag her round the corner of the building to the entrance, hissing, "We've just got to go for it!"

As we round the corner, the bored-looking soldier, now

on his own, looks up at Jessica and nods in recognition. She walks past him and hurries across the marble floor to the lab. Then to me, he says, "Identification. Hey! You can't bring your dog in 'ere—it's a medical facility!"

But I don't wait. "Not my dog, sorry," I say as Mr. Mash trots past the soldier and into the building, stopping to sniff the statue of Edward Jenner and trotting on down the long corridor toward the lab.

The soldier has blocked my way. "I need to see your ID," he says. He's being more aggressive, but he's only a couple years older than Clem. That realization makes me bolder.

"Sorry, I left it in the lab," I say.

"Don't care. No one gets in 'ere without official identification."

Over his shoulder I can see a person walking toward us, his bowlegged pace even more obvious than ever. "Jackson!" I shout. He grins and holds up his hand in greeting, unaware of the urgency of the situation.

"You've got to help me," I say to him. "I . . . I've lost my ID."

Jackson is level with us now and gives an apologetic smile. "Well, if it were down to me, Miss Santos, it wouldn't be a problem. But you know how it is now." He jerks his thumb at the young soldier. Then he looks at me quizzically.

"Is something wrong, Georgie?"

"Yes, Jackson!" I'm practically screaming. "*Everything's* wrong, and I'm trying to put it right, but I've only got a few minutes." I remember what Other Me said to Jessica before. *Mum.* "If you ever, *ever* believed me, believe me now, on the life of my mum, I swear, Jackson, you have to . . ."

I think it's the mention of my mum that does it. Jackson holds up his hand as though he's swearing an oath.

"I'll vouch for her, Private. That's Georgina Santos."

The soldier curls his lip and sneers. "Listen, old man. I don't care if she's the queen of . . . *Oh my God*, what is *that*?"

We follow his gaze. Running toward us from around the corner is Other Me, pursued by countless scorpions of all sizes, still led by Buster.

"Out of the way!" Other Me screams. "Let me in!"

There's no stopping her. She has only about a ten-yard lead on the scorpions, and there are more of them now. Lots more.

The soldier says nothing but moves aside from the doorway and cocks his gun, shouting into a radio attached to his collar.

"*Guard Station Two Eighteen! Two Eighteen! Request immediate backup. Repeat: immediate backup. Situation critical!*"

There's a burst of deafening gunfire, aimed at the scorpions, as Other Me, fear etched on her face, draws level with us and gasps, "Shut the door! Quick!"

The soldier turns to us and yells, "Do as she says! I'll deal with them!" and opens fire again. A couple of the scorpions crash to the ground, leaking black stuff. Still the rest of the shiny black horde advances and he yells into his radio again: *"Giant scorpions, sir! Thousands of 'em!"*

They are now so near I can smell them: a rank, acidic smell. They're so closely packed that their hard shells are scraping against each other, and before the door slams shut I shout out to the soldier, "Come back in—they'll kill you!" but he's still firing: *bang, bang, bang, bang-bang-bang.*

There are loud, unearthly screams coming from the dying scorpions as they're hit, but still others advance. There are just too many for one gun and, as the door slams shut, the last thing I see is the young soldier kicking out at Buster before disappearing under a wave of shiny black, swearing and groaning.

Alerted by the gunfire, Jessica is running toward us from down the corridor, shouting, "What's going on?"

Mr. Mash stands in the middle of the marble floor, his feet slightly splayed, the hackles on his back standing up in anger. Other Me is leaning with her back against the double doors, panting hard. The scorpions are scratching at the doors.

"Georgie!" screams Jessica. "Get away from there!"

"They're . . . they're going to get in. Somehow. They're

strong and smart," Other Me gasps. I remember what Dr. Pretorius told us about how quickly they could learn.

"My time's running out," I say. "I've got to get to the lab!"

"Jackson. Can you help?" says Other Me. Jackson is looking between the two of us, trying to work out why he's seeing double.

"Don't worry about it," I say. "We'll explain later." Then I scream as a black scorpion leg smashes through the glass pane of the door. "They're getting in! Come *now*!" I grab Other Me's hand and run toward Jessica and the laboratory corridor.

I turn back to see Jackson clambering onto the Jenner statue, lugging a large fire extinguisher behind him. From outside comes rapid gunfire as more soldiers arrive. Another glass pane smashes loudly, and seconds later, a scorpion the size of a cat drops to the marble floor and starts scuttling toward the statue.

"Good luck!" I shout.

Our shoes squeak on the marble, and Mr. Mash is ahead of us, his claws going *click-clack* on the floor. He's staying close to me, even though he can't see me. To our left is the familiar long window showing the laboratory with its robots and conveyors and endless computer screens.

The scorpions are now streaming through the windows, dozens and dozens of them, their feet a hideous cacophony of clattering and clicking, scuttling and rattling along the stone floor, their tails quivering and aggressive, their acrid smell catching in my throat.

"Get the lab door!" shouts Other Me.

Jessica is swiping her security pass at the laboratory door's entrance control, but she's doing it too fast and pushing at the same time. Meanwhile, there are scorpions massing round the plinth bearing the statue of Edward Jenner, and Jackson is standing in Jenner's lap, aiming jets of fire-extinguisher foam at any of the creatures that try to scrabble up the stone base.

"Go on! Get off, ye little devils! Take that!"

Then I see him: Buster. He's twenty yards away, down the corridor, but he turns his upper body and tilts his head. He starts to come toward me and a chill of fear runs down my neck.

He recognizes me.

"Quick, Mum!" shouts Other Me.

"I'm trying!" wails Jessica, jabbing frenziedly at the door panel.

Buster is getting faster and closer, his coal-black pincers clacking with aggression and his tail quivering.

He has drawn back his stinger to strike when the lock springs open and we fall through the door. Mr. Mash is barking loudly and lunges forward, seizing Buster's front leg between his teeth. The scorpion lets out a squeal and the giant sting arches over his back and plunges into Mr. Mash's thigh.

No!

Mr. Mash howls in pain and lets go. As Buster pulls back, ready to strike again, there's a split second for me to reach out and drag Mr. Mash by his collar into the lab. Slamming the door behind me traps Buster's tail as it aims another strike, and it waggles menacingly while I lean on the door. A second later, the weight of the door crushes the tail and it snaps off, twitching horribly on the floor as the door slams shut.

Poor Mashie is twisting in pain, whimpering and turning his head to try to locate the source of the sting and lick it, but he can't reach. I long to comfort him, but I have to leave him.

"Where is it, where is it?" I shout as Jessica opens a big fridge door, and a cloud of ice steam seeps across the floor. Seconds later, she passes a box to Other Me, who rips it open and offers me a tiny glass bottle.

"You've come a long way for this," she says.

Other lab personnel have gathered round us, drawn by the noise and the disturbance. An older man with white hair says, "What on earth is happening out there, Jessica? What in God's name are you doing?"

"Not now, Arthur," she says with such force that he stops talking and watches.

The bottle. It's tiny, but I'm supposed to swallow it whole. Not the contents: the whole bottle.

I try.

I put it in my mouth and I try to swallow it.

And I can't.

It's a little cylinder about two centimeters long and I gag every time I try. I'm sobbing with frustration, as time is running out.

Outside in the corridor I hear shouts, then a Klaxon alarm goes off at a deafening volume. Through the window, the corridor is filled with giant scorpions; then there's a loud *whoomph* as a smoke bomb explodes, followed by gunshots as the soldiers try to deal with the scorpion invasion.

Inside the lab, people scream at the gunshots and fall to the floor, and I'm desperately trying to swallow the little bottle. I get it to the back of my throat, but I keep gagging. It's scratching the flesh of my mouth, and I'm sobbing with frustration.

It's all over.

I've failed.

So many people are going to die.

Chapter Seventy-One

"What's happening?" asks Other Me, her voice rising in pitch with fear at the chaos surrounding us.

"It's no good," I say in despair. "The scorpion sting I got bridged the RL–VR gap. It means anything inside me can pass through the wall." I'm panting and not explaining myself very well.

"*Which wall?*" wails Other Me, looking around as if there was an actual wall.

"Don't you remember? The virtual wall between you and me! Between this and a year ago!" I yell. "But it has to be *inside* me. I can't just, you know, carry it."

"So . . . so swallow it! Try again!"

"I can't. It's just too big."

In my pocket, my phone goes *ping pong*.

Out of time.

I slump to the ground to await the blackness of the dome.

Mr. Mash limps over to me and my double, his long tongue hanging out.

I wait.

Then suddenly Other Me grabs Mr. Mash's collar and leaps to her feet. "He's just been stung!" she shouts. "Victoria sponge! Jackson's Victoria sponge!" She reaches into her shoulder bag and pulls out a squashed paper bag.

"Mashie! Mr. Mash! Look what I've got for you!" she says, and without asking she snatches the glass tube from my hand, shoving it into the center of a sticky slice of sponge cake. She pushes it toward Mr. Mash's muzzle.

He sniffs it. Then, without chewing, he swallows it whole.

I hear, "Good luck!" and look up to see Other Me and Jessica clutching each other in a tight embrace, waiting for me to go.

"Georgie! Georgie! Quick!"

I'm holding Mr. Mash as everything goes black, and then, through the fog of my brain and the agony of the headache, I can hear someone shouting. I'm retching and convulsing and scrabbling at my helmet with my fingers.

I recognize the voice. "Georgie! Georgie! Are you all right?"

It's Ramzy.

Above me, the pin lights of the dome come on.

Chapter Seventy-Two

He's standing at the edge of the circular floor, and I crawl toward him, sweat running down my neck, the taste of vomit hot in my throat. There's a rhythmic thumping noise coming from somewhere, and I hear, "Open up, open up now!" shouted through a megaphone.

"The police are coming in with a battering ram downstairs," says Ramzy. "Did you get it?"

I can't speak, but I point at Mr. Mash, who is himself retching. He's bleeding badly from the scorpion sting and I half push, half drag him off the floor and through to the control room where we both collapse. It's only been ten minutes but it feels like *much* longer. In the corner of the control room is Sass, still in the beach robe, still staring at us in wonder.

"Are you OK?" she asks, but I'm too exhausted to answer.

Dr. Pretorius sits in her desk chair, breathing shallowly. Her dark skin has turned a grayish brown and her eyes are slits behind her thick glasses.

"Tell me . . . tell me you got it, kid. Tell me that all of this has been worth it—*please!*"

From downstairs, we hear the door being bashed in.

I look over at Mr. Mash, whose neck is stretched forward as he vomits up the glass tube. Fishing it out, I hold it up, and it seems to take all my strength to lift it, but I do, and a smile breaks out on the old lady's drawn face.

It's a full smile: the first I have ever seen her make, and her pale eyes crinkle at the edges. She nods.

"Good work, kid." She closes her eyes and her head drops.

"No!" I cry. "Don't die!"

She opens her eyes again. "Don't be ridiculous. I'm not gonna die on you. The job ain't done yet, kid."

The computer monitor is still showing the news program: it's chaos on the street outside, with sirens and flashing blue police lights. On-screen, Aunty Nush is in the cab of a truck, facing the metal doors of the loading bay, and a reporter is saying, ". . . *dramatic scenes here in Whitley Bay as the aunt of one of the children is about to break down the doors of the Spanish City . . .*"

"No, Aunty Nush!" shouts Ramzy at the screen, but it's too late. His aunt fires up the engine.

"Can you kids still carry me?" says Dr. Pretorius. "'Cause we're runnin' short on time. Get me into that beach robe!"

Sass quickly takes it off and helps Dr. Pretorius into it.

"OK—now socks. Quick! Ah, forget it. What difference will it make anyhow? We gotta go."

I can barely drag myself to my feet, let alone carry another person, but somehow Ramzy and Sass manage to get Dr. Pretorius down the metal stairs into the loading bay at the point when the first deafening crunch happens.

Aunty Nush has driven into the doors.

The big metal doors bow inward but don't give way. It won't be long. Sass squeals in fright.

"There it is. Get me in. It's fully charged, but who knows how far a solar battery will take me at nighttime?"

The copter-drone sits in the center of the concrete floor, and holding Dr. Pretorius on each side, we drop her into the chair as the metal doors take another massive bashing by the front of the truck outside. One more bash, and they'll come crashing in.

"Stand back!" shouts Dr. Pretorius. The blades of the drone start to whir and the noise in the loading bay is tremendous. "Here—take this!"

She tosses Ramzy a rectangular cassette, the size of a book, that she popped out of Little Girl before we left the control room.

"What is this?" he shouts over the din as the drone begins to hover, lifting Dr. Pretorius a yard off the ground.

"It's only my whole life's work, kids. Thanks to you, I

know that it works. That's good enough for me. Do with it what you think is right."

There's a pause in the din, one of those odd moments when everything goes quieter in the midst of chaos. Outside, the crowd is breathlessly awaiting another attempt to smash in the doors, and the truck's engine noise dips slightly before revving up again.

In the second or two of calm, Dr. Pretorius looks at me as fiercely and as intensely as anyone has in my life. Her lips are moving but I can't hear. I lean in so she can croak into my ear.

"You done good, kid. All of ya. And that stinkin' mutt. And, if anyone asks, tell 'em I ain't all bad." Then she smiles her half-smile. "Ha!"

There's another huge bang and the doors of the loading bay finally crash forward under the impact of the truck. There's a cheer from outside, and the truck backs up, leaving a huge open space. I can see TV cameras, and crowds of people, and police officers. Camera flashes are almost blinding me.

Then the crowd gasps as the copter-drone rises up a little more and hovers in the center of the storage area as Dr. Pretorius adjusts the controls. Someone shouts, "It's her!"

Then the door of the truck opens, and Aunty Nush's large figure appears as she climbs down from the driver's seat. I look across at Ramzy, whose mouth is hanging open.

Aunty Nush's face is a picture of pure fury, her eyebrows clumped together into a fierce hedge, and she stomps toward Ramzy, clenching her fists. I cower and put my hands up to my face to cover my eyes. Ramzy's flinching too.

She strides past him toward the copter-drone, her long cloak fluttering in the downdraft from the copter blades. Without warning, she stretches up and grabs one of the arms of the copter-drone, and it lurches to one side. She screams something at Dr. Pretorius and uses her other hand to try to hit her. Dr. Pretorius's eyes widen in fear, and she powers the copter blades some more till they whine in protest, trying to lift up and away from Aunty Nush.

"No, Aunty! No!" yells Ramzy, rushing forward and grabbing her arm, but that just pulls the copter-drone down farther till it's tilting alarmingly to one side. "Let her go!" Then he shouts something, and there's a loud exchange between them.

Aunty Nush's face suddenly softens, and she says something that could be, "Really?"

Ramzy nods. What he says sounds like, "Error! Error!" but clearly means, "Yes! Yes!"

Aunty Nush looks up at Dr. Pretorius, and when their eyes meet, she slowly lets go of the copter-drone. It rocks and surges toward the roof, then stabilizes. Dr. Pretorius eases it forward, through the bashed-in doorway and into the air above the astonished crowd.

On the ground, Ramzy and Aunty Nush are embracing. She is stroking and kissing the top of his head while tears stream down her fat cheeks and they turn to look at the copter-drone.

Dr. Pretorius looks down, gives a little salute, and I like to imagine that she says, "So long, folks!" but it's too noisy to hear. Instead, she gets higher and higher and then the drone banks off to the right, over the road, over the beach, and over the sea, becoming a speck in the twilight.

And she's gone.

Then my arms are round Mr. Mash, and I'm covered in blood from his scorpion wound, and people are shouting around me.

"Stand back!" they say. "The dog's infected!" Nobody will come closer: they stand around in a circle, and I see Dad's face pushing through to the front.

"It's all right!" I hear myself saying. "It's all going to be all right."

And there's Jessica. I want to hold up the glass bottle and shout that I have the cure, but all the people standing around will see, and it'll be on television, and I think of all the explaining I'll have to do, so I just hold it in my fist.

And of all the people that are standing around, not daring to touch me in case I'm infected, it is Jessica who steps forward. She crouches down and puts her arms round me and whispers, "Did you get it?"

As we hug, I slip the little vial into her hand and say, "I got it."

Then Dad is there, hugging me, too, and Clem. Ramzy is hugging his dad now, and Sass and her mum are hugging as well. Mr. Mash is motionless beside me.

The last thing I say before I pass out is "Can we get him to a vet? He's been stung by a scorpion . . ."

Chapter Seventy-Three

When I come round, I'm in the hospital again. Dad is sitting by my bed.

"Hi," he says.

I blink a few times, then say, "Mr. Mash?"

Dad nods slowly. "Very sick. But he's gonna be OK. Did you say *scorpion*?"

I'm not even sure what I remember. I gulp down a glass of water that Dad hands me, and say, "Did it really happen?"

"It really happened," says Dad gently. "At least . . . *something* really happened. You can fill in the details when you're ready. Right now, you just need to rest."

"The cure? Jessica got the bottle?"

"Oh yes. It was analyzed two days ago and tested yesterday and full production started last night, so—"

"Two . . . ? H-how long have I been asleep?"

"Medically induced coma, Georgie. Three days. We thought we'd lost you." His chin wobbles a bit, and I see him clench his jaw. He grins to disguise it. But a tear leaks out anyway and tumbles down his face, splashing on his round tummy.

"And the other dogs? Everyone's dogs?"

"No more killings, Georgie. The cull was suspended yesterday when the cure was announced. You've done it. I don't know how, but you've done it. They're calling it a million-to-one chance."

As I close my eyes again, Dad's words go round in my head. *A million-to-one chance. A million. Chance. Million . . .*

Then I sleep some more.

Chapter Seventy-Four

**SPANISH CITY SIEGE FUGITIVE
STILL WANTED BY POLICE**

Link to reclusive billionaire still "unproven"

---

*Dog Plague mastermind
is victim's stepmum*

WHITLEY BAY: One week after the dramatic Spanish City siege, the elderly woman who escaped in a self-piloted drone remains on the run and wanted for questioning by the police.

She was known as "Dr. Pretorius" to the children she had allegedly kidnapped. Police are investigating the possibility that she is in fact the Norwegian tech billionaire Dr. Erika Pettarssen who disappeared five years ago.

A spokesperson for the Pettarssen charitable

foundation, which provides funds for developing technology in poorer nations, said they had had no contact with her.

The local children at the center of the siege were lured to a hi-tech games laboratory by "Dr. Pretorius," where they tested virtual-reality games with an advanced form of transcranial direct-current stimulation device built into a bicycle helmet. One of the children—Georgina Santos—was taken to the hospital suffering headaches and vomiting. She is expected to make a full recovery.

The laboratory was located in the iconic dome of the 1910 Spanish City entertainment complex. Police computer experts say that all the disks that might contain clues about the games being developed had been wiped by the time they arrived.

In a startling twist, Georgina's father's partner—pictured at the scene cradling the blood-soaked girl—is Jessica Stone, the bio-botics technician who is being credited with identifying the nanobiotic molecular antidote—the so-called cure for Dog Plague.

The two events are not believed to be connected.

Chapter Seventy-Five

I'm still in the hospital and my memory is still fuzzy. I want to keep asking people stuff like "What happened to the scorpions?" and I woke up once, saying, "Are the soldiers still outside the hospital?" And then my mind just goes blank for ages.

Mimi the doctor is nice, but she thinks I'm "confabulating" again, and it's difficult to know what I'm remembering right and what is wrong.

Then Clem turns up on his own. He's shaved his stupid beard off, which makes me smile because he looks more like the Clem that I remember, but it's only when he sits down that I know why the words *million* and *chance* have been kicking around in my head.

When I ask him about the Geordie Jackpot, he gives a rueful smile.

"Campervan," he says. He had emptied his pockets to get the keys, and his wallet containing the winning ticket got fried with the rest of the campervan's interior. To give him credit, he doesn't actually seem that disheartened. "What you never had you never miss," he says, but I wonder if he's been practicing saying that.

Clem was lucky. Thanks to the panic over Dog Plague, he was only given a police warning on the night everything happened. He expects he'll have his learner's permit confiscated, but it could have been worse.

"Why has the beard gone?" I ask him.

"Got a date, haven't I?" he says, blushing a little, which is so cute! My brother is actually very good-looking when he's not all oily and beardy.

"Who?" But I already know the answer.

"Anna Hennessey. She saw me on TV apparently. Sass went home all upset and told everyone about the chase in the van, and, well . . . I think she reckons I'm a bit of a bad boy."

"You?" I scoff. "She'll be disappointed."

He grins. "Yeah, well. Maybe I can persuade her to go for nice guys!" He pauses, then says, "Thanks, Pie-face!"

Chapter Seventy-Six

I'm back home now.

Ramzy, according to Dad, has been hiding with his dad and Aunty Nush to escape the "media circus." Apparently, they had had journalists and bloggers and everyone knocking at the door at all hours and wanting to interview Aunty Nush about bashing the door in, and she has no interest *at all* in talking to anyone.

But things have calmed down now, and most of the journalists have gone, Dad says, so after a couple of days Ramzy comes to see me. And Mr. Mash, of course, who's got one of those cones on his head to stop him licking the scorpion wound.

Ramzy goes nuts when he sees it. "Hey! That's like Timmy in the Famous Five!" he says. "He had one on all through *Five on a Secret Trail* because he cut his ear chasing rabbits!"

I smile. It's good to see Ramzy again, and we head down to the beach with Mr. Mash, who now has Dudley's collar disc clinking next to his own. That was Ramzy's idea.

On the way, he shrugs off his little backpack and takes out a book. "Speaking of the Famous Five," he says. "Remember this?" I look closer and it's not a book at all. It's a heavy white rectangle, disguised with a Famous Five book cover. I shake my head.

"Have I seen it before?" I ask.

"It's her life's work. She gave it to us to look after," says Ramzy. "But I think you should keep it. You never know if she'll be back."

The beach, once again, is full of dogs, and Mr. Mash runs to the shoreline to bite the white tops of the waves. The weather has turned cooler and we sit on the stone steps looking out at the dark blue sea as the salty breeze whips up little flurries of sand.

"Hard to believe it really happened, isn't it?" he says, and I can't think what to say. Perhaps it's because I find I'm forgetting so much of it, as if there are holes in my mind that the memories are falling through. I tell this to Ramzy and he says, "Good job *I* can remember, then."

He really seems unaffected by it all, which I'm glad about, but a little jealous at the same time.

"I told you about meeting myself, didn't I?"

"You did. What were you like?"

"I was OK," I say. "Expensive sneakers, though. And a cool watch."

"That's the Geordie Jackpot. That's what happens when you *don't* make the difficult decision to save the world. The ticket doesn't get burned in a freak campervan explosion."

We stay there for a bit, looking at the horizon. "Where do you think she went, Ramzy?" He doesn't answer. He's on his feet and walking toward the Spanish City.

"I've got an idea."

Five minutes later, we're being scowled at by Norman Two-Kids as we look around his shop, while Mr. Mash waits obediently outside.

"You buyin' somethin' or not?" he says.

"Just browsing!" says Ramzy cheerfully. Then softly, to me, he says, "Look at the cameras: there, there, there, and there."

There are security cameras everywhere, pointing in every direction, including one directed straight at the Geordie Jackpot terminal.

"Excuse me, sir," says Ramzy to Norman. "But if I were to purchase a Geordie Jackpot ticket . . ."

"Hey, I remember you. Go on, get lost."

"Just one question: do the tickets have the time of purchase written on them?"

"Course they do. But you're still not buyin' one. Go on—clear off!"

Chapter Seventy-Seven

As for Jessica . . .

Well, that's two of us in the family who have now met the king. He came up on a "private visit"—no press, no photographers, no warning—and he brought his Jack Russell terrier, called Tigger, who's quite old now but super cute. Jessica invited me and Mr. Mash too. The king wanted to thank the people who worked at the Jenner laboratory, and spent ages talking to Jessica.

Then he shook my hand. As he bent down to pat Mr. Mash, he moved in close, murmuring so that no one else could hear.

He said, "I've just been told the most *extraordinary* story involving a very brave dog and something called a Future-Dome. Is it true?"

I nodded and found myself saying, "Yes, sir." I've had enough of lying.

"Well, your secret's safe with me," he said, and then he winked. "Jolly well done, both of you!"

We've been getting on quite well, actually, Jessica and I. I think it was seeing her and Other Me in the future, how Other Me called her Mum. I've thought about it a lot and I have worked something out.

Danger and horror and difficulty often bring people closer together. That's what must have happened with Jessica and Other Me. Living through everything that led to the world that I saw must have made them trust each other and *like* each other.

And so it came to me as I was taking Mr. Mash's cone off for the last time. Why not allow that to happen, anyway?

I thought of my Wisdom of the Dogs poster. *Like people in spite of their faults.*

Dad loves Jessica. So I will too. At least I'll try.

She has been nice. St. Woof's is still closed down, so Mr. Mash has been living in the barn, but seeing as it's the school holidays, I have plenty of time to hang out with him, and he's not lonely. Jessica's allergy is not her fault. She even suggested the other day that Mr. Mash might be able to stay so long as he didn't come in the house. There's a shed in the garden that we could turn into a fabulous doghouse. (Ramzy has already drawn up plans, obviously.)

Clem has been in touch with the Geordie Jackpot people. He got an email back from them.

Dear Mr. Santos,

Thank you for your email. We have an established procedure for lost ticket claims, and we investigate all such claims thoroughly.

We will be examining the videos taken within the shop where you say you bought the ticket, **Narayan Supreme Stores**. If we can establish that you bought the ticket, then we will begin the process of verifying whether you are, in fact, a Jackpot winner.

Yours sincerely,

Ms. J Knight

Geordie Jackpot Claims

Clem's in a good mood, although he's nervous. He finds out tomorrow if the Geordie Jackpot investigation will make him a winner. He hasn't told anybody else.

It's still a secret between him and Ramzy and me. And possibly Anna Hennessey, and therefore possibly Sass, and therefore possibly everyone else in the world. It doesn't really matter to me, but I hope Ramzy gets his share. I can't forget how upset he was when I was dismissive about it all.

I get a pang of shame when I think about how he couldn't admit how little money his family has.

I want his life to be as full of adventure as he deserves—and it's looking pretty good.

In fact, everything's looking pretty good.

Later that same day, we're walking along the beach with the Spanish City ahead of us. There's me, and Clem and Dad and Jessica, and Mr. Mash (of course). We're going to have tea at the Polly Donkin Tea Rooms to celebrate Dad and Jessica's engagement (the wedding to be performed next year by the Reverend Maurice Cleghorn).

I'm smiling to myself when Jessica hangs back and comes alongside me.

"What's the smile for?" she asks, smiling herself.

"It's a secret," I say.

And then I add, for the first time, "Mum."

Epilogue

All of that happened last summer.

All through the winter, and into the spring, I would look at Mum's tree bent over the skyline, and I would feel that something wasn't right.

Something was left unfinished. And today I'm going to finish it.

Dr. Pretorius's disk cassette is still disguised as a Famous Five book. I have wrapped it in plastic, and sealed it with packing tape, and put it in an old tin and melted candle wax around the rim of the lid.

It's very early on the morning of Dad and Jessica's wedding and I'm the only one up. Mr. Mash and I walk up to Mum's tree with a spade, and I dig a deep hole underneath the branches while my dog watches.

It's the first of May. There's a clear blue sky, and a light breeze is shaking the boughs, which are heavy with pearly-white cherry blossom. The blossom is due to drop at any time now.

It's perfect.

I place the tin with the disk in the hole and fill in the soil, stamping on it while Mr. Mash sniffs the ground curiously. I look back at our farmhouse, and across the fields to the silvery strip of sea; then I check around that no one's listening. I've never done this before, but I've heard Dad talking to the tree as if it's really Mum.

"Mum?" I say out loud. "I don't know if anyone can ever create the dome again, but I'm leaving this here for you to look after. Just in case, you know."

It feels strange, talking out loud, but Mr. Mash is listening, with his head tilted to one side, and so I carry on.

"I wish I could have saved you, too, but it doesn't work like that. But we saved other people, so you know . . ."

I stop for a while.

Then I say, "Were you helping me? I think maybe you were. That's what mums do, isn't it?" I'm remembering how I thought of Mum's song, before deciding to bust Dr. Pretorius out of the hospital, and Other Me didn't, and how that seemed to be the difference between our timelines.

I pause for a bit and look up through the branches. Finally, I say, "Talking of mums . . . You'll always be my real mum, but . . . I kind of have a new one now. I hope that's OK. Shall we call it the Big Experiment?"

That's it. I sigh deeply and contentedly and prop the spade

over my shoulder. "Come on, Mashie," I say, and start to head back down the path. Mum's song—the one from *Chitty Chitty Bang Bang*—is playing in my head and, at that moment, the breeze picks up, and a blossom petal floats past me. Then another, and another, till Mr. Mash and I are enveloped in a cloud of white as a strong gust shakes all the blossoms from Mum's tree, casting them onto the path before me.

Mashie's jumping up, trying to eat the petals, and I know then that everything's going to be all right.

Acknowledgments

It is nice for authors to imagine that we are the only ones responsible for producing books, but this is a long way from the truth. I owe thanks to so many people, especially Nick Lake, whose wisdom and tact could be a model for all editors; also Samantha Stewart and Jane Tait for helping this story through its later stages; and countless others—some of whom I never even meet—whose job it is to get this book into your hands.

Thank you.

About the Author

ROSS WELFORD worked as a business journalist before becoming a freelance writer and television producer. His debut novel, *Time Traveling with a Hamster,* was called "smart, engaging, and heartwarming" in a starred review by *Booklist* and was named both a New York Public Library and Bank Street College of Education Best Children's Book of the year. He is also the author of *What Not to Do If You Turn Invisible* and *The 1,000 Year Old Boy.* Ross lives in London.

Don't miss the remarkable story of the thousand-year-old boy. . . .

There are stories about people who want to live forever. This is not one of those stories. This is a story about someone who wants to stop. . . .

Alfie Monk is like any other nearly teenage boy—except he's a thousand years old and can remember the last Viking invasion of England.

Obviously no one believes him.

So when everything Alfie knows and loves is destroyed in a fire and the modern world comes crashing in, Alfie embarks on a mission to find friendship, acceptance, and a different way to live . . .

. . . which means finding a way to make sure he will eventually die.

An astonishing and funny novel about a girl who—by disappearing—will write herself into your heart forever . . .

Twelve-year-old Ethel Leatherhead only meant to cure her acne, not turn herself invisible. But that's exactly what happens when she combines herbs bought on the Internet with time spent in a secondhand tanning bed. At first it's terrifying to be invisible . . . and then it's fun . . . but when the effect doesn't wear off one day, Ethel is thrown into a heart-stopping adventure. As Ethel struggles to conceal her invisibility, she unravels the biggest secret of all: who she really is.

Al Chaudhury has a chance to save his dad's life—but to do it, he must travel to 1984. . . .

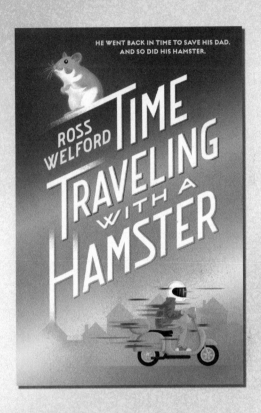

My dad died twice. Once when he was thirty-nine and again four years later, when he was twelve.

On his twelfth birthday, Al Chaudhury receives a letter from his dead father. It directs him to the bunker of their old house, where Al finds a time machine (an ancient computer and a tin bucket). The letter also outlines a mission: travel back to 1984 and prevent the go-kart accident that will eventually take his father's life. What could possibly go wrong?